FOOTSTEP ON THE STAIR

FOOTSTEP
ON THE STAIR

Rosemary Anne Sisson

This first world edition published in Great Britain 1999 by
SEVERN HOUSE PUBLISHERS LTD of
9–15 High Street, Sutton, Surrey SM1 1DF.
This first world edition published in the U.S.A. 2000 by
SEVERN HOUSE PUBLISHERS INC of
595 Madison Avenue, New York, N.Y. 10022.

British Library Cataloguing in Publication Data 683367

Sisson, Rosemary Anne, 1923-
    Footstep on the stair
    1.   Love stories
    I.   Title
        823.9'14 [F]

        ISBN 0-7278-5467-4

Typeset by Hewer Text Ltd
Edinburgh, Scotland.
Printed and bound in Great Britain by
MPG Books Ltd, Bodmin, Cornwall.

In memory of my mother's cousin, Thea, and her mother, Belle, whose story this partly is.

Prologue

In the summer evenings of her childhood when the golden light pressed against the drawn curtains of the small back room and the children's voices echoed out of the scent of the new-mown grass in the next garden, Thea would lie in bed holding her breath and waiting.

Sometimes, so intently did she wait and listen, that she seemed to hear the front door opening, and the small, dull sound of a bowler hat on the hatstand, and footsteps on the stairs. But they never came any further than the landing outside her room. Once she had got out of bed and run bare-footed across the linoleum and opened the door. But there was no one there, and suddenly she was afraid and ran back to bed, jumping in under the thin cotton sheet and worn blankets and faded eiderdown, her heart beating wildly as though she had been on the edge of discovering something, and was glad that she hadn't.

Long afterwards, when it was all over, and the mystery was solved, and the expectation, after its fashion, satisfied, she would look back into the house in Abbot's Green as though into a doll's house, and see there the four unreal figures of that childish game. There was Emily in the kitchen, creaking in her basket-chair by the fire, which even on the hottest day burned red between the bars, and resting her black-stockinged legs on the wooden seat of a kitchen chair while she read 'Peg's Paper'. There was Nan, with pins in her mouth, fitting patterns and material on the dressmaker's dummy and searching for the one piece of paper pattern which had always

1

floated down under the table. Nan was not Thea's nurse but her grandmother, only, since 'Nan' was allegedly the first word the infant Thea had uttered, Nan it had been ever since.

There, too, in the doll's house was Thea's mother, Belle, sitting by the window, sewing, and looking, with her red-gold hair and violet eyes, out of place in that shabby sitting-room, as though an exotic foreign doll had been placed among the ordinary English ones, good-humouredly submitting to their companionship, but always remaining slightly withdrawn.

And upstairs in the tiny bedroom lay the silent, motionless little girl doll, watching and waiting, with that secretive look on her face.

"How strange," Thea would think in after years, "that they never asked me what I thought, and that I never told them."

She could not remember when or how she had learned that her father was dead. It was as though he had always been there, part of her childhood, ceremonially absent. Death in Abbot's Green was at once dignified and slightly improper – like a Bishop who had said a rude word. People in Abbot's Green would never have said that to lose a parent was inexcusable carelessness. They did behave, however, as though death did not happen to respectable people. It was this drop of the voice and faint portentousness which Thea always connected with death, and she used it herself when she went to school and walked home with her small, self-important friends.

"*My* father is dead," she would say. "He died when I was a baby."

Then she would see in their faces that slightly shocked but very respectful look, and it was as though she and her father were in partnership, his unassailable deadness being set up against their families' prosperity, and she, like a princess, claiming from him her regal inheritance of mortality. It would even seem to her – and to her little friends, too – that their fathers were rather plebeian and unimaginative in being still alive, and that hers had done the aristocratic thing.

It was only when the house was quiet and she lay all alone in bed that she would imagine that she had, after all, that other kind of father who would open the shiny walnut-stained front door, put his bowler hat on the hatstand and come up the stairs to say good-night. And then her heart would beat fast in her flat, bony, little girl's chest, as though whatever was most desired in life was, when it actually occurred, most to be dreaded. But, that silent footstep on the stair, was it life or death?

One

T hea's first memory in life was of the thick red tablecloth, reaching nearly to the floor under which she sat as a child, and played, and crooned little songs to herself, and listened to the conversations of the grown-ups. Sometimes she was a queen, the footstool her royal throne, and she dispensed justice to two plaster dolls, a ragged teddy bear and a reluctant kitten. Or she would cook meals upon the footstool and serve them, still upon the footstool, to her former subjects. They all bowed low to her. They were only too ready to bow low. The difficulty lay in persuading them to remain upright. But her favourite game was to pretend that she was on a desert island, and that this was her hut. Storms, hurricanes and tempests flung themselves upon that hut. Lions attacked it, bears snuffled at its door, fierce natives hurled their spears at its inviolate walls. As long as she stayed inside, she was safe. The more violent the dangers, the more pleasing was her sense of security. Sometimes she would lift the corner of the tablecloth and put her small head out, withdrawing it with a gasp of terror, and then curling up in the very centre of the hut and whispering, "Safe, safe, safe!"

Thea always played underneath the table, when she was little, because the top of the table was occupied by dressmaking. She had once asked her mother why she and Nan did dressmaking for a living.

"Well, Grandfather's business failed, and –" her mother hesitated, then finished – "and the shock was so great to him that he died."

"He did?" Thea was impressed. She had a picture in her mind of water coming out of a tap and then suddenly stopping. She had also a dramatic vision of someone who had been watching the tap coming to Grandfather and saying, "Your business has failed," and of that dignified gentleman putting his hand to his watch-chain and falling dead. It was only many years later that she discovered that Grandfather's dying had been a long, weary, heart-breaking process, that he must first go bankrupt, that his wife and two daughters must move to a poorer house, and a poorer one still, that he must make another venture and lose what little money had been salvaged, that he must have a nervous breakdown, become violent, and then suicidally depressed, before he could die, slowly and sadly, leaving his wife worn out and nearly destitute. But, to the small Thea, there was a pleasing briskness about the story. Grandfather's business had failed, so he fell dead. It was very simple, and very suitable. She nestled closer to her mother, for it was near her bedtime, and Emily would be calling her in a minute.

"And then?" she asked.

"Then Nan decided to take up dressmaking, because it was the only way she could think of to make money. Aunt Ruth was only quite young then, you know."

Thea tried to imagine Aunt Ruth as young, but could not. "As young as me?" she asked.

"No, not quite as young as you."

"Oh." Probably Aunt Ruth had never been as young as that. "And then?" she asked, inexorably.

"Then I got married, and went away. Aunt Ruth married Uncle Edward, and then I came back, and brought you with me, and here we are." Her mother laughed, and added, "That's the end of that story, and I can hear Emily calling you."

"Oh, no, Mother, not just yet. You haven't told me when Emily came."

"Why, Emily has been with Nan for years, ever since she

was first married. When Emily first worked for Nan, she had two maids under her."

"I wish Nan had kept one of the other maids," sighed Thea.

"Thea, what a wicked thing to say!"

"But, Mother, Emily's so cross."

"I know, darling, but she doesn't mean half she says. Besides, she's been good to Nan."

"She's cross with Nan, too," Thea protested.

Her mother chuckled softly, and answered, "Nan understands. She knows what Emily means." She took Thea on her lap, saying, "You must try to love Emily, darling. She's fond of you, really, only she doesn't show it. Will you try?" Thea buried her face in the rich red-gold hair, and sighed, "Yes," but privately thought the task of loving Emily an impossible one, and, throughout her childhood, was convinced that Nan was as frightened of Emily as she was herself. Nan, she thought, was in the position of a man who has bought a fierce watchdog and cannot persuade it to let him near his own property. She barked as furiously at her mistress as she defended her from outsiders.

Nan's small, shabby house was in North London, in a suburb, not far from Alexandra Palace. It was not a beautiful place – few suburbs are. But, when the may tree at the corner of the road was in blossom, and scattered its scarlet petals far over the pavement, when the laburnum tree next door bloomed, when the roses in the front gardens put forth their fragile heads to gladden passers-by, Thea thought that there could be no greater beauty anywhere. There was a solitary thrush, too, who would perch beside the kitchen window in the evening, and sing as though he were the last bird left alive and must voice the joys and sorrows of all men and of all ages. Thea would lean out of her bedroom window, thinking that the thrush was poised high above the world, and that all motion, all breathing stopped, while he sang his song of delight and piercing sorrow.

In the summer, she loved to sit in a little house which she had made for herself among the few bushes which Nan fondly called 'The Shrubbery'. Thea would lean against the fence, quite hidden by the dark leaves, enjoying the scent of the sun upon the hot, rough wood, and the musty, dusty smell of laurel bushes. Sometimes people would walk along the pavement outside, quite unaware of the small girl who sat still and silent within a few feet of them. Thea liked to feel that she wore an invisible cloak, as though she shared a magic secret with herself, and the scraps of conversation which came clearly to her, however unimportant, became suddenly exciting and illicit.

In the autumn, the plane trees shed their bounty of crimson and brown leaves freely on to the pavements, as the may tree gave its petals in the spring, and Thea loved the whisper and chatter they made as she shuffled her boots among them. She never tired of the yearly challenge of the chrysanthemums; mad, ragged heralds of winter, who lifted their tawny heads in rebellion above the parsimonious confinement of the narrow front gardens in which they were planted.

And in winter came the pleasure of the lighted windows. Walking back from dancing school, swinging her bronze slippers in her hand, Thea would try to dawdle past those gay squares of arrested life, where a lighted lamp, an outstretched arm, a child's head, acquired a romance, a wonder not their own. It seemed to Thea that the people in those golden windows lived only for that moment during which she looked in upon them. They had never existed before. They would never move after she had been urged crossly away by Emily. Only for that moment would they laugh or move or sit in the lamplight, within the picture frame. Thea often wondered if, when Nan and her mother were too engrossed in their work to draw the heavy red curtains of the sitting room, those who passed the window thought of them only as unreal figures in a coloured picture.

Thea enjoyed the dark winter evenings beside the fire, with

hot toast, and the lamp lit early, and the small room close and intimate, while the wind murmured in vain against the windows. Sometimes, when they were not too pressed with work, Nan and Thea's mother would read aloud in turn, while Thea drew illustrations to the stories: golden lions, or purple sea-monsters, or red houses falling perilously down a green hill. She never could decide whether she liked these winter fireside evenings best, or the summer days, with tea in the garden and the butter melting in the sun and occasional games of ball with her mother, who would catch up her skirts and run and laugh like a girl.

Everything Thea did and thought in her childhood was unfailingly linked with her mother. Yet it was her mother who lent to the quiet pleasures and customs of the suburban life a touch of uncertainty and insecurity. She never became part of her surroundings, never fitted into the obscure uniformity of Abbot's Green society. She trimmed her hats herself, yet there was always a breath of daring about them. Her dresses, her jackets and costumes, were of cheap material, yet they had a style and dash which were faintly unsuitable in that small street and humble occupation. Like the chrysanthemums, Belle Lawrence seemed to raise her head in protest against the narrow bounds of her life. The very silence of that protest made it more violent.

"I suppose Mrs Lawrence has had a very gay life," said Miss Luke to Nan one day, her sharp little nose quivering like a mouse's.

"No more than most of us, when we were young," replied Nan, with unwonted sharpness, and then, looking at Miss Luke's face, felt remorseful. Miss Luke lived next door, and long years of spinsterhood had left her with an eager, searching look, more hurtful than acidity. She had an invalid mother, and was in the habit of confiding to all her acquaintances that she had "given everything up for Mother". But Miss Luke's real story was more cruel than the fabulous tale of self-sacrifice and service. No one had ever wanted her. She had grown from thin, plain girlhood, to lean, flat-chested middle-age, without even the bitter satisfaction of unrequited love. Miss Luke had never been in love, never been loved, and she looked out upon Belle Lawrence's glowing beauty and self-assurance with an odd mixture of pleasure and jealousy.

"I mean," she added hastily, "she dresses so cleverly. But I suppose she gets that from you."

Nan glanced down at her shabby dress and smiled inwardly, but made no reply. She knew that Miss Luke was longing to ask why Belle had returned home only three years after her marriage, why she had returned alone, but for the frail baby, why, if she was a widow, she had not worn mourning, and, of what illness her husband had died. Nan reflected, with quiet satisfaction, that, slight as was her own dignity, yet it had been sufficient, for eight years, to prevent the ladies of Abbot's Green from asking her these questions. They had hinted, suggested, hesitated, but they had never asked.

So, Belle Lawrence went out to tea, helped with her mother's infrequent *At Homes*, played tennis at the local club and worked hard at dressmaking, finding her pleasure in watching her puny baby change into a slender, silent little girl, with delicate features, soft, fair hair, and great hazel eyes which made Belle frown and sigh at the bitter-sweet memories they evoked. Nan's eyes were grey and Belle's a deep blue, but Thea's glowed brown and green and golden out of a small, pale face.

Thea, engrossed and happy, as only a child can be, with the everyday happenings of their quiet life, never wondered whether her mother was contented. The daily, seasonal and yearly events which she knew and loved were like fenders about her. Her life was a little ship, sailing upon a calm and infinite ocean, manned by a familiar and unchanging crew. When she first realised that her mother hated dressmaking, hated Abbot's Green, hated the little, dark house, the shock and distress to her was great.

One of Nan's richest clients was Mrs Harmon, a woman of wealth but no breeding, to whom people were divided into

three classes – her equals, to whom she gossiped, her superiors, of whom she gossiped, and her inferiors, whom she
ignored. Nan annoyed her, because she was not sure how
to treat her. Nan lived in a small house and did dressmaking,
but she had once lived in much the same style as Mrs Harmon
herself. Nan was polite, but not obsequious. She wrote out a
bill for each piece of work, and accepted money, yet Mrs
Harmon never quite liked to speak to her as she would to a
tradesman, or a servant. She usually compromised, and used
the tone of a charitable parish visitor, condescending and a
little domineering. She mistrusted Belle, as much for her
beauty as for her easy manners, and ignored Thea completely.
One afternoon, she was particularly insufferable.

"It is so difficult to keep good servants these days," she said
to Nan. "Don't you find it so? Really, the gels of today expect
too much money for too little work." Nan, on her knees
before the lady's daughter, pinning the hem of a new winter
dress, replied meekly, "They do."

"But, of course – that's not quite straight, I think. No, to
the left. Oh, I see, you haven't pinned it yet – of course, I
suppose your daughter does most of the housework."

Belle stitched industriously, her eyes upon her work.

"Well, we have an old family servant," Nan answered, in a
hushed voice. "She's so attached to us," she added apologe-
tically.

"Really," said Mrs Harmon, offended. "I should have
thought . . ." She paused. "That bodice doesn't seem to fit
at all, does it?"

"I haven't quite finished it," Nan explained.

"Oh, I see."

"It's very uncomfortable," said young Miss Harmon,
whom Belle always called The Horrible Child.

Nan silently continued to fit the dress.

"I suppose you will soon be retiring," continued Mrs
Harmon. "I suppose Miss – er – Mrs – er – your daughter
will be taking over the business."

11

Thea, sitting by the window, saw her mother start and look up, and then turn quickly to her stitching again. Nan said in a hurried way, with an anxious glance at Belle, "Oh, I like the work. I've always enjoyed sewing."

"Really?" said Mrs Harmon offended again.

There was a brief pause, broken once more by Mrs Harmon.

"How much will this dress cost?" she asked, and Belle bent closer to her work.

Nan named the price, simply enough.

"Well, I consider that very expensive," said Mrs Harmon, the light of battle shining in her eyes. "After all, it's only a child's dress, and I only come to you out of—" She stopped, but continued, "After all, I could go to a larger establishment if I chose."

Nan still fitted the dress, only with a faint flush under her thin, lined cheek. "There is a lot of work in it," she explained, gently.

"Well, I'm sorry, but I think that it is too much." The Horrible Child tugged at the dress, scattering pins on to the threadbare carpet. Nan drew the dress off and bent patiently down to pick up the pins. There was a short silence, before she said quietly, "Perhaps it will be best if you pay whatever you think is right."

"Very well," said Mrs Harmon, graciously accepting the confession of defeat. "When will the dress be ready? I must have it by next week."

"I'll have it ready for you by Thursday," Nan answered, with the faintest sigh, and turned to button Miss Harmon's coat.

Later, when she returned to the room after seeing Mrs Harmon's carriage drive away, Nan said wearily, "I wish people who could afford it would pay what things are worth. I was depending on that extra money."

"We don't want *her* money," said Belle, with suppressed fury.

"Well, the trouble is, we do," said Nan, smiling a little through her anxiety. "Mrs Drake didn't like her jacket and would only pay half what I wanted for it. It was just as she ordered it, too. I knew it wouldn't suit her. Then, Mrs Fairs has decided to go on wearing her black, instead of having a new one." Nan smiled outright here, and so did Belle, for Mrs Fairs' black satin was a standing joke. She had worn it on best occasions for ten years, for nine of which she had spoken of having a new dress made. But Nan's next words were spoken seriously enough, and effectively sobered Belle as well. Thea, sitting behind the curtain, realised that they had forgotten that she was in the room. "I'm afraid Thea's dancing lessons will have to go for the time being."

"No!" cried Belle, with unexpected violence.

"But, my darling—"

"No, no, no! Whatever else goes, not that."

"But, it's an extravagance. And she doesn't even like it much."

Belle stood up, and flung her sewing on to the floor. She held on to the edge of the table, as though to steady herself, and her voice trembled. "She shan't grow up like that brat next door. She shan't be an 'Abbot's Green girl', with an empty brain and no social graces. I hate this place, and if I stay here much longer, I shall go mad. At least Thea shan't live here all her life. I hate the people, with their miserable 'conversation'." She mimicked savagely the semi-genteel, slightly cockney, suburban accent. " 'Turned out nice again, hasn't it? I shouldn't wonder if we had rain again, though. The days are droring in, aren't they?' I hate their beastly little houses, each one exactly like the next, and all furnished in the same carefully correct way. It's like living with a flock of sheep – only they're more stupid than sheep."

Thea drew further back behind the sheltering curtain. Her heart was beating heavily, as though she had been running. Belle went on, with a sudden final burst of fury, like the last

13

thunder of a storm, "If I don't get out of this drab, dirty, deadly place, I shall go mad."

Nan was trembling too, but when she spoke it was in a calm, understanding voice. "Darling, I know how you feel. Why not go away for a holiday? Take Thea and go and stay with Aunt Mary for a while."

Belle came round and put her arms round her mother's neck, resting her fresh face against her mother's cheek. "Mother, dear, I'm sorry. I didn't really mean it. You know I like being with you. It's only that . . . Anyway, we've had fun while we've been here, haven't we? And if Thea has to stop her dancing lessons, well, she has to. She *doesn't* like them, either." She chuckled in the husky, wicked way which Thea loved. "If she weren't so light, she'd sound like a herd of elephants. She does her best as it is. We'll give her some extra French coaching in the spare time." She picked up the dress, smoothing it out rather ruefully, and glanced at Nan, and then laughed. "Mother, don't look so worried. I'm all right now. I feel much better for that outburst. I shall be able to talk of Mr Winter's rheumatism with new interest and enthusiasm."

Nan smiled at that, but still with the two lines on her forehead emphasised. "I'll go and make some tea," she said. "It's Emily's afternoon out."

"I'll come and help you." They went out together, Belle's hand on her mother's arm. Thea waited until they had gone into the kitchen and then tiptoed out of the room and up to her bedroom. There in that narrow little room, with her childish ornaments about her, she lay on her bed and cried, slow, hot, reluctant tears. She did not know why she was crying, but felt that the warm safety of her childhood had deserted her, that into her calm and steady way of life had crept an uncertainty and a threat of violence which filled her with dread. For, if her mother was not contented, then nor was she, since she loved her mother more than anything in the world. She did not know that this same content, for which she

14

wept, was the sweetest gift of childhood, and that, losing it, she was no longer a child.

Thea only cried for a few seconds and then sat on her bed, looking out into the garden. A light fog was swirling silently over the grass and, through it, a lighted window in the house at the end of the garden glowed with a faint mystery, like the glimmer of a lighthouse over a grey sea. Where the road curved inwards, Thea could see the street lamps shining like storm-tossed galleons, the flicker of the gas giving the illusion of the rise and fall of high waves. Michaelmas daisies still bloomed in the flower-beds, pale and ghostly, and yet somehow gallant, defying at once the fog and the winter, yet blending into the subdued colours of the scene. They had not the magnificent rebellion and incongruity of the chrysanthemums, but, with a stauncher fortitude, endured the chill weather and comforted the weary, until they made way for the bright spring flowers.

At tea that day, Belle was very merry and very sweet-tempered, and they all laughed together in cheerful companionship, with the red curtains drawn close against the gloomy evening. But each of them kept a secret from the others, and, in the weeks that followed, Thea often would see Nan looking at her daughter with an anxious, apprehensive speculation. She, too, watching Belle with new carefulness, became aware of something of the tumult and revolt which lay hidden beneath that white forehead and smiling mouth. Sometimes, as the winter closed pitilessly in upon the dark streets, Belle would sit at the window, her work fallen in her lap, her hands clasped tightly, staring at the wet road and the damp, dead garden with madness and loathing – a prisoner looking for the first time at her fetters. Sometimes her discontent would show itself in pettishness and irritation, but usually it was silent and hopeless.

The time passed by for Thea much as it always had, with school, and homework by the fire, and only the release from the shuffle and curtseying of the dancing lessons to remind her of that black afternoon. But the days ran away under her feet swiftly and perilously, like a ball under the feet of a circus clown. It took only an eddy of swirling fog in the gathering dusk to bring into her mind a frightened questioning and doubt.

Two

"Thea," said her mother one day, "how would you like to go and stay with Aunt Mary for a little while?"

"With you?" cried Thea, joyously, "Oh, yes!"

"No," answered Belle. "I wouldn't be coming."

Thea looked up sharply. "Then I don't want to go."

"Just for a week or two," her mother pleaded. "You'd like it and Aunt Mary has asked you so often. It would be good for you to be with people your own age, too."

"Couldn't you come?" said Thea, softly, looking wistfully up into her mother's face.

For a moment, it seemed that Belle faltered and hesitated. Then she said briskly, "No, but I'm sure you'll enjoy it, and it will be nice for you to get away for a little while."

"I don't want to get away—" began Thea, but her mother caught her up and whispered, with an entreaty which Thea didn't understand, "Please, darling, I want you to go." So, for Thea, the matter was decided.

The preparations were made during the last two weeks of the term and, on the day before she was to go, Nan took her to pay a visit to Aunt Ruth. Aunt Ruth was her mother's sister, but Thea found it hard to believe. Aunt Ruth had colourless hair, a pale, lined face and a mouth which permanently turned down at the corners. Aunt Ruth had a quiet, toneless voice, more penetrating in its moaning complaint than any shouting. And Aunt Ruth always had some new grief to voice. Either 'the girl' had broken her best glass, or Edward had burnt a hole in her best carpet, or soup had been spilt on her best

17

table. It was as though a malignant fate stalked around her house, marking her favourite possessions with a large notice saying, 'Please break, stain or otherwise irreparably damage', and this edict always seemed to be obeyed.

Aunt Ruth lived in a neat little villa, not far from Nan's house, and everything about her was neat. The very flowers in her garden seemed to bloom more tidily and stand up straighter. In the summer and spring, Aunt Ruth was usually to be found kneeling on the path in a gardening apron and gloves, digging up blades of grass with a mournful energy, knowing that they only grew to spite her, and would thrust their impertinent shafts up again as soon as she had finished.

Today, however, she was awaiting her visitors in the sitting room, with a small fire which burnt in a tidy, obedient way in the spotless hearth. She greeted her mother with a kiss on the cheek and then stooped to say, "Hello, Thea. Aren't you going to kiss me?" Thea never knew why she said this, since they always exchanged a mutually unenthusiastic embrace, but, realising that no reply was expected, she merely raised her face and kissed the air beside Aunt Ruth's left ear. Aunt Ruth had no gift for entertaining children, and was as much embarrassed in talking to them as they were by her, so Thea, the first greeting over, knew that she was free to wander round the room, looking at the ornaments and staring out of the window. Behind her, her Aunt was embarking upon her Jeremiad.

"Edward's got a dreadful cold," she began. "I didn't get a wink of sleep last night. He was coughing the whole time, and blowing his nose."

"Poor Edward," said Nan, tactlessly.

"Poor me," protested Aunt Ruth. "I couldn't sleep at all. There's no need for him to make such a noise over it. Then I had to get up early for the sweep."

Thea turned to listen at this. She always looked forward to the sweep's visit, when she would go and stand on the lawn and await the black, sooty head of the brush, thrusting forth out of the top of the chimney like a jubilant adventurer. She liked the sweep too, with his rolling eyes and shining white teeth and dusty black face and hands. She never thought of him as being white underneath, like any ordinary mortal. Sweeps were born like that, to have kisses blown to them from ladies' hands, carrying their sooty uniform from house to house, and sending their ragged brushes pushing up towards the sky through dark passages. But Thea might have known that the sweep would have cast no glamour over her Aunt Ruth.

"He made the most dreadful mess. I was hours cleaning it up, and the girl—"

"But, didn't you spread sheets in the rooms?" asked Nan.

"Yes, Mother, but you know how that soot gets *everywhere*, and the girl—"

Here 'the girl' opened the door and carried in the silver teapot, Aunt Ruth's most valued wedding-present. There was always a painful silence while 'the girl' was in the room. Aunt Ruth didn't approve of talking in front of servants and apparently even a remark about the weather might be passed on to the neighbour's 'girl' to your detriment. So they waited in awkward silence until tea was ready, and the door had hardly closed behind the trim young parlourmaid, before Aunt Ruth continued "—is simply no good at cleaning. I think she'll leave soon. She says there's too much to do, and I know I'm working all day. She left a caterpillar in the lettuce today, and Edward was so upset. He was green and furry and sat up and waved. It was disgusting."

"Edward sat up and waved?" asked Nan, wickedly. But Aunt Ruth did not even smile.

"No, the caterpillar, of course."

When tea was over, and Thea had eaten as little as she dared, because she was afraid of dropping crumbs or making her fingers sticky, Aunt Ruth said, in her odd, abrupt way, "Thea, would you like to see The Book?"

"Oh yes," cried Thea, with real delight, for this alone made her visits to Aunt Ruth worth while. So she was sent to wash her hands and on her return found the great book of 'Morte d'arthur' laid upon the table. How this book came into Aunt Ruth's possession had always puzzled Thea. Presumably it was her uncle's, but it was strangely incongruous in that house of neat commonplace. It was a beautifully bound volume, with illuminated capital letters and coloured illustrations. Thea would begin at the first page and go solemnly through the book, searching for Sir Launcelot. All other pictures were rapidly dismissed, but she would linger long over this, her own knight, and had been known to weep over the picture of his death. At first, Aunt Ruth used to plague her with exhortations to be careful, not to tear the pages, not to bend the back, but seeing the awe and reverence with which the little girl touched the magic volume, even Aunt Ruth was satisfied, and she and Nan could talk freely, knowing that Thea was far away in that land of gentleness and violence, of beasts, ogres and fair ladies, of love and undying hatreds.

But, on that afternoon, even this book could not deafen Thea's ears to the words spoken of her mother. Leaning over a picture of Elaine, the Fair Maid of Astolat, with Sir Launcelot gazing at her from the bank of the river, she was thinking that the Fair Maid had hair of much the same colour as her own, and that she would like to die by floating down a river in a barge, with sorrowing friends upon the verge, when she heard Aunt Ruth say plaintively,

"But why must it always be Belle?"

Thea, keeping her eyes upon the page in front of her, was instantly alert.

"She hates being here," Nan answered. "She always did."

"What about the child?" asked Ruth, glancing at the intent figure by the table.

"She will stay with me."

"Belle's always the same," said Ruth, with sudden subdued anger. "She's always had the best of everything."

"But for Father's trouble—" Nan began, but Ruth interrupted.

"Yes, I know, but for Father's trouble, I could have had what she did. Why couldn't I be the eldest, and have all the nice clothes and the parties? She's always been the lucky one, and now, just because there isn't much going on here, she must go and look for some amusement elsewhere."

"There'll be duties attached."

"Oh, yes, I daresay!"

There was a brief silence, before Nan said, gently, but with a hint of reproof in her voice, "Belle hasn't always been lucky, you know."

"Hasn't she?" said Ruth, and this time there was something very like hatred in her tone.

"It will only be for a time," said Nan, after another pause, "and the money is very good." She glanced at Thea, with sudden anxiety and, raising her voice, said, "Well, we must be going. Thea leaves tomorrow, to stay with Mary." Thea, with the baffling subtlety of children, continued to appear engrossed in her book, turning over pages with eager care. Nan, reassured, said in her low tones, "Belle will be in to see you before Friday." Thea, staring sightlessly at the dead Guenevere, was wondering with sick apprehension where her mother was going and when.

Three

A fter lunch the next day, Thea set off for the station with her mother. She wore her second-best white frock, with the white lace petticoat underneath, and her mother had coaxed her fine hair into ringlets with loving care. She wished, though, that she had a coat and hat other than her school outfit, and that her clothes were not packed in the battered and shabby Gladstone bag which had belonged to Grandfather. Her slim black legs dragged slowly along, until Belle was forced to hurry her.

"We shall miss the train," she said.

"I wish we could," Thea answered, choking a little.

"So do—" began Belle, and stopped herself. "You'll enjoy it, darling, I know you will. Think what a lot you'll have to tell us when you get back."

When at last they were upon the platform, and the nose of the train appeared in a distant tunnel, they turned to each other and clung wildly together. Thea realised that she had never before been away from her mother, even for a night. All her love for her seemed to have gathered in her throat, stifling her. She clung speechlessly and desperately, wishing that the moment of parting could last for ever. She heard her mother whisper, "Thea, oh my Thea," and, as they drew apart, saw that her eyes were full of tears. But the train had stopped, and in a minute she was in a carriage, with the bag beside her. The door was slammed, and she leant out of the window, with a dazed, unbelieving look on her face, as the train drew out of the station. Her mother stood on the platform, a tall, graceful figure, in the blue costume, with the large, elegant hat on her glowing hair, waving and smiling, with tears in her blue eyes.

As she sat down in the carriage, Thea felt her breath coming fast and her lips beginning to quiver. She glanced quickly round at the other occupants, a stiff lady in the far corner, and a white-bearded old gentleman, with a great deal of watch-chain, opposite her. She pulled out her handkerchief and pressed it against her mouth, trying vainly to quell the storm. But great sobs kept rising in her throat. As fast as she swallowed one, another took its place, while the tears slid uncontrollably down her cheeks. She mopped them up as best she could, feeling that no true lady would behave with such little consideration for other passengers as to cry in a public conveyance, but could not entirely stifle her grief, and she felt that the stiff lady in the corner was going stiffer than ever with strong disapproval. Suddenly, a deep, gruff voice said, "Here, take this." Looking up, she saw a blur of white, red and gold, representing the old gentleman's beard, face and watch-chain, and a lower blur of white which resolved itself into his handkerchief. He took her small square of linen away from her, put his own larger vessel into her limp hand, and said, "Have a good cry and get it over. Much better." Thus advised, Thea made no further effort to restrain herself. She bowed her head, buried her face in the wide and fragrant handkerchief, and cried with a wild abandon that had something of pleasure in it. At last, she blew her nose thoroughly, wiped her eyes, and handed the handkerchief back to the old gentleman, murmuring shy thanks. He eyed his property thoughtfully, and said, "Hm, much better," with his eyes twinkling behind his pince-nez spectacles.

Thea sat then, with a feeling of adventure and excitement. She had never met any of her cousins before, and felt some apprehension at the thought of a family of children, accustomed as she was to being solitary, but she enjoyed the independence of visiting them alone, and fully expected to like them, since she nearly always did like people. It was only as the stations flashed past her, and she knew that she must soon get out, that she was beset by her old enemy of shyness. Who would meet her at the station? If it were one of her cousins, would she be expected to kiss her? Supposing it was the boy, James, surely she wouldn't be expected to kiss him? She twisted her hands in her lap, forgetting all homesickness in these new fears.

When she arrived at Enfield, the old gentleman, with courtly gallantry, handed her out and lifted her bag down for her and, thanking him, she was taken by surprise when a clear voice said, "Are you Thea?" She looked round, to find a tall, handsome girl, with dark hair tied back with a large black bow, who, as she nodded, said, "Come along. I'm Lydia." There was no question of kissing, for Lydia took her by the arm and hustled her along with an energy that barely left her time to pick up her bag and bring it with her. At the barrier, Lydia, in a sudden fluster, remembered Thea's ticket and seemed much relieved to find that she still had it. She set off at a brisk walk up the hill, while Thea panted along beside her. Lydia's skirt reached nearly to her feet, showing the smallest possible amount of trim black ankles without entirely concealing them. She seemed to be on the verge of putting her hair up and letting her dress down and becoming a young lady. Only a certain loudness of voice and awkwardness of movement betrayed the fact that she was still at school, and not yet 'out'. Her manner towards Thea was so very maternal that Thea, though grateful for her kindness, felt insulted.

"This is Windmill Hill," Lydia remarked, "You know what a windmill is, don't you?"

Thea's heart swelled with indignation, but, "Yes," she whispered.

"That's right," Lydia encouraged her, "that's right." She continued to talk, kindly and brightly, while Thea trudged at her side, feeling an agony of embarrassment, and answering in single words. Once, when Thea changed the heavy old bag from one hand to the other, Lydia asked if it was heavy, but

Rosemary Anne Sisson

Thea replied that it wasn't and they went on faster than ever. At last, when Thea was scarlet-faced with weariness and shyness, they turned in at the gate of a large house built of red brick, with white paintwork that gleamed in the sun, a shining brass door-knocker, and a garden which was green and golden and cream-coloured with an abundance of spring flowers.

"We're home now," said Lydia, and Thea, looking with pleasure at the big, comfortable house, so kindly in the sunshine, felt that this was really a home.

As they approached the house, a boy came round from the back and paused, seeing them.

"This is James," said Lydia, bending down to look into Thea's face. "Say 'hallo', Thea."

"Go on," cut in James, unexpectedly, "Thea's not a baby. Don't show off."

Lydia straightened her back, changing in a moment from maternal kindness to fierce annoyance. She stamped her foot. "You beast!" she spat at him. "It's always the same when I try to help Mother. No one appreciates it."

She turned her back with a swirl of skirts, flung open the front door and rushed inside, slamming it behind her. Thea gazed after her in startled consternation.

"Oh dear," she said, "I'm afraid—"

"You don't want to mind her," said James, cheerfully, "she's always Getting Up."

"Getting Up?" queried Thea.

"Well, that's what Nurse says. She says Lydia's always Getting Up."

"Oh, I see."

The regarded each other, smiling with an immediate understanding. James had dark hair and grey eyes, a lean, well-cut face, and a mouth which tended, even then, to curve into a faintly sardonic smile, as though he had already begun to laugh at himself, at his fellow-beings, at the doings of the world he lived in. Thea's heart went out to him at once. He

26

seized her bag and led the way inside, saying only, "Mother's resting. I'll take you upstairs."

Thea wanted to ask him, as they went together up the wide staircase (very different from the narrow stairs at Sunnyside) whether Aunt Mary was ill, for Nan never rested unless she had one of her headaches, but she was still breathless and shy and, after two flights of stairs, when they came into a big, airy room, James announced casually, "This is Thea," and disappeared once more upon his own affairs.

Thea, aghast at his desertion, found herself confronted with a small, neat person, in spotless white apron, veil and cuffs over a dark blue dress; a gentle-looking and plain-faced woman. Behind her, wide-eyed and silent, was a little girl, rather smaller than Thea, round-faced, plump and pretty, with big blue eyes, curls about her shoulders and a finger in her mouth.

"Well, Thea," said Nurse, in very brisk tones for so gentle a person, "This is Janey." Thea could think of nothing to say.

"I'll go and see about tea," said Nurse. Janey clutched at her skirts in vain. The two children were left standing looking at each other in silent dismay. Nurse looked back round the door.

"Take Thea to the night-nursery and show her where to wash her hands." Janey heaved a sigh of relief. Action was easier than conversation.

The night-nursery was nearly as large as the nursery and looked out over the garden on to fields. A big bed near the window was Nurse's, and two small beds were for Janey and the visitor.

"Do you sleep alone?" asked Janey, as Thea stood looking at the pleasant view, so different from the grim rooftops and dusty windows which peered in at their house.

"Yes, I do now," replied Thea, "though –" with a momentary tremor – "I used to sleep with Mother."

"I wish I slept with Mother, or alone." Janey glared resentfully at the stiff white coverlet of Nurse's bed. She

27

put her finger in her mouth again, regarding Thea thought-fully. "Mother says that Aunt Belle is very beautiful."

"She is, oh she is!" cried Thea. Tears rushed into her eyes but her pale little face was suddenly glowing, and she clutched Janey's hand with rare and unexpected emotion. Like most shy people, Thea was slow at making friends. She had developed, moreover, from living with grown-ups, a critical and detached habit of observation. She was accustomed to sitting in the room while Nan's clients called, perfectly silent, entirely self-effacing, as she carefully examined their clothes, their features, their manner of speech, and passed judgement upon them. But towards Janey, Thea felt immediately a strong and warm liking. Before they turned away from the window, she knew that Janey was her friend.

When they returned to the nursery, they found the big square table already laid for tea, with high square stacks of bread-and-butter and a single, solid home-made cake. In the corner of the room, a small boy was sitting on the floor, surrounded by odd screws and pieces of tin. "That's Andy," said Janey casually. The small boy remained engrossed in his occupation.

"What's he doing?" asked Thea.

"Oh, taking something to pieces. He's always taking things to pieces."

"Andrew," said Nurse, who was finishing laying the table, "come and say 'How do you do' to your cousin."

And now Thea began to realise that Nurse's gentle and sweet countenance was a snare and an illusion, for Andrew meekly put down three screws, a nut and a spanner, got to his feet and came over, wordlessly extending his hand. "How do you do?" said Thea, gravely.

"Very well, thank you," he replied, and started back to his corner.

"Andrew," said Nurse, who had her back turned, "don't start playing with that again. Go and wash your hands."

"But, I've only got to—"

"Andrew!"

Andrew went, without more argument, and Janey looked after him with amused affection.

"What does he do," asked Thea, "when he's taken them to pieces?"

"Why, then he puts them together again."

"He's awfully young to play with things like that, isn't he?" said Thea, looking at the bewildering confusion in his corner.

"He's got Concentration," said Nurse, severely.

Further moral teaching was prevented by the entrance of Lydia, with James close upon her heels. Lydia was very cold and distant, mindful of the recent quarrel, until Nurse said, "Now then, Lydia, don't you start Getting Up with me." Then she relapsed into a sulky child. James, hungry and noisy, was immediately subdued by Nurse and sent to clean fingernails found to contain a liberal supply of garden earth. Andrew's return was heralded by a shrill whistling, reminiscent of a train at a platform. This subsequently changed to a wailing noise, interspersed with angry protests.

"Andrew, stop that noise," cried Nurse, going to the door, and speaking only slightly louder than usual.

"She fed my rabbit," he roared, rubbing his fists in invisible tears. "I saw her. She fed my rabbit."

Behind him, came a thin little girl, a few years older than Janey, looking a little dazed by the noise, as well she might.

"I didn't," she protested, "I didn't."

"I saw her from the bathroom," shouted Andrew, "I saw her."

"Did you, Charlotte?" asked Nurse, calmly.

Charlotte sighed. "I only pushed a lettuce-leaf through," she said. "It looked sort of hungry, so I gave it a lettuce-leaf. It liked it."

"It didn't," Andrew shouted, hiccuping still with unseen tears. "It didn't like it. It hated it. It wasn't hungry."

"It's nothing to make a fuss about," Nurse said. She turned

29

to Charlotte. "Why did you do it?" she asked, sternly. "You know he doesn't like it."

"I didn't think he'd see," said Charlotte, pouting and unrepentant.

"I'd know if I didn't see," Andrew said, darkly. "I always know."

"Be quiet, and don't be silly," said Nurse, repressively. "Sit down, all of you. Tea's ready. Thea, will you sit here."

"Andy doesn't often get cross," Janey remarked to Thea, under cover of the general movement, "but when he does, he's awful." She regarded her brother with the same fond pride that Thea had noticed before.

When they were all seated and the silence occurred which should take place in all families at the beginning of a meal, when everyone concentrates without interruption upon the satisfying of hunger, Thea looked round at each member of her new companions in turn. She noticed that they were all dark, except for Andrew, and that he was further remarkable for a pair of very beautiful eyes. They were large and brown, not with the liquid softness of spaniel eyes, but glowing with golden lights, lively and wide awake. Of them all, Charlotte was the only one who did not look vigorous and healthy. She was angular and white-faced, with shoulders that tended to droop, despite Nurse's constant reminders. Charlotte alone was a plain child. James and Lydia were handsome, Janey was pretty and Andrew had that quality, which cannot be analysed, of charm. There was something attractive in his smile, with the two large front teeth, which reminded Thea of pictures of baby rabbits. His voice, when he was not in a temper, was sweet and soft, and his fair hair fell away from a high, wide forehead. Thea noticed that all the family were more tolerant of his faults than of each other's, that they treated him with a fond indulgence. She noticed also that Nurse was very strict with him, and never realised that this was intentional and politic. She noticed that James ate with a wholehearted enthusiasm, that Charlotte ate very little, that

Janey seemed to consider eating a welcome but serious duty, that Andrew, with a dreamy look upon his face, put in some useful work, and that Lydia, in a graceful, ladylike way, ate quite as much as anyone else, if not a little more. Janey, in the first pause for breath, glanced round the table and then remarked sadly, "James can eat more than I can, but he still stays thin."

"That's because I'm energetic," replied James. "You don't run about enough."

"Don't speak with your mouth full," put in Nurse, "and, Charlotte, take your elbows off the table."

Thea removed hers swiftly and glanced furtively at Nurse. That admirable woman poured out milk, without so much as a twitch of her lips.

"Lydia eats a lot and keeps thin, too," Janey said, with the air of continuing her last remark. She could carry on a monologue, despite any irrelevant intervening comments.

"Never you mind about whether you're thin or not," said Nurse. "It's whether you're healthy that counts."

"I'd rather be thin than healthy," said Janey, mournfully.

"You shouldn't be so wicked," Nurse replied, closing the matter. "You count your blessings."

Thea sat listening to the conversation, looking out of the window past Lydia's head at the wide road and the bare plane trees, with a feeling of unreality growing upon her. When had all this happened to her before? When had she sat in that big room, with the white cloth spread for tea? When had she sat with this family, listening to this talk? She stopped eating for a moment, and it was as though everything stopped. The clock stopped ticking, the voices came from far away, she was poised in eternity, and all that happened was strange and familiar and ancient as Time itself. Then Nurse spoke, and all she said was, "Will you have some more milk, Thea?" but the spell was broken, the clock was ticking, and Thea was in the room again, an ordinary little girl, visiting her cousins, with the magic moment gone.

"Dad's going to take us to the Tower of London, tomorrow," said Janey.

"Us?" queried Thea.

"All of us."

Thea gasped. She nearly said, "Won't it be very expensive?" but bit it back in time.

"Queen Elizabeth built it, didn't she?" said Lydia, with a casual show of knowledge, which was immediately spoilt by James.

"No, silly, because Walter Raleigh was shut up there."

"Perhaps she built it for him."

"No, it was built ages before then."

"I expect Christopher Wren built it," put in Janey, hopefully. The other two shouted with laughter.

"Well, he built a lot of things," she said, quite undisturbed. "Dad said so."

"King Arthur built it," said Charlotte, as one stating a fact.

"He couldn't," answered Lydia, "because he didn't exist."

"Yes, he did," Thea said quickly, and then blushed, and wished that she had kept quiet. "I've got a book . . ." she began, and then realised that it was not quite true and stopped in painful confusion. James broke in quickly, as he always did when someone was in trouble.

"Of course he existed, but I don't think he built the Tower."

"I expect it was Edward the First," said Lydia.

"William the Conqueror," suggested James.

"*I* built it," announced Andrew, emerging milkily from his mug, and was told by Nurse not to be silly.

"Who did build it, Nurse?" asked Janey of the oracle.

"You should learn that from your history books," replied Nurse, and Thea saw Lydia and James exchange an amused glance. She herself thought that it was probably the work of that diligent fellow, Julius Caesar, but had not the courage to say so.

"May I have some more cake, Nurse?" asked James, too casually.

"No, you know you're only allowed one piece."

"But it was a very small piece."

"Are you hungry?" asked Nurse. James hesitated. If he said "yes", she would tell him to eat bread-and-butter. If he said "no", she would say that he didn't want any cake. He wisely kept on firm ground, and repeated, "It was a very small piece." Nurse silently cut him another piece of cake.

"Nurse!" cried Lydia, outraged.

"No business of yours," said Nurse, shortly. "You had a big piece to begin with."

When tea was finished, and Nurse had piled the cups and plates on a very small tray and carried it away, Janey said with importance.

"Now we'll go and see Mother."

Thea was prepared to go straight downstairs, but found that she must first wash her hands again, comb her hair, and smooth out her dress, following Janey's example, and was informed that "Mother likes us to look nice." It occurred to her, however, that this ritual was undertaken more upon Nurse's behalf than her aunt's, since they were seized upon by the small tyrant, on the stairs, and minutely inspected, before they were allowed to continue.

The drawing room was, like the rest of the house, large and airy, but full of furniture, of odd little tables and chairs, of china ornaments and miniatures and photographs. Aunt Mary sat in front of a small fire, sewing, and her voice, in reply to Janey's knock on the door, was sweet and low. She looked up and smiled as they advanced, saying, "Thea, dear, how nice to see you." The fragrance of her soft cheek, as Thea bent over to kiss her, was like primroses new-picked from green woods, and she pulled Thea gently down on to a stool beside her, and asked about Nan, about Belle, about Thea's school and friends.

"Mother," said Janey, suddenly, "is Aunt Belle your sister?"

"No, dear, my cousin."

"Then you're not really Thea's aunt?"

"No, if she liked, she could call me Cousin Mary," she answered, smiling.

"Then, Nan—" began Thea, puzzled.

"My mother was Nan's sister." She looked at the two frowning little faces. "Nan is my aunt."

"Goodness," said Thea, and fell into deep thought. How was it that Nan and Aunt Mary's mother, starting from the same family, had fallen into such different ways of life? How was it that Aunt Mary could sit in this spacious, gracious, quiet room, sewing a fine embroidered cloth, while her mother was imprisoned in the dark little sitting room, stitching eternally at Mrs Fairs's black, or at other hated garments? She remembered Nan's thin, lined face, her grey hair, wispy and untidy, her shabby old grey dress which she wore 'for best', her red, pricked fingers with the permanently-installed thimble. Aunt Mary's face was as smooth as a girl's, her forehead without a crease, her dark hair beautifully piled on her head, with natural little curls on the brow. She wore a lavender silk dress with sleeves puffed above the elbow and with fine lace draped over the shoulders and the front of the bodice. Her hands were small, white and smooth, with a ruby ring and two more diamond rings as well as her wedding ring. Watching the golden rose spreading its petals over the white linen, the delicate fingers smoothing the silk, Thea felt a sudden stab of disloyalty to the dark little room at home, to the red curtains, the threadbare carpet, thick always with a shedding of pins, to the unfinished garments behind the door, to harassed, weary Nan, and to her mother, so beautiful, so dear, so shut in. Why could not their house be light and clean and airy, without that perpetual smell of cooking, creeping incorrigibly from the too-near kitchen? Why could it not look out on to a garden gay with spring flowers, breathing fresh breezes from the fields beyond? Why could not her mother be the gracious mistress of a large house, with a noisy, friendly, loving family, with a life made permanent and secure by dear and unfailing ties? There was a short silence as she thought of all this. The flames whispered in the hearth, birds twittered outside the window, and Aunt Mary's budgerigar sang in its cage. From upstairs, as from another planet, incalculably distant, James's voice called, "Nurse!" But, *Why?* thought Thea, and *Why?* and *Why?* and still the birds sang in the fading evening light.

Back in the nursery, Janey began to introduce Thea to the Bloggs Family, who inhabited the huge dolls' house. It was while they were trying to seat Miss Edwina Bloggs at the dining table, that Nurse called Janey. Born, clearly, of a Brobdignagian line, Miss Edwina persistently overturned the dining table, which was perhaps unnecessarily small, or kicked her father in the face with unfilial violence. Consequently, Janey said, "Coming," and forgot the summons, while they wrestled with the refractory young lady. It was not until they had persuaded her to sit down, and were retrieving Mr Bloggs from under the table, whither he had weakly slid, that Nurse appeared in the doorway of the nursery, saying quietly, "Didn't you hear me call you?" Janey scrambled to her feet looking scared, but said peevishly, "I was just coming."

"Go and put your things away in the night-nursery," said Nurse, adding over her shoulder, "and you won't be going out tomorrow with your father. He doesn't like disobedient children." She went out, and Janey sat down suddenly upon the floor, while Thea looked at her helplessly. Lydia had been reading at the table, but she came over to Janey immediately and knelt down beside her, saying in a new voice, "She doesn't really mean it, Baby. She'll let you go." Janey's face was slowly puckering, and she only waited to say, "She does this time," before dissolving into a deluge of tears.

James, coming in at that moment, said in surprise, "What's up?"

"Nurse says," Thea explained, uncertainly, "that Janey can't go tomorrow."

He whistled, and looked at Lydia. "Does she mean it?" he asked. Lydia nodded over Janey's head, and then said briskly, "If I were you, Baby, I should go and put the things away, so as not to make her any crosser." Janey trailed sadly away, and Lydia, still on her knees, looked up at James. "She meant it, all right," she said.

"Ask Mother to do something," James suggested. Lydia nodded.

"I'll go and ask her now."

"Don't look so miserable, Thea," James recommended, "Mother will do something."

Thea was puzzled. Before tea, Lydia had called James a beast, they had wrangled over who built the Tower, and Lydia and Janey had had a brief but fierce passage of arms over Janey's kitten, who had been sharpening its claws on Lydia's knitting. Yet now these quarrels, which would have overshadowed Thea's evening, seemed to be entirely forgotten. She noticed that Charlotte, in the corner, was assisting Andrew with an intricate piece of machinery, her long, straight, black hair falling over his shoulder. It was all incomprehensible.

A little later, they were all once more in the nursery, Nurse darning socks in a grimly distant manner, as though she knew that public opinion was against her. Janey and Thea were listlessly ordering the affairs of the Bloggs family, of whom Albert Bloggs had died suddenly and was about to be buried with full military honours. They both felt that they were burying all Janey's worldly hopes. The door opened, after a quiet knock, and Aunt Mary came in. Nurse stood up, and said, very politely, "Good-evening, Madam," while the children chorused a glad greeting.

"Have they all been good?" she asked, smiling as though sure that they had.

"All except Jane, Madam," replied Nurse, still frigid.

"And Nurse says," choked Janey, "that I can't go out tomorrow."

"Oh, Janey," said Aunt Mary, gravely. "Well, perhaps if you are *very* good all the rest of the evening, Nurse might let you go, as Thea's here. I should be very good and see." She smiled at Nurse, and came further into the room, looking at Lydia's book and James's, at Charlotte's painting and at Andrew's odd little junk-heap. Janey's hand crept out and clasped Thea's. Nurse continued with her darning. Aunt Mary turned back towards the door, and, as her eyes met Thea's, she smiled in a meaningful, amused way, before saying, "I'll come and see you when you're in bed."

After her departure, Janey insisted on resurrecting Albert Bloggs and celebrating his birthday, while Nurse, still grim, took Andrew off to bed five minutes before his proper time. When she summoned Janey and Thea, their eager obedience was pretty to see, and they prepared for bed with a docility that was as rare as it was efficacious. Nurse kissed Thea goodnight, in a cool, businesslike way, and turned to Janey.

"Nurse."

"Well?"

"Can I go tomorrow, Nurse?"

"I shall have to see."

"Oh, *please*, Nurse."

"Very well, if you're a good girl."

"Oh Nurse, oh, thank you."

"But, no talking, mind, when I turn the gas out."

"Oh no, Nurse."

She extinguished the light and left them. Janey soon went to sleep, exhausted by sorrow and joy. Thea lay on her back, her legs straight out, looking at the thin streak of light through the curtains. She could hear the water running in the bathroom, where Charlotte had been overtaken by the insatiable monster, Bedtime. An unnatural hush from the nursery showed that James and Lydia hoped that Nurse might forget them, a hope ever-renewed and always unavailing. The ugly little dark house seemed a long way away. Nan and her mother would be sewing under the bubbling gas and, in a little while, Emily would be coming in to lay the table for supper. She saw, quite clearly, her mother's face, concentrated upon her work, with the little lines of humour round her eyes, and the framework of soft, shining red-gold hair. She would be missing Thea and worrying about her, and the little room upstairs would be empty when she went to bed. Janey's deep, regular breathing accentuated Thea's loneliness, and tears of homesickness were close to her eyes when the door opened and a shaft of light fell across the dark room. Aunt Mary came softly in, her dress rustling, and bent over Thea, who suddenly reached up with her arms and clung to her with a catch of the breath, and was held close and petted in gentle embrace. Then Aunt Mary tucked her in and said, quite in the way of her mother, "Go to sleep now, dear," and she turned over and sighed in contentment, hardly hearing Janey's half-waking murmur of "Goodnight, Mother." In another moment, it was morning, Nurse was drawing the curtains and James and Lydia were wrangling loudly over the bathroom.

Four

Feeding the rabbits was a ritual that took place every morning after breakfast. In term-time, it was hurried through, and the care of James's grey Angora fell to the lot of Janey, but in the holidays it became a meeting place, with discussion of plans for the day, and mutual advice for feeding and medicine. Recriminations were temporarily laid aside, and an armistice was presided over by the beady eyes and twitching noses of ruminating rabbits.

"My rabbit's called John Cassius," announced Andrew, pointing to a wary creature who, shrinking back into his hutch, seemed to indicate that food could be too dearly bought.

"That's a funny – I mean, why did you call it that?" asked Thea.

"Dad named him," Andrew answered proudly. "He just looked at him and said 'John Cassius has a lean an' hungry look,' so I called him John Cassius." It was many years before Thea saw the joke, and when she did, she cried instead of laughing.

Andrew drew the mournful animal out of its refuge and hugged it to him, fondling its drooping ears. "He's a very 'fectionate rabbit," he said, looking up at Thea with his great brown eyes. "He likes being kissed." The rabbit submitted to a wet kiss upon its nose and, on being restored to its hutch, fled into the farthest corner and sat down with its back turned. Thea felt that only its physical peculiarities prevented it from putting both paws up to its ears and hunching its shoulders.

Andrew regarded it fondly. "You see, he's sorry I've put him back," he pointed out. Thea was grateful for the information. She would never have guessed it from the rabbit's behaviour.

Uncle Robert had only come home late the night before, after they were in bed, and departed early for his office in the morning. He was to return directly after lunch, to take them on the promised expedition. Thea's first impression of him, as he awaited them in the hall, was that he was a very upright man. He was tall and broad-shouldered, and held himself very straight and square. She subsequently realised that he was not merely upright in carriage. James once said of his father that he was always asked to take the bag round in a strange church. Thea thought of this as rather a fine epitaph. He was, above all, a just man. He might be hard sometimes, but he would never be prejudiced or unjust. Thea was at first considerably in awe of him, with his black beard and imperial and heavy eyebrows. But she soon noticed that his blue eyes had a kindly twinkle in them, and learnt that very often when he spoke gravely, he was joking, and that it was safe to laugh. He treated all the children with a serious consideration. He never talked down to them, or was heavily jocular. If he made a joke, it was not at their expense, but for their amusement, even if the jokes were often beyond their comprehension.

In after years, Thea used to look back upon that day with an awed wonder that she could ever have been so happy and so carefree. Occasionally, she would think of her mother, and wish that she were there but, for the most part, it was as though she had never had any family but this one, as though Uncle Robert was her father, and these were her brothers and sisters. No one who has grown up as a member of a big family could realise the wistful, pitiful envy with which such a position is regarded by an only child. The advantages of a number of relations are so familiar that they are taken for granted, or, indeed, overlooked, obscured by the more obvious disadvantages of loss of privacy or brutal misunder-standing. With your family there is no need to keep up appearances, and no use in it. They know your very thoughts, your faults and virtues, and love you neither for your faults nor your virtues, but because you are yourself.

Something of this Thea perceived on that sunny spring morning, as she slipped unobtrusively into their fellowship. Like a wild creature, conscious of a safe refuge, she effaced herself silently and thankfully in her surroundings and from that comfortable obscurity enjoyed the excitement and variety of the day's expedition. Always, looking back on those few hours of delight, she saw, as a symbol of her happiness, Andrew, in his sailor suit and navy-blue stockings, with the absurd round cap pushed back on his fair hair, skipping eagerly along to keep up with his father's long strides. On the train, in the cab, in the Tower itself, it was Andrew, his golden-brown eyes wide and astonished, who lingered clearly in her memory. Missing him for a moment, they turned back and found him standing in front of a Beefeater, regarding him with a bright, pleased look, though in perfect silence, while the magnificent figure, serenely conscious of the picturesque, if unusual costume, gazed back at him with calm approval. When Lydia, running officiously to bring him along, took him by the hand, he started and, turning readily to her, said in a high, loud voice, "Isn't he beautiful?" and even the impassive countenance of the great man relaxed into a smile. When he had carefully examined the dungeons, Andrew said to their guide, with a judicial air, "Rabbits wouldn't like it."

"Wouldn't like what?" asked the man, bewildered.

"Down here," Andrew explained. "Too dark."

"It wasn't meant for rabbits," the man protested, with the aggrieved air of an innkeeper, whose accommodation is being criticised.

"No," Andrew agreed, calmly, "rabbits wouldn't like it."

The man opened his mouth for further defence of the apartments, but closed it again with a silent acknowledgement

41

of defeat, while Lydia looked embarrassed and even Uncle Robert was barely able to conceal his amusement.

When they had thoroughly explored the Tower and considered it architecturally, historically, and from such practical viewpoints as whether you could defend it from attack and where the boiling lead would be stored, or where was the most strategical point for a charge of gunpowder, were a new Guy Fawkes to transfer his attention to it, Uncle Robert led them to a tea-shop, where he had hot buttered toast and rich cakes spread before them, and sat back with a glint of mischief in his eyes to watch them demolish it.

"Janey will be sick," threatened Lydia; as her sister embarked upon her fourth cake."

"I doubt it," replied Uncle Robert. "I have a higher opinion of Janey's capabilities than you have."

James and Thea began to laugh, while Lydia looked annoyed and Janey licked her fingers and opened her eyes in placid surprise.

"In fact," Uncle Robert added, looking thoughtfully at his younger son, "I should have thought that Andrew was imperilling his digestion rather more."

"Oh, Andrew's never sick," Lydia answered disgustedly, and Andrew, partially embedded in a doughnut, nodded his confirmation.

After tea, the children were all sleepy and, once installed in the railway carriage on the homeward journey, there was little more conversation. Andrew climbed on to Lydia's lap and settled down to sleep. Charlotte, who had eaten less than anybody, was white-faced and feeling sick. Such is the unfairness of human rewards. James took her to the window and stood talking to her to make her forget it. Thea leant against her uncle with a drowsy sense of well-being. She was only partly woken from her doze when he lifted her on to his knee and rested her head against his shoulder. She smiled up at him with the simple friendliness and trust of a sleepy child, closed her eyes again, and went to sleep in earnest, the whirr and chatter of the wheels upon the railway lines blending slowly into her slumber. Only, as she slid into unconsciousness, was she aware of the strong gentleness of his arm about her, and of a wish that this were her father, that the safety and comfort of his protection were hers by right.

The day after their visit to the Tower of London, it rained. It was the sort of rain that could not be ignored. It came down in a steady and determined way which indicated its intention of continuing to fall all day, and probably during the next night. The children, disconsolate and cross, huddled in the nursery, glaring up at the grey sky, and scowling at the puddles on the path. They had intended to go out and fly their kites, and nothing else would satisfy them. It was in vain for Nurse to point out that they could fly their kites on the next day. Like all grown-ups, she could not understand time. To a child, there is no tomorrow. There is only today. So the children sat and stared at the rain, feeling that life held no joy but that of flying kites, and that they could only be flown on that one day.

"I know," said Thea, suddenly, remembering their conversation at tea on the day of her arrival, "let's play at being King Arthur's knights."

The others considered the proposition, singly, and then in council, and pronounced it good.

"James had better be Launcelot," Thea said, unblushingly.

"I'll be Guenevere," announced Lydia, scorning to admit that she had had designs upon the Greatest Knight herself.

"Oh no, you can't be!" cried Thea, wildly.

"Why not?"

Thea was silent, scarlet in the face.

"Thea ought to be Guenevere," said Janey, "as she's the visitor."

"I'm the oldest," began Lydia.

"I'm Elaine, the Fair Maid of Astolat," Thea stated firmly.

The others looked at her, puzzled and uncertain.

43

"Then why can't I be Guenevere?" asked Lydia, preparing to pick up her skirts and sweep out of the room in wounded majesty.

"You can be, it's only—" Thea stopped again, close to tears.

"That's all right then," broke in James, quickly. "Janey, what will you be?"

Janey, after a lot of thought and promptings, chose the gentle Tristram and Charlotte startled the assembly by choosing to be Mordred, the traitor.

"I'm King Arthur," said Andrew.

"You can't be—" Lydia began, but James said cheerfully, "He might as well be. King Arthur never does anything. He just sits on his throne and sends the knights out, and listens to their stories."

The nursery thundered to the hooves of chargers, the high challenges to single combat, the ferocious clamour of tournaments. Guenevere was rescued from countless towers, and Mordred perished a dozen times. The Fair Maid, dangerously poised upon two rush-bottomed chairs, floated down to Camelot, and thereafter made herself useful as a spare knight, a spare lady, La Belle Isolde (dying gracefully on Tristram's crumpled pinafore) and Sir Bedevere, flinging a real sword, stolen from over the dining-room mantelpiece, out over the mere. And over it all, smiling benevolently from a chair on the nursery table, sat King Arthur, a crown upon his head and a black and sooty sceptre in his right hand.

"Why didn't you want Lydia to be Guenevere?" asked James of Thea afterwards, when Lydia had disappeared to visit relations with her mother. Thea, staring out at the wet garden, hesitated.

"It doesn't matter," James said, seeing her undecided. "I only wondered."

"You'll think it's silly," said Thea. "It was only that . . ." She looked at his gentle, kind face and smiled. "My aunt's got a book," she explained, "with pictures in it of all the Knights. There's a picture of Elaine, and she's sort of like me, only

44

much nicer, of course. And there's a picture of Guenevere, and she's got hair that's just the colour of Mother's, and I always think of her as Guenevere. Her eyes are the same colour too, and she's, oh she's beautiful."

"I see," said James, and Thea felt that he really did understand.

"It was silly," she said. "It was just that for the moment, I didn't want anyone else to . . . to take Mother's place."

"And did King Arthur look like Andrew, holding the poker?" asked James, teasingly, and Thea, laughing, forgot her distress.

On the next day, they went and flew their kites. Thea awoke in the morning with an uncomfortable feeling that something was resting on her feet. Nurse was pulling the curtains as usual, and, as the clear light fell across her bed, she could see a strange shape, a brown parcel, variously pointed.

"Nurse!"

"Yes, Thea?"

"There's something on my bed."

"Is there?"

"Do you know what it is?"

"I should open it. Perhaps it's for you."

So Thea untied the string, and pulled off the paper, and sat gasping at the sight of a blue kite, with a long string of multicoloured streamers for a tail, and a big notice with 'For Thea, from Aunt Mary and Uncle Robert' printed on it and attached to the end of the tail.

"Oh, Nurse! Oh Nurse, isn't it wonderful. Oh, isn't it beautiful! Is it really for me? Can I keep it?"

For a moment, Nurse disappeared, and in her place was a gentle little woman, who smiled and put her arms round Thea, saying in a voice somewhere between amusement and pain, "Of course you can keep it. It's a present."

Then Janey woke up and admired the kite, and Nurse reappeared, saying briskly, "Come along now, get up. You'll be late for breakfast." But between Thea and Nurse was a secret understanding, such as could never exist between Nurse and her charges.

"Mrs Fitt always comes on Saturdays," said Janey, as they walked back from the hill, their kites limp and tame in their arms, all their mad leaping and wildness stilled.

"Who's Mrs Fitt?"

"Our dressmaker," Janey answered.

"But, what's her real name?"

"That is her real name, honestly." Janey laughed at Thea's incredulous face. "Maybe that's why she became a dressmaker."

Thea smiled, but she could not help wondering if Mrs Fitt would be like Nan.

The dressmaker was not, in fact, like Nan in appearance or in manner. She was an ugly, sharp-faced woman, who, like many of her profession, dressed herself very badly. But she was painfully and perseveringly bright.

"How are you, Mrs Fitt?" said Nurse, rather absently, as she sorted out clothes for alteration.

"Oh, not too bad. I can't complain. We're as young as we feel, you know."

"And your husband?"

"Oh well," answered Mrs Fitt, with more determined brightness than ever, as though she were afraid that she might not sound convincing, "he's doing pretty nicely, thank you, considering. Things are never so bad that they couldn't be worse. Of course, he's very weak still, but they say the darkest hour is before the dawn." By this time, Mrs Fitt had pulled a dress over Janey's head, and the pins in her mouth impeded her speech a little, but not seriously.

"Everyone's very kind, and every cloud has a silver lining, as the saying goes. And I always say, a friend in need is a friend indeed. What did you want done to this? Taken in a little here, yes? And let down a little. Miss Janey, you're getting thinner and taller, not that you want to be too skinny, but there, it's always the way, we always want what we haven't got."

As Mrs Fitt paused for breath and to replace pins in her mouth, Nurse managed to say, "Stand still, Janey," before the dressmaker began again.

"There's a little place wants mending here, a stitch in time saves nine, you know. Well, as I was saying, troubles never come singly, for my aunt has just died, a little lower in the waist, don't you think? And then they always say that one funeral means there'll be another soon, and my mother's been very poorly lately, but still, there's no use looking for trouble. Never cross bridges before you come to them, my poor father used to say."

Thea, listening to this ridiculous flood of speech, felt unreasonably annoyed. She felt that Mrs Fitt was in some way making Nan, and even her mother, look foolish, that Mrs Fitt might be taken as the pattern for all dressmakers. Still the woman went on talking, with the familiar dressmaking terms mingled with an account of her professional triumphs, ("Mrs Fitt, she said, I don't know how you do it, I really don't.") and of her sister's boy, whose head was "a mass of curls", and of countless other members of her family, who seemed to Thea to be tiresome folk, much given to painful illnesses and to quarrelling with their neighbours. Nurse, keeping a wary eye upon the progress of the fitting, said, "Really!" or "Well, I never!" at intervals.

When Mrs Fitt had gone downstairs to have her lunch, Thea asked Nurse what was wrong with Mrs Fitt's husband.

"He's paralysed," Nurse replied, briefly.

"But – was he always paralysed?"

"No, only a few years ago. He had an accident, and he hasn't been able to work since."

"Oh, Nurse, how dreadful." Thea felt shocked, and in a strange way, indignant. Mrs Fitt wasn't the sort of person to have a trouble of that sort. She was too foolish, too trivial. Tragic people should be dignified and fine. La Belle Isolde

47

could be tragic, or the Fair Maid of Astolat, or Guenevere. But, Mrs Fitt . . .

"You wouldn't think it," she said, tentatively, to Nurse.

"No, she bears up wonderfully, considering," Nurse answered, but absently again, as though she had said it rather too often. "Her father's just died, too," she added, "so she has to help to support her mother as well."

"You wouldn't think that such a thing would happen to . . . to *her*," persisted Thea.

Nurse paused, and looked at her. "Things like that can happen to anyone," she said grimly.

Thea was silent, considering this. She had always thought that there were people who were set aside for tragedy from the beginning. If the lives of quiet, ordinary people could be thus overturned, who was safe? Need one not be great to know tragedy? Was obscurity not enough to ensure immunity? She thought of Nan and her grandfather. She remembered her mother, and the dim shadow that lay upon all mention of her father. What can one do, she thought, to be safe? Aunt Mary, she thought, was safe. Nothing had ever touched her. She was sheltered by her staunch and loving husband, by children who adored her. This family at Enfield lived in a magic circle, protected and secure. She was herself for a brief time within that shelter, but she would soon leave them for the defencelessness and uncertainty of her own life. Fear of the unknown future held her trembling once more, a grey fog swirling before her.

Five

" Rabbits haven't got much ambition," James remarked, lazily tickling the grey Angora under the chin with a blade of grass.

"John Cassius has," began Andrew.

"For goodness sake shut up about your beastly rabbit," cried Lydia. "No one's interested in it."

"But he's—"

"No, I agree," James broke in. "Shut up about it, Andy. No one wants to talk about it, except you."

"I expect they all think that when they grow up they'll escape and live in green fields," Thea suggested.

"I don't think so," said James. "I think they just like living in hutches and eating what they're given." He shuddered. "Just think of living in a hutch all your life."

"You might say that we live in hutches all our lives," said Lydia. "After all, houses are only like hutches with two storeys."

"I shan't live in a hutch all my life," James said energetically. "I shall go to sea."

"Dad wouldn't let you," said Lydia. "Besides, I wouldn't like the Navy much. And ships are like hutches."

"Pooh, I wouldn't join the Navy – too much ordering about. I shall run away and go aboard a merchant ship. And we'll sail right round the world, and fight with pirate ships in the . . . in the Caribbean Sea, and battle with storms round the Horn, and drop anchor off the South Sea Islands."

"Merchant ships don't carry guns," said Lydia, but James

did not hear her. The throb and quiver of the ship lay beneath him, a grey and white path churning in her wake. There was the taste of salt on his lips, and the wind flung itself against his body. His lean brown face was still and intent, his grey eyes shone with distant visions. He was Sir Richard Grenville, the little "Revenge" leaping at his command between the great Spanish galleons, until she lay in the unnatural calm under their bows. He was Drake, he was Raleigh. His hands were upon the wheel and the ship fought like an unbroken colt under his touch, the wet canvas roaring above.

"Well, I shall be a great writer," said Lydia, impatient of these idealistic dreams. "I shall be famous and very rich."

"What will you write about?" enquired James, swallowing the anchor, and speaking with deceptive innocence.

"I shall write about . . . about . . ." Lydia paused. What would she write about? She pretended not to see James's happy grin. "I shall write about everything!" she cried, flinging out a hand and hurting her finger against the corner of the rabbit hutch.

"I should," James advised, kindly. "Don't leave anything out."

"What will you do, Thea?" asked Janey. Thea hesitated, and then replied quickly, "I don't know, what about you?"

"I shall get married," said little Janey, firmly, "and have four children, two girls and two boys, and I shall have two kittens."

"Oh, have two children and four cats," James begged. "And I'll take them to sea with me, and drown the kittens in the Spanish Main, and maroon the children on a desert island." He was laughing now at himself as well as the others, the sardonic compression back in the corners of his mouth.

"What will you do, Charlotte?" enquired Janey.

"I don't know," she murmured, dreamily. "I don't know. Something."

Thea turned and looked at her. Charlotte was sitting with her hands clasped round her knees. As she spoke, she put one hand between the young curves at her breast, as though to still a beating pulse, or a sudden pain. She had lost one of her hair-ribbons and the long black tresses fell over her shoulder, shading her face, lending to it an unexpected charm, so that, with the black hair and the fine bones of her face, the thin black eyebrows and dreaming eyes and the hollow paleness of her cheeks, she looked for a moment like a beautiful enchantress.

"You never know what Charlotte's thinking," said James, watching her. Charlotte started, as though aware that she was giving away a secret. She shook back her hair and said impatiently, "What's the good of making plans? Nothing ever happens as you want it to." She hunched her shoulders again and clasped her knees, with the sulkiness back round her mouth, her face sharp and plain. "And if you plan things," she added, "they don't happen, but if you don't –" she paused, and then finished, as though to herself – "if you don't, they might."

James is right, thought Thea. You never know what Charlotte's thinking. The others played and talked and squabbled in familiar fellowship, James and Janey, Lydia in a strange alliance with Andrew, but Charlotte walked alone. She was not unfriendly or rebellious, but remote. She joined in the family activities readily enough, but silently and in her own fashion. Who but Charlotte would have chosen to play the part of Mordred, the traitor knight? Who but Charlotte would have tied her kite to a fence and lain the whole afternoon on her back, still and rapt, watching it leap and curvette against the blue sky, while the others ran and laughed and shouted? Yet the others never wondered at her or questioned her behaviour. She was Charlotte. They took her for granted, as they accepted Nurse, or Mrs Fitt, or Thea herself. One of their unspoken rules was that each of them was entitled to a certain privacy of thought and opinion. It was possible to live, as Charlotte did, a remote and mysterious existence within the communal life of family activities. They took no notice of her now, as she sat, like the eternal spirit of childhood, clasping her knees and dreaming high, strange dreams in the spring sunshine.

Towards the end of the fortnight, Thea's thoughts turned, steadfast as the needle of a compass, in the direction of her home. She loved her cousins, especially James and Janey, and she was happy, busy and amused. But there was room in her heart only for her mother. The dark little house, the lone- liness, the constant anxiety about money, all this was as nothing, while she was with her mother. As the time of her departure drew near, her longing to see her mother increased. The whole family came to see her off at the station, except for Uncle Robert and Aunt Mary. She hated to leave them but once the train was on its way, southward bound, there was no thought in her heart except of her mother. What would she be wearing, how would she look? Thea could see her, standing on the platform, smiling, with her blue eyes alight with pleasure. She would open her arms and Thea would run into them, and they would be together again.

The train drew in at Abbot's Green. Thea dragged her bag out on to the wooden platform, too much occupied in looking for the dear, familiar figure to shut the door behind her. A porter jostled her, slamming the door. On the platform stood Nan, alone.

"Where's Mother?" cried Thea.

"She didn't come to the station," Nan answered, kissing her.

"Oh, Nan, is she ill?"

"No, no, of course not. Where's your ticket, dear?"

Thea surrendered her ticket and allowed herself to be led down the steps and out into the street. There was a puzzled look on her face, as though she had just woken up after walking in her sleep, and was wondering where she was. The vague fear which had troubled her since her last visit to Aunt Ruth, and which she had pushed away from her, became stronger. She answered Nan's questions, still with that abstracted look on her face. When they reached the house, she pulled her hand away from Nan's and ran up the garden path and inside. The sitting room was empty. She came out and found Nan hurrying after her.

"Where's Mother?" she cried. "Nan, where's Mother?"

"My dear," Nan answered, trembling, "she's gone away for a little while."

"But where?"

"To France. She had a chance of more pleasant employment and—" Thea waited for no more. She jerked away from Nan's restraining hand, crying wildly, "No! No, no, no! She couldn't, she just *couldn't* go away and leave me!"

"Thea, dear, she had to. You know how she always hated dressmaking. This way, she'll be able to save some money, and then, when you're a little older, you can go out and join her."

"No," said Thea, in a breathless, cold little voice. "No." She did not hear what Nan was saying. She knew that this was what she had feared and refused to believe, and she still tried not to believe it, as though, if she denied it often enough, it would not be true. She still half expected her mother to come in, having found that she could bear the separation no more than Thea, having gone only a few hours' journey away.

"When did she go?" she asked Nan, with sudden intentness.

"Last Friday, dear."

Then Thea knew suddenly that it was true, that she was alone, deserted, abandoned by her mother who had never failed her. She was crying in the dark, and no quick footsteps came up the stairs, no loving arms held her safe. There was only a chill, empty fog about her, and a pain in her chest, and despair such as she had never known. There was no faith or safety in the world, only treachery and pain.

The next few weeks had for Thea some of the quality of a nightmare, with moments of horror interspersed with periods of vague, misty discomfort. Sometimes, at school or doing her homework, she would pause and wonder why she felt so unhappy. Then she would remember, and the dull pain was sharp, the tenderness became agony. The greatest bitterness of this time was the realisation that her mother had been packing and booking her passage and saying her farewells while Thea herself had been cheerful and unconscious at Enfield. It spoilt the memory of those carefree weeks. She felt that she had been cheated into laughing and gaiety, that a trap had been baited at the end, and that she had fallen into it more heavily for being so unprepared. It was useless for Nan to say, with pathetic repetition, that Belle had only gone to France, that she would be home again in a year or two. To Thea, France was further away than Fairyland. One could reach Camelot in an afternoon, one could, in a breath of time, be aboard the Hispaniola, anchored off Treasure Island. Wonderland lay but through a looking-glass. But France was a thousand miles away, over the water, out of all reach. To her, it was as though her mother was dead. She never expected to see her again, and sometimes, as she sat at meals in sullen silence, she was holding in her mind, fiercely, as though pressing on a wound, her last picture of her mother, standing on the platform, smiling and waving, with tears in her eyes.

For Nan too these were weeks of torment. She hardly knew the sunny, contented, good-tempered little Thea, in this sullen, brooding child, who stared at her as at an enemy, and sat for hours in her room, doing nothing, only staring out of the window with old, sad eyes.

"If only she'd have a good cry and get it over," said Emily, and Nan replied anxiously, "I'm afraid she has more of her father in her than we thought. Belle would never have taken it like this."

"Miss Belle would've had a crying set-out that took the roof off," said Emily, approvingly, "and then all over and done with."

In the end, it was a little thing that broke the storm. Looking in her drawer for a handkerchief, Thea came on one which did not belong to her. She raised it to her face, and smelt immediately her mother's scent. As the fragrance of the handkerchief leapt up at her, Thea stood motionless for a moment, and then screamed as though someone had hit her, and burst into violent sobs. Nan, running upstairs, found her lying on the floor, the handkerchief clasped to her cheek, crying without any restraint. She held her close and soothed her, while Emily, who had heard the uproar, stood at the door, wiping her own eyes on a tea towel.

"Nan," said Thea, one day, "when did my father die?" They were sitting in the small patch of stones and grass, called alternately 'the lawn' and 'the rockery', which, with 'the shrubbery', comprised the garden. Nan was sewing as usual, while Thea, learning to knit, was manufacturing a garment whose width varied from row to row in an interesting way, and was moreover remarkable for occasional lace-work of a novel design.

"Your father?" answered Nan, vaguely.

Thea, thinking that she was trying to gain time to think, repeated with a little impatience, "My father, Nan. When did he die? He is dead, isn't he?"

"Yes," Nan replied. "Oh yes, he died, when . . . when you were born."

"Where, Nan?"

"In London."

"Oh." Thea looked at her. She was concentrating her attention earnestly upon a simple piece of hemming. "Did you like him?"

She started and looked up. "Did I . . . ?"

"Like him, my father?"

"Yes," said Nan, doubtfully.

"But . . ." Thea prompted.

"But, I liked some other men who wanted to marry your mother, more than him."

"What were they like?" asked Thea.

55

Nan smiled reminiscently and put down her work. "Well, there was Arthur Jervis. Your mother met him at Aunt Mary's house."

"Was he handsome?" asked Thea, hopefully.

"He was a fine-looking man," Nan answered, defensively. "He was very kind and affectionate and had plenty of money, a good position, and was generally respected."

"But, Nan, you shouldn't marry for money."

"Your grandfather," said Nan thoughtfully, "always used to say, 'Don't marry for money, but marry where money is.' " She was silent for a moment, but presently took up her work again and continued. "You mother liked Arthur, but she never could help teasing him. He was a little quiet, you know, and rather slow to see a joke. But I think she would have married him after a while."

"And?" Thea was spellbound by this new story.

"Then your mother met your father at a dance."

"What was she wearing?"

"She was wearing her blue silk. It was one of my dresses made over, but it suited her beautifully. She went with Arthur Jervis, and he'd given her a spray of white roses, though they were really out of season."

"Oh, lovely!" Blue silk gown, white shoulders, white roses, blue eyes and shining red-gold hair.

"Yes, she was looking very pretty," said Nan. "She was dancing a waltz with Arthur Jervis, when your father came in. He waited until it was over, then walked straight over and asked your mother for a dance, without even an introduction."

"And did she give him one?"

"Well, she might not have. Though . . . But, anyway, poor Arthur said something, and she deliberately crossed his name off her card for the next dance, and wrote Tom – your father's name – down instead. Arthur was very upset." Nan shook her head, but laughed.

"Was Father handsome, Nan?"

"Yes, very handsome," Nan replied, suddenly sober.

"What did he look like?"

"He had dark hair, and fine hazel eyes—"

"Like mine?" interrupted Thea.

"Yes," answered Nan, and fell silent.

"What happened then?"

"Well, he called quite often to see your mother. Arthur Jervis did too." Nan began to smile again. "It was very difficult, with them both coming in so often, and with your mother not able to make up her mind which of them she would marry. Arthur used to sit and glower, while Tom was talking and laughing, and paying pretty compliments. Arthur never could pay compliments. If he as much as told your mother that she looked nice, he said it as if he were ashamed of it. Tom could always make us laugh, and your mother likes laughing, you know." Was there a hint of bitterness in those words?

"And what happened in the end?" asked Thea, eager for the happy ending of the fairy-tale.

"Then your mother accepted Tom Lawrence," Nan answered shortly, "and they were married soon afterwards."

"I expect she was glad that she did," said Thea, thinking how dreadful it would have been if her mother had married the wealthy, respectable, dull Arthur Jervis. Nan made no reply. In the evening sun, her face looked very thin and white, the lines emphasised. She was frowning down at her work, and her eyes looked tired, her whole attitude one of weariness. With all the humour gone from it, her face looked old and discouraged.

"Was he poor, Nan?"

"Who?"

"My father."

"Yes, he never had much money." She got up, folding her sewing. "Come on, Thea, time for bed."

When Thea had bathed and said her prayers and been kissed good-night, it was still light, and she sat up in bed, looking out at the sunset sky, pale blue, with clouds like pink powder-puffs, and enviously watching Elsie Winter next door, who was allowed to stay up later, and was still playing in her garden. Considering the story she had just heard, she thought that her mother was like the princess in the fairy story who always chose the swineherd, rather than the prince. But her mother, she felt, had been cheated, since her swineherd, though as charming as all fairy-tale swineherds, had not discovered himself to be a prince in disguise, nor taken her away to a fairy palace, nor, apparently, happened upon a magic store of rich jewels. She thought of her father with longing. If only he had not died! She pictured him, like a younger Uncle Robert, or an older James. She thought of him laughing and making her mother laugh. She leant over to her looking-glass, and gazed into her own eyes, trying to see in them a glimpse of that handsome young man who had danced into her mother's life. Her pale little face stared back at her gravely, the soft, light hair standing out stiffly in curler-rags, to the detriment of all beauty. She smiled at herself then, and lay down in bed. The shrill voice of Elsie Winters came from far away, and she was soon asleep. But from that evening, she played a new game with herself. She would pretend that her father was alive, and in the house. Sometimes, she would talk to him, but mostly she was content to imagine that she heard his footsteps on the stairs, that he was coming to say good-night to her. Or, she would pretend that he was kept late at the office, and that she was waiting for him to come in. She would lie quite still in bed, listening for the sound of the front door opening, and his deep voice in the hall, and his quick step. At times, she so nearly believed in the game, that her heart would beat faster as she waited for him. Only one thing troubled her. The face of her father must remain shadowed. He had hazel eyes, like her own, but for the rest he bore only a resemblance to James, even to the half-mocking smile and the cleft chin.

Six

"You'd better tell the child," said Aunt Ruth, "if she doesn't know."

"Oh, she doesn't know," Nan replied, looking at Thea, engrossed but watchful at the table.

Doesn't know what? thought Thea, warily, turning over a page.

"I think you'd better tell her," said Aunt Ruth, getting slowly up from the imitation-Regency couch, and holding a lacy shawl about her. "She might begin to wonder—"

"I will if you like," Nan replied, "but children are very unobservant, you know. They just don't notice."

Thea, feeling increasingly that someone was trying to cheat her, tried to think what she should notice, but gave it up. Everything seemed quite normal, and Aunt Ruth's list of grievances had been even longer than usual. "The girl thinks that she can do what she likes just now. I have to go out into the kitchen sometimes when I don't feel like it, just to show her that she can't."

"Don't do too much, my dear," advised Nan, "let the house go for a bit."

"Oh, I can't, Mother. She broke my best vase today, and threw it in the dustbin without telling me. Fortunately, I heard something clink, so I went and had a look. And there it was, all covered with tea-leaves."

"Was that the purple one with the green vines?" asked Nan, with a twitch of the lips.

"Yes, my *best* one."

"But so ugly, I always thought."

"Yes, Mother, but it was a very *good* one," said Aunt Ruth, reprovingly. "Luckily, it was only broken into three pieces. I shall have it mended."

"How very lucky," Nan answered dutifully, but with a most undutiful twinkle in her eyes.

"Thea," said Nan, on the way home, "one day soon, Aunt Ruth may have a little baby."

"A boy baby or a girl baby?" asked Thea.

"We aren't quite sure yet," Nan answered. Thea was silent, considering the matter. She would never have expected Aunt Ruth to decide to have a baby. Surely it would break things and knock things over, especially if it was a little boy.

"I expect she'll have a little girl," she suggested.

"Why do you think so?" asked Nan, with interest.

"Well, they're quieter, don't you think? They don't break things so much."

"That's why I hope it will be a boy," Nan replied, half to herself.

Thea, not understanding, continued with her own thoughts, the red leaves shuffling under her feet. At the corner of the street, the first sharp wind of winter swept gustily down, whirling the tumbled glory off the road, flinging the red and gold and brown up and down together in a spiral of colour. Nan flinched against the cold blast.

"It's nearly winter," she sighed. "And it gets dark so early."

"I like winter," cried Thea. "Oh, look, there's a window with a light in it." She pulled Nan along to look at the coloured picture, and went on, "Besides, there's muffins and hot toast, and roasted chestnuts and, maybe, snow."

Nan smiled. "Oh yes, winter's nice," she answered, "but I like summer better." She began to plan her budget, thinking that even if Thea's winter coat would last another year, she must still get her a new pair of shoes, and that perhaps she herself did not really want a new jacket for the cold weather.

60

She buttoned her thin coat about her, and walked with her head bent against the wind, while Thea danced along with a scarlet leaf clutched in her hand.

There are moments in the lives of all of us upon which we dare, not look back, moments of pain which after ten years are still sharp. But there are times of happiness, too, which lie more heavily and more dangerously upon the memory, which strike more cruelly to the heart in after years.

On the day that Belle Lawrence returned to the house ironically named 'Sunnyside', Thea knew that she had nothing left to wish for. She hung about her mother, like a small, loving puppy, content only to look at her, to touch her dress and watch for her smile. Belle was moved and distressed by this devotion, feeling in it some reproach to herself, but Thea thought nothing of the separation or of the parting which was again to come. It was enough that her mother was home, and would be with her until after Christmas. The house was gay with laughter, Nan was cheerful, and contentment descended upon Thea like a divine peace.

One evening soon after her return, Belle and Nan went to spend the night with Ruth, much to Thea's disgust. On their return, they told Thea that Aunt Ruth had a baby son. She was pleased, but more pleased that they were home again. When Nan returned to Aunt Ruth, Thea and her mother spent a happy afternoon together. Emily had toasted some muffins and made some cakes, and they sat by the fire in perfect contentment, talking and laughing while the rain fell steadily outside.

"I do love you, Mother," said Thea suddenly, when tea was cleared away, and her knitting had been admired. Belle fell to her knees beside her daughter and took her in her arms.

"Darling," she said brokenly, "we shall be able to be together soon. When you leave school, you can come out and join me. It's best to do it this way, and make a little extra

61

money. We don't want to live in this dreadful place all our lives, do we?''

"I like to be wherever you like to be," answered Thea, and Belle looked troubled, as though it was not the reply she had hoped for.

"You'll like it out there," she said, pleadingly. "It's like living in a different world, all colours and sunshine and beauty, instead of this dirt and rain." She glanced at the window, where the drops rattled out of the darkness like spears flung by an invisible enemy and slid down the wet panes of glass. "I'll draw the curtains," she said, and, rising, went to pull the heavy red plush, pausing only to peer, shuddering, into the gloom.

"Nan hates the winter too," said Thea. Belle turned sharply to look at her, but Thea's face was open and innocent still of all reproach. "I rather like winter," she added, "sort of shut-in and safe."

"I hate being shut in," answered Belle, shaking her shoulders like a disobedient child, "and who wants to be safe?" Thea was silent. "I'd rather live on top of a mountain and be in danger of falling off every minute of the day," cried Belle, "than live in a valley and be safe. Besides, it's a mistake to feel too secure. It is when you feel most safe that you are in the greatest danger." She leant against the mantelpiece, gazing into the fire, and Thea wondered if she was remembering Tom Lawrence, but dared not ask her. They were both startled when the front doorbell rang violently. They listened to Emily's voice in the hall and heard a man answering her. Belle went out, to find Uncle Edward, wild-eyed and breath-less, who said simply, and with a certain fine dignity in his distress, "Belle, will you come at once?"

"Of course," replied Belle, after a second's pause when she seemed about to ask a question. "I'll get my—" She turned, to find Emily beside her, holding her hat and coat. As she thrust in the hat-pin, she said to Edward, with a catch of the breath, "Are we in time?" and he answered, "I think so," Then they were gone, and Emily and Thea were left standing in the dark hall, listening to the jingle and rattle of the cab, driving off into the rain and the wind.

Some hours after Thea had been in bed that night, she woke up to find a bar of light falling across her room from the half-open door, and to hear voices coming from outside. She slid out of bed, and crept across the room. She could just see her mother sitting on the stairs. She had her hat in her hand and was stabbing her hat-pin into it, slowly and insistently, while she spoke without looking at Emily who stood below. Her voice was very weary.

"It doesn't seem fair, does it?" she said, as Thea held her breath to listen.

"Now, Miss Belle," said Emily, very gently, "don't take on so."

"Poor Ruth," Belle went on, still staring at her hat and jabbing the hat-pin, "Just when she had what she wanted, and could have been happy."

"Miss Ruth wouldn't never have been happy," cut in Emily with something of her usual sharpness, "She wasn't the happy sort."

"She was always so envious of me," said Belle, and smiled crookedly. "If Father hadn't lost his money, she might have been a different person. It seems hard that this should happen just when she had something I hadn't – a son. It might have made all the difference to her. She might have been happy for the first time in her life."

"I don't think Miss Ruth was born to be happy," Emily repeated obstinately.

Belle laughed shortly, and flung her hat down with the pin skewered through it and stretched her arms above her head.

"Born to be happy?" she said, "are any of us? Look at Father and Mother. Look at me. We're not a very lucky family. I don't know what chance Thea has."

She put her hands up to her hair with a sigh, and began taking hair-pins out and letting down the rich coils as though they lay too heavily upon her head. The gas flared and bubbled above her, and Thea's bare feet were cold on the linoleum. She rested the sole of one foot on the instep of the other, and leant against the wall which was chill through her nightdress. The wind suddenly threw a shower of rain against the windows, and she had to strain her ears to hear her mother's next words, spoken with her arms still bent up to her head.

"She knew that she was going to die. The last thing she said to Mother was that her best vase was being mended, and that Mother should call and hurry them up. She told Edward not to wear that shirt again, because it wanted mending." Belle laughed on a broken note that turned swiftly into tears. She put her face into her hands and wept bitterly, with her hair falling about her shoulders. Emily came quickly up the stairs to put her arms round her, murmuring, "There, Miss Belle, there. Don't take on so." But Belle only shook her head, crying through her tears, "Poor Ruth, poor Ruth." Thea thought that it was a fitting valediction to her aunt. Poor Ruth.

The next morning, Thea's mother told her that Aunt Ruth was dead. It was typical of Belle that she used no such euphemism as 'passed away' or 'fell asleep', with which fearful relatives try to smooth the abrupt finality of death.

"Because of the baby coming?" asked Thea. The two events seemed to her to be connected.

"Yes."

"And is the baby all right?"

"Yes, the baby is quite well. The doctor made a mistake, and so Aunt Ruth died."

"What will happen to the baby?" asked Thea, looking forward to the possibility of the baby living at Sunnyside.

"I don't know, but I expect his father will look after him."

"But, Uncle Edward can't look after a baby, can he?"

"His sister will have to come and live with him," cried Belle, with a vehemence which Thea did not understand. "Nan has enough to do, and I can't help."

Thea had wondered for a moment if her mother might perhaps stay at home and help care for the baby – but only for a moment. Her mother must return to the blue skies, the blossoming trees and the sunshine where she loved to be. Abbot's Green was well enough for Nan, or for herself, but not for her mother. How could a butterfly dwell contentedly in a matchbox?

When Nan arrived home that afternoon, looking more pinched and weary than ever, she said that Uncle Edward's sister had arrived and taken charge of the house and the new baby. She and Belle avoided all discussion of Aunt Ruth, but, later in the evening, they began to talk of 'what to wear'. Thea was puzzled by this at first, and then shocked as she realised that they were speaking of mourning clothes. Death was not in itself so dreadful a thing, but there was something sordid about the discussion, so soon after the event, of whether that navy-blue coat, already dyed, would dye again to black, or whether the black hat would 'do', if the necessary heavy veils were bought for it.

"I'm afraid I must dye the dress you brought me," said Nan, and Thea thought of the new dress which her mother had brought from France, and trembled.

"Your navy-blue serge is *very* dark," Belle insinuated.

"Oh no!" cried Nan, more roused than Thea had ever heard her, "not against black! I must have a black dress."

"Thea needn't," her mother said, and the child held her breath.

"Oh yes, I think so."

"No," said Belle, flatly, "I don't approve of children in black. She won't be going to the funeral. We'll get her a black band to wear on her arm."

Thea was relieved when it was so decided. The black band was sewn, and she felt rather important when she pulled it up her arm. Elsie Winter was impressed, and Thea put on a mourner's visage and remarked that it was her *only* aunt, as though that made her death a more memorable one.

"Will she have a funeral with plumes on the horses' heads?" asked Elsie, awed.

"I expect so," Thea replied, smugly. But as she gradually realised that she would never see Aunt Ruth again, she began to remember her kindness, the presents she had given her, her odd, shy, abrupt way of trying to amuse Thea when she went to tea, and the readiness with which she used to lend Thea The Book – a loan now made permanent through her will. Thea was seized by a hatred for the hypocritical black band, and tore it off her arm, burying it in her chest of drawers, far behind her summer combinations and petticoats. Nan, of course, noticed its absence, but Thea, blushing at the lie, said that she had lost it, and Nan promised to make her another, but forgot.

"Thea," said her mother that evening, when Nan was out of the room, "when I die, don't bother to wear black for me."

"Mother!" she gasped, horrified.

Belle looked up, surprised and smiling. "We all die, sooner or later, and I shall probably die before you do. Black won't suit you at all."

"But don't you have to wear black when someone dies?" asked Thea.

"That depends on who it is. Unless Nan were still alive, I wouldn't want you to wear it for me. I'd rather look down from the clouds, or Heaven, or wherever I am, and see you looking nice, than loaded with black draperies."

Thea began to smile.

"And don't let them put lilies all over the grave," Belle went on, still half-laughing, half-serious. "I hate lilies. They always remind me of funerals."

Thea laughed outright at that, and Belle added, "And don't let them put any moral teaching on my tombstone, such as, 'When this stone you pass by, think how soon you might die.'

I always think it's such impertinence, for people to hand out moral advice, just because they're dead."

"Mother," said Thea, after a moment, "what do you think happens to you when you die?"

"I don't know, darling. I think you get to an odd sort of heaven in time – not crystal and gold harps, but all the best of what you love on earth, with no pain or fear or anger. Is that what you think?"

"I don't know. I don't somehow feel that there is a heaven."

"There must be," said her mother, "to make it up to the people who've been unlucky on earth. There just must be."

Thea knew that she was thinking of Aunt Ruth, and perhaps all the family who were 'not born to be happy'. Belle gazed into the fire for a long time, her fingers closely entwined, the nails turning white under the pressure. Thea thought that she looked older than ever before, and felt, as she watched her mother, a still, chill fear. How could she go on living, if her mother were to die? Then Nan came into the room, and Belle straightened her shoulders and smiled at Thea, and the fear was forgotten.

Seven

Time, which overshadows all human affairs, is suitably
mad and unreasonable. Our childhood, which is so long,
so slow, so unending, becomes, in retrospect, but a summer's
day, sweet, cloudless, and all too short. The discovery that we
are grown-up invariably takes us by surprise. And, from the
time of our eighteenth birthday, the years slip away like leaves
off a tree in an autumn gale. So it was with Thea. She had
waited so desperately and longingly for the time when she
should be grown-up and able to join her mother, yet she was
startled beyond reason to find herself sixteen years old, with
school behind her and the prospect of a journey to Monte
Carlo before her.

It was decided that she and Nan should pay a visit to
Enfield, where Lydia was to be married, and that Thea should
travel from there with Uncle Robert, who had business in
Paris and had offered to escort her there, and thence put her
safely on the train south. Thea had not visited the family at
Enfield since her first journey there as a child, and she almost
dreaded to return to the place where she remembered such
happy and golden days. For the magic circle was broken.
Andrew, the spoilt, the beloved, their pride and delight, had
run heedlessly into the road and under the hooves of a fast-
moving cab, and so out of the family life in a breath of time
upon a summer's afternoon. Thea remembered her wild
incredulity when Nan told her of the accident. "It couldn't
happen to him. It couldn't happen to them," she had cried,
and remembered Nurse's grim comment, "Things like that

can happen to anyone." But it was more than a tragic end to a
hopeful and endearing young life. It meant that there was no
enchantment in the Enfield family, and no security in their
circle. A horse and cab, and a rolling ball, could shatter the
staunch fabric of their world as easily as a doctor's error could
destroy Aunt Ruth, who was not born to be happy.

The first change Thea noticed at Enfield was in the house. It
was not as trim and shining as she remembered it. The paint
needed renewing and the brass knocker was dim. She found
Janey comfortably unchanged, plump and friendly and placid, with that hard rock of independence and intelligence
beneath her gentle ways which made her respected by the
other members of the family.

Lydia, already cut off from the rest by her approaching
marriage, was further withdrawn by the loss of Andrew. He
was the only one who had preferred her company to any
other, who had loved her uncritically and warmly. With James
she had always squabbled, Charlotte viewed her distantly and
Janey tolerated but laughed at her. She had given Andrew
protection and advice, and the feeling that he turned to her
first in any trouble had checked her egotism, softened her
imperious impatience. Now angry and bitter, Lydia looked
upon the world and upon her fellow human beings with ready
antagonism, determined only to marry well, to have a big
house and plenty of money and to have children – above all to
have a son. She was rude and contemptuous towards her
future husband, who seemed to like it.

"If I were Tony," said Janey, thoughtfully, "I wouldn't
marry Lydia."

"She's very beautiful," Thea remarked.

"No, not exactly beautiful." Janey corrected her. "Lydia's
good-looking, but not beautiful." She was right, thought
Thea. Lydia was a handsome girl, but her features were
too strong for beauty.

"If I were Lydia," Charlotte put in, "I wouldn't marry
Tony."

"Oh, Tony's all right," said Janey, "I rather like him."

"So do I," agreed Charlotte. Thea and Janey waited for her to qualify her statement, but Charlotte always preferred obscurity to verbosity. She, who had been a plain child, was now a gawky, unattractive girl. She wore her hair in one big plait, turned up at the back of her neck into a long knot, which James irreverently called a door knocker. The ankle-length skirt and shirt-blouse, which on Lydia had looked so graceful, on Charlotte seemed awkward and shapeless. Yet there was about her an air of expectancy, of dreaming virginity, which partly redeemed her pale face and long nose and uncouth movements. She still retained that suggestion of mystery, of a carefully-kept secret, which had so intrigued Thea seven years before.

Nurse, bereft of all her charges, still remained, sewing and helping in the house, unable to leave because of her devotion to her mistress, but querulous and sharp-tempered because she loved children and was miserable without them.

"Don't you miss having children to look after?" Thea asked her on the first evening of her arrival, perching on the nursery table while Nurse darned a pair of James's socks.

"Yes, I do, Miss Thea, but I couldn't have gone to another family after this one. I was too fond of them all. They all had such strong personalities, you know, and were so different. I did try another place once, after Andrew . . . But I couldn't take an interest in the children. Dear little things they were, too, little girls, and very pretty and obedient. But it was no good. I felt homesick all the time."

"These weren't very good children," Thea remarked, laughing.

"Oh, they weren't too bad. Andrew was the naughtiest, by a long way. That was why I was fondest of him, I expect. But the others didn't give much trouble, no more than children ought to."

"I didn't know he was your favourite," Thea said.

"Oh well," Nurse replied, hastily, "I never had favourites.

71

It doesn't do, you know, with children. But if I *had* had favourite, it would have been Andrew."

"I was very sorry to hear about . . . about it," said Thea, awkwardly.

"Yes," said Nurse, in her unemotional way, "it was a pity. It was a pity for Master James, too."

"Where is James?" asked Thea. She had been too shy to ask after him before.

"At the office. He doesn't get home much before six, or a bit after."

"The office! James works in an office?"

"Yes, didn't you know?"

"No, I didn't know. He always used to say that he'd go to sea."

"I never knew the boy who didn't," Nurse answered, caustically. "It won't hurt him to do some real work, for a change. Now that there isn't as much money as there was, it's right that he should work."

Ah, James, James, thought Thea, is this the end of your dreams? Is this the salt spray and the kicking wheel, the excitement and delight? Must all our dreams end like this? Nurse bundled her darning together and looked at the battered alarm-clock on the mantelpiece, the one Thea remembered from her last visit.

"I must go down and help with the dinner," she said. "We haven't as many in the kitchen as we did have." She rose from the creaking basket-chair, for so many years her chair of state, and went out, leaving Thea thoughtful and disturbed. How was it, she wondered, that each generation looked back upon its childhood as a happier time? Was it that the world was gradually becoming a less kindly place? Or did children not see the ugly things of life, only the happiness?

The basket-chair creaked suddenly, in the disconcerting way such chairs do, and Thea started, and was relieved to find it still unoccupied. She looked round the deserted nursery, tidy and empty as it never had been in the old days. Andrew's corner was bare and clear. The residence of the Bloggs family was closed, and dust was thick on the roof. Thea opened the front of it, which squeaked protestingly at being made to work after so long a vacation. She almost expected to find the Bloggs family disporting themselves, free from their former taskmasters. But they were all motionless and inanimate. Mr Bloggs, smaller than she remembered him, sat opposite his spouse at a dining table which bore two empty dishes, as though they had finished their meal and must wait, like good children, to be told to get down. Fanny Bloggs sat at the piano, her hands at her sides, as though waiting for inspiration, while the young giant, Edwina, leant against the wall beside her, defying her to play another note. Only Albert Bloggs was in a somewhat unconventional pose, doing a handstand in the kitchen sink, watched with admiration by the cook. These little bits of stuff and sawdust were once alive to me, thought Thea. They once moved and spoke. Half-ashamed, she restored Albert to the dining room and set the cook to work at the kitchen range. She laid the table with a pink blancmange (of somewhat more solid proportions than most blancmanges) and a diminutive dish of fruit, then brought Fanny from her musical labours to join in the feast. Edwina, as troublesome as ever, she was forced to leave leaning against the dining table and threatening to tip her father off his chair. She looked in on them for a moment, before she shut the door upon them, with an absurd envy. Lucky little dolls, shut in their wooden box, motionless and undisturbed.

From downstairs, the old grandfather clock struck six in his high, clear tones. Thea knew that she must go downstairs and join the others. She looked round the nursery once more, and the sun threw a golden beam into Andrew's corner, as if it were searching for the intent little figure, the yellow head and baby-rabbit smile. Thea sighed, shivered and turned away, closing the nursery door behind her, gently, to shut in the childish ghost, busy upon his own affairs, unchanging and

73

unchanged in a household where all had changed. As she reached the top of the last flight of stairs, the front door opened softly and James came in, a taller James and dressed in ugly city clothes, high, stiff collar and hard hat. But the same James, oh surely the same James! Thea would have run down the stairs to greet him, but paused before the air of secrecy and furtiveness about his entrance, almost as though he hoped to enter the house unobserved. As she hesitated on the top stair, Uncle Robert came out of the drawing room, shutting the door behind him. He stood still, regarding his son, while James, putting his umbrella in the stand and hanging up his hat, said with an air of calm politeness, "Good-evening, Father."

Uncle Robert ignored this, and said in low, distinct tones, "I called in at the office for you this afternoon. I had a message for you."

James inclined his head and waited, with the same exaggerated politeness.

"You weren't there," said Uncle Robert. "At four o'clock, you had already left the office."

"I had some business," said James, but something of his assurance had left him.

"It won't do, James," Uncle Robert went on, and there was more of an edge in his voice. He's losing his temper, thought Thea. Oh, James, do be careful. "When are you going to stop behaving like a grocer's assistant, running after cheap girls all the time, and playing truant like a contemptible schoolboy?"

"I wish to God I were a grocer's assistant!" cried James, and his voice too was rising. Thea thought that it was as though they were rehearsing a play. They had said this, or something like it, often before. "At least it would be better than that damned office."

"How dare you swear at me!" shouted Uncle Robert.

"And the girls," said James, softly, as though to himself, "are not cheap, definitely not cheap. In fact, rather expensive."

"If you are about to say that you have spent your salary and your allowance and are in debt again," said Uncle Robert, "I shouldn't trouble. I am not giving you a penny more while you consistently refuse to work."

James said nothing to this. His handsome face relaxed into a look of sullen anger which hurt Thea more than his violent speech. Uncle Robert was about to speak again, when Aunt Mary came out of the drawing room, leaving the door open behind her. Looking into the room, Thea could see Nan and Janey and Charlotte, talking together in cheerful companionship. She thought that James, silent and sulky in the hall, was like a lost soul.

"Robert, I think it's about time we dressed for dinner," said Aunt Mary. "We have guests, you know," she added, in gentle reproof. She went over to James and kissed him. "Hallo, James," she said, "your cousin is here, and Nan. You must have forgotten they were coming." She took his arm and led him into the drawing room, and Uncle Robert followed, unwillingly enough, but with a slight lightening of his black cloud. Dear Aunt Mary! still the peacemaker, though even she had lost some of her tranquil happiness. Probably, Thea thought, that was buried in the child's grave in an Enfield churchyard. She came downstairs, slowly and reluctantly, and went into the drawing room to meet the new James.

The next morning, Thea and Janey, as by common consent, wandered out into the garden.

"Oh, the rabbits!" cried Thea, dismayed. "You haven't any rabbits."

"No," answered Janey, "We . . . we hadn't time to feed them." Thea wondered what had happened to John Cassius. The old swing was still suspended beneath the arbour, and Thea cautiously sat down on it, pushing the ground away with one foot. Nurse's voice called, "Miss Janey, your mother wants you," from the house.

"Oh, bother!" said Janey. "I don't expect she does. I expect it's Nurse. Still I'd better find out. I won't be a minute." She ran lightly indoors and Thea remained, pushing herself gently to and fro.

She was startled when a voice behind her said, "Hold tight!" and James, pausing until she was more firmly settled, began to swing her vigorously. Thea laughed delightedly, as she climbed and dived, her feet together and a light breeze lifting her long hair, still down her back but tied back with a bow instead of being in ringlets. After a while, James left her to finish the momentum, sitting on the rockery to watch her, and smiling at her flush of excitement.

"Did you come out to feed the rabbits?" he asked, as she came to rest. "We gave them away some time ago."

"I miss them," Thea answered. "They were nice to talk by."

James laughed. "That's a funny way to put it." Then he sobered and said, as a sudden thought came to him, "How long ago were you here?"

"Nan and I were talking it over. It must be seven years."

"Oh, then that was before . . ." He stopped, and finished, "You must find a great difference."

"I'm different too," Thea replied, indirectly.

"Are you?" teased James. "You look the same to me."

Thea looked at him gravely. He was thinner, she thought. There was an hollowness in his cheeks, and that faint, but unmistakeable sullenness round his mouth, which the cleft chin seemed to emphasise. He was still very handsome, but he didn't look happy.

"Well?" said James, smiling, but with some anxiety.

Thea blushed, a weakness of which she was always ashamed. "You're thinner," she said.

"I shouldn't be," James said. "Goodness knows, I never take any exercise now, or play any games. I just sit at an office desk and add up figures which mean nothing at all to me, and which come to a different total each time I look at them."

"You don't like it?" asked Thea, hoping to give the impression that she knew nothing of the family recriminations.

"Like it!" cried James. "My God, like it! I would rather clean . . . clean . . ." He came to a stop, and then went on, with a belated flash of more suitable inspiration, "clean out stables."

"Are the people pleasant?" asked Thea.

James affected to consider. "Well, there are three clerks, called, as far as I can gather, Bunk, Podgy and Spook. They take a distant interest in horse-racing, and constantly enquire after each others' 'fillies'."

"Do they own some race-horses, then?"

"No, it appears that this is the delicate way in which they choose to refer to their lady-friends."

"How very rude!" cried Thea, insulted.

James grinned. "Their taste is not irreproachable. Then there's an aged Member of the Firm, called Mr Bancroft. He appears in the office at nine o'clock and suddenly disappears at five o'clock. I rather believe he locks himself up in his desk with the private papers."

"You don't like him?"

"My dear girl," said James, pityingly, "do you conceive an affection for a ledger or a balance-sheet or a desk?"

"But, why do you have to do it, if you hate it?" said Thea.

James frowned, and the momentary return to his sardonic good humour gave way to the new discontented pout.

"Well, Father's business hasn't gone very well lately. His partner absconded with a lot of the firm's money, and, of course, Father had to go and make it good."

"Of course," agreed Thea. Upright. The sort of man who was asked to take the bag round in a strange church.

"Yes, that's all very well," said James, crossly, "but it meant paying out much more than he could afford and we've been short of money ever since. It's hard on Mother and on the girls." He paused and added very softly, as though ashamed of it, "It's hard on me, too."

"I'm sorry," said Thea, inadequately.

"Everything's gone wrong with us lately," said James,

sighing. "Ever since *that* happened to Andy, things have gone wrong. And, of course, Father always thought that it was my fault. So it was."

"Your fault?" asked Thea, shocked. "How could it be?"

"He was with me when it happened," James explained. "I let go of him and he dropped the ball and ran after it and . . ." He stopped abruptly and bit his lip, as though he were sorry to have said so much.

"I'm sorry," said Thea again. "But it wasn't your fault. It was just . . ."

"Oh well, I never got on well with Father anyway," said James, shrugging his shoulders. "And of course he adored Andy. But then all of us did."

Oh God, thought Thea suddenly, if you exist, how could you do this to James? How could you take that eager, friendly, hopeful boy and turn him into this thin, cross, discontented young man? Oh James, oh James.

Janey came down the path, swinging her hat by the ribbon. "It's nearly time for church," she said.

James leapt to his feet. "I must fly, or I shall get caught."

"Oh James, you'd better come this morning," cried Janey, "it'll please Dad."

"Nothing would please him."

"But you don't even try."

"The rôle of prodigal son suits me too well."

"You'll only go and visit Betty Holiday, and promise to take her out tomorrow."

"I shouldn't wonder."

"You can't afford to."

"My money is as the widow's cruse," replied James, with a flourish. "See how well my illustrations fit in with the spirit of the Sabbath."

"Perhaps she'll be at church, like us," said Janey, in forlorn hope.

"Knowing Betty as I do," said James cheerfully, "I doubt it." He walked round the house, put one hand on the top of the gate and vaulted over. Janey looked after him anxiously, and then back at Thea.

"He's so silly," she sighed. "He just tries to annoy Dad."

"He never calls him 'Dad' now," remarked Thea. "He calls him 'Father'."

"He has ever since Andy was killed. Dad said something to him then, something about having no sense of responsibility and thinking only of himself. James never forgave him. It wasn't fair, either. James isn't like that at all. He never has any money because he's so generous. He just gives it away to anyone who's hard up."

"But if it isn't his to give," began Thea. "I mean, if he then has to borrow for himself . . ."

"I know," said Janey, laughing a little. "He gives his own first and then he borrows, and gives that, too. He spends a lot, and he always has lots of girls. He makes dates with about four on the same evening, and fits them all in. But, of course, it's expensive," she added, judicially.

"What's gone wrong with him?" cried Thea, puzzled.

"He never could keep money. And Dad's so careful about money matters and likes everything in order. Then, James hates this office."

"But, why does he have to do it?"

"What else can he do?"

"There should be something that he's *meant* to do, something he'd like. Uncle Robert can't just put him in this and leave him, knowing he hates it."

"He was in another business before this," Janey said, sadly. "Dad says he'll never settle down to work. I don't believe he will. I'm so afraid he'll make a mistake in the books or something like that and get himself into trouble. I don't know what will happen to him if he doesn't settle down soon. It worries Mother so."

"But he's such a gifted person. He's clever and everyone likes him. It can't be right for him to be so unhappy."

"I don't know," said Janey. "He's weak, that's the trouble.

Dad's so strong that he doesn't like it. James can't refuse people, and he can't make himself work. He and Dad have rows all the time, and they're both right. Dad expects too much, and James gives too little. It's dreadful loving them both, and seeing both sides." She sighed, and Thea thought how fair-minded she was. Devoted to her father, adoring James, she could yet see where each of them had failed and how their relations with each other had become so unhappy. For the first time in her life, she was glad that she had no family but her mother and Nan.

"Perhaps James will find something he likes and settle down soon," she said.

"I hope so," Janey answered, shaking her head, "because if not . . ." She broke off, crying, "Heavens! it's time we went. Come and get your hat on."

Thea left the swing swaying on its ropes, and they went together through the garden and past the empty space where once the rabbits had ruminated in their own aloof fashion. Thea was thinking with grief that you could never go back in life to what was past. The days and weeks and years went by, and you could never recapture them. You thought to tread the same ground again, but it never was the same. It was like walking upon an eternally revolving stage, but, move as you would, you could never reach the place you had started from.

Eight

T hea had never been to a wedding before. Janey, who had
already been bridesmaid twice, assured her that it wasn't
much fun.

"The great thing is to have plenty to eat," she said. "As far
as I can see, people only go to weddings to eat, look at the
presents, and look at other people's clothes. They go to have
their own clothes seen, as well."

"How horrid!" exclaimed Thea.

"Oh, I don't know," said Janey, tolerantly. "They enjoy it,
and it doesn't hurt anyone." She added after a moment's
thought, "They bring wedding presents too."

"I think a wedding ought to be more – more sacred," said
Thea shyly, surprising herself.

Janey looked across at Lydia, smiling and self-possessed,
and at the stupid, amiable face of her husband. "Ye-es," she
agreed, doubtfully. "There's Charlotte rubbing her left ear,"
she cried, suddenly. "That means I must hand out the lobster
patés." She rushed away, leaving Thea uncertain of what she
ought to do, feeling conspicuous, standing there alone, but
too shy to help feed the guests. She watched Janey taking the
silver dish to two smartly-dressed women nearby. They both
smiled at her with many expressions of delight. "Oh dear,"
one of them exclaimed, "aren't they rather big?" She looked at
the patés carefully, and then smiled at Janey again, while her
hand hovered over the dish, dropping aimlessly, but uner-
ringly, upon the largest. The other woman murmured, "I
shouldn't really, but they look so delicious," and selected the

81

second largest. As Janey moved on, Thea heard one of the harpies remark to the other, "Rather vulgar to have so much food." "These are far too big," the other agreed.

Thea shuddered. There was something degrading in inviting such guests to one's wedding. Surely it was possible to ask only the people dear and familiar, and forgo the entrance fee of a silver wedding present which the unwanted brought with them. She looked back, as Janey had, at Lydia and her new husband. Was there nothing between respectable Arthur Jervis and a dangerously beguiling Tom Lawrence? For the first time in her life, she pondered upon her own shadowy future husband. Would she ever marry, and if she did would she choose a man of worth and possessions, or a dear undependable man such as – well, such as James? She searched the room for James, but could not see him in the throng.

Close by, she heard one of the guests she had watched before saying, "That must be poor Belle's girl." Thea was shaken by sudden rage. How dared they speak of 'poor' Belle! How dared they talk of her with that tone of pity, they who had nothing, no grace, no beauty, no gaiety or humour! She clenched her fists and turned towards the window, to hide her emotion. She could feel the hated hot blush stealing over her face, but still the high, hard voices spoke on, loud enough for her to hear them speaking of her dress, her hair, her looks, "*So* different from poor Belle. Must take after her father."

At last, Charlotte came to enquire if they had all they wanted, and they moved away in her wake. As they went, Thea heard the elder remark, "Such a plain girl, isn't she?" "Almost ugly," the other supplemented, looking after Charlotte's thin, stiff figure, more awkward than usual in the ruffled pink, which seemed to accentuate her corners. Thea was surprised by the sudden defensive affection with which she regarded Charlotte, moving through the crowd with the smart, scented critics behind her.

Thea began her interrupted search for James once more. If he were near, surely he would come to rescue her, standing so solitary and embarrassed. She saw him at last, leaning over a tall, well-dressed girl who sat at the far end of the room. He was looking down at her with an air of intimacy, of amused interest that filled Thea with unreasonable jealousy. Looking at the assurance of the girl, the familiarity of James's attitude, Thea felt more lonely than ever, more pitifully young and inexperienced and unwanted. As she watched them, she became aware of someone standing near her, but did not turn her head, and was startled when a voice spoke to her. She jumped and found a stranger offering her a sandwich. Blushing hotly, she refused, but still the man lingered, holding the dish with embarrassment, as though afraid he might drop it.

"You are a sister of the bride?" he asked at last.

"I . . . no, I'm a cousin." Oh, go away. Do go away.

"I am a stranger here," he said, and now Thea noticed a faint accent in his speech. She shot a quick look at him, and looked back to James. "My name is Paul Bruner," he added. Thea felt that she should tell him her name, but hesitated a few seconds too long, and then could not break the silence. At last, she forced herself to ask, "Are you from abroad?" Perhaps he was French, she thought, and might know her mother.

The stranger laughed pleasantly, and answered, "Ah, I can never pass as an Englishman. My accent is not good enough. No, I am German." Thea looked up at him then, long enough to notice his light-brown hair, friendly brown face and blue eyes. "I . . . I've never been to Germany," she stammered, in a desperate attempt to avoid a silence.

"You would like it," he answered, with new animation. "I come from Berlin. You must persuade your uncle to bring you over on one of his visits. Berlin in the spring is beautiful."

"Yes, I should like that," said Thea. "I'm going to France next week," she added, proudly.

"To France?" he asked, with something like dismay in his voice.

"Yes, my mother is there."

"I see. But later you must visit Germany." He smiled down at her. "What do you suggest I do with these sandwiches?" he asked, his eyes twinkling. "I can persuade no one to eat them."

Thea laughed, feeling suddenly at ease. "I should give them to Charlotte," she suggested, her diffidence almost vanished.

"Charlotte is the beautiful sister of the bride?" he asked.

"No, no," began Thea, and stopped. "I mean, Charlotte is that one there, with her hair up."

Paul Bruner followed her gaze, and said, "Yes, that was the one I meant. The bones of her face are beautiful, like a Grecian statue."

"I never thought of her as beautiful," said Thea, thoughtfully.

"One day she will be, I think," replied Paul Bruner. Thea looked at Charlotte with this new idea in her mind, and was about to turn back to him, when she noticed the brunette alone on the couch, James no longer at her side. Then she found James coming towards her, picking his way through the chattering guests. She was afraid that, seeing the stranger beside her, he might not come to her, so she stepped forward, away from Paul Bruner, and smiled at James as he drew near.

"Janey's looking for you," he said, "and you're to come and have some champagne. They're going to cut the cake, and I'm instructed to see that you have a large piece of sugar-icing." He winked at her, adding, "It's like going through a chicken-run at feeding time. Here, I'll go first and blaze a trail." He seized her hand and turned back into the crowd, and Thea followed him readily. Then she remembered the stranger and realised her rudeness. She glanced over her shoulder, but the German had turned away. She could see only his back and the curve of his brown cheek. Moreover, James was holding her hand, forging steadily through the noisy groups. She went with him and forgot her new acquaintance, nor did she see him again before he left.

"When I get married," said Janey, "I shall ask only the people I really want."

"Think of the wedding presents you'll lose," said James, mockingly. They were sitting in the nursery, the four young people, making a late meal of pastries and jelly and cake, which James had foraged from the party. The last guest had departed, the small, informal dance was over and they sat with the comfortable feeling of weariness, satisfaction and hunger which follows a party.

"Did you see Mrs Dunbar?" asked Charlotte, a rare dimple in her cheek.

"Is that the one with the hat like an ornithologist's night-mare?" enquired James.

"Yes. She said what a plain girl I was."

"Charlotte!" cried Janey indignantly. "What did you say?"

"Oh, she wasn't addressing me. She was talking to someone else I didn't know. The other woman said I was ugly. I was just fetching them some champagne," she added.

"Was *that* why you told me to give them the second-best champagne?" cried James, laughing.

"Naturally," Charlotte replied, calmly. "I didn't think that they deserved the best."

James chuckled. "Perhaps that'll teach them to be more cautious, if not more charitable."

"I can't imagine Lydia married," said Janey, after a moment. "It seems funny that someone can be part of a family for so long, and then one day she suddenly isn't part of it any longer."

"Oh, she's still part of the family," said James, but care-lessly, as though the subject did not interest him very much.

"No, not really. After people are married, you never really know them again. They're . . . they're set apart. They live together for the rest of their lives, and no one else really knows what they think, or what they say to each other, or how fond they are of each other."

"Unless they get divorced," suggested James.

"Oh, our sort of people don't get divorced. They're too cautious. I think it's rather frightening to be tied to one person for the rest of your life. Just think, it might be for seventy years!"

"I think it's rather nice," said Thea shyly, "to think of having one person who belongs to you for always, that you belong to for always, and someone that you can depend on. It's rather comfortable."

"If it's the right person," put in Charlotte, in a low voice. They were all silent for a moment, thinking of Lydia and her new life-companion. Thea wondered if they were remembering the other gap in the magic circle, Andrew the beloved. She leant out of the window, pressing her forehead against the iron bars, placed there to curb the suicidal instincts of children. Sitting there, gazing up at the sky, she felt once more that sensation of falling into eternity, as she had felt at that first nursery tea, with the firelight glinting on the brass bars of the fender.

"Who am I?" she thought. "What am I? What am I doing in this world? To what end do I exist?"

It was as though a match should ponder upon its existence, during the brief instant of its ignition – and yet the purpose of a match seemed more obvious than the purpose of a human life. The immensity of the world frightened her – so large a dwelling for one person – and the multitude of other dwellers filled her with dread. A terrifying unreality was upon her. She moved her hand, yet it was not there. She sighed, and the sound was already lost. Time had vanished in the shifting sands of past and future. Then she knew that of all perilous thoughts, one must keep from one's soul the knowledge that it is alone, and for ever, that no one else can ever know the thoughts and aspirations, the temptations and convictions of those who are most dear and close. One must cling to the nursery bars of companionship, of little, familiar things, which hold us back from the dread chasm. The glimpses of eternity must be brief as lightning, lest they strike us to the earth, and blind us with their brilliance.

She drew her head back, and looked at the others, feeling a warm relief in finding them so comfortably familiar, as though she had been on a long journey away from them. Yet James was only just lighting the cigarette he had taken from his case as Charlotte spoke, and Janey was even then taking breath to reply.

Nine

T he chatter of the train and the rattle of a loose blind
formed into a little singing voice which said in Thea's
ears, "I'm going to see Mother, I'm going to see Mother." She
was entirely happy, she told herself. She was utterly contented. But she knew that it was not so. Behind the glad
jumping of her heart, she could feel a sensation of discomfort,
such as may greet us when we wake up with an unpleasant day
before us. Yet there was nothing before her which she
dreaded. There had been nothing to distress her in the
journey, in the night in Paris, in the dinner with Uncle Robert
at an open-air table of a café, with stars above and Parisians
wandering distractingly by in the street.

Paris had excited and delighted her, and Uncle Robert had
been kind and amusing, even teasing her a little, as James
might have done. She had enjoyed the crossing, and the train
to Dover, knowing that Uncle Robert had charge of all
arrangements and of the baggage, and that she had nothing
to do but smile at him and do as he suggested. So what could
be causing her this uncomfortable feeling? Ah, as if she didn't
know all the time that it was Nan, the sight of Nan's face as
she kissed her goodbye, her drooping shoulders as she stood
on the platform, waving and smiling! Nan had been wearing
her best clothes, and Nan in her best always seemed to Thea a
little pathetic. As they drew near to Abbot's Green station, she
had begun to gather her luggage together, her suitcase, her
umbrella, the handbag in which Thea had watched her fumble
for so many years, always so pitifully empty. Her black-gloved

87

hands were a little unsteady, but her fine grey eyes were clear, her thin face, in which some little trace of her former beauty remained, was calm. As she kissed Thea, her calmness slipped from her for an instant and Thea could not forget that look of pain and despair before she drew back quickly and straightened her hat, that hat which she had trimmed and re-trimmed for so long, and which was now gaily decked with glossy blue feathers. Uncle Robert opened the door for her and handed her out, and Thea saw him grip her hand for a moment in silent comfort before he re-entered the carriage.

"Goodbye, Thea, have a lovely time, dear. Give my love to your mother."

"Oh, Nan. Goodbye, Nan." How could you thank someone for inexpressible service, for unfailing kindness? How could you, on a railway station, apologise for years of thoughtlessness, of blindness, of ingratitude? Oh, Nan, forgive me. Oh, Nan, I'm sorry. The train puffed away from the platform. Nan turned suddenly away, as though she could smile and wave no longer. Thea saw her turn to pick up her suitcase, and then stop to unbutton her glove, in which she always kept her ticket. Then she was out of sight. Thea pictured her walking wearily back to Sunnyside, to the dark room, the unfinished dresses and jackets, to Emily, and a solitary meal. Thea's sense of guilt was mingled with wistful resentment. Could nothing ever be perfect? Must happiness for one person always mean grief for another? The unfamiliar countryside slipped by her almost unnoticed, as she saw Nan's tall, thin figure in the shabby summer costume, her grey hair bundled up beneath the too-gay hat, and her eyes hurt and troubled.

Thea's first impression of her new home was given by a palm tree growing actually on the platform. This incredible sight filled her with delight. She thought of a palm tree growing on Abbot's Green station and chuckled to herself. As she opened the carriage door and prepared to look for her mother, she was beset by a conviction that she had done this before, disastrously. She remembered suddenly the day on which she had returned from that first Enfield visit, to find no Mother, only Nan. She alighted and stood half-dazed by the babble of French voices, the shouts of porters. Then she saw her mother, searching among the passengers. Belle wore a cream-coloured costume, with cream roses pinned to it. Her hair was even more burnished than Thea remembered, under a modish, light straw hat. Her eyes met Thea's and she ran towards her with her arms open. Thea flung herself into them, and suddenly there was no noise, no babble of foreign tongues, no jostling passengers, only a world of two people, held closely in each other's arms, with the evening star poised above them in the first dusk.

The car stopped in front of a narrow doorway, and Thea was conscious of a feeling of sharp disappointment when she found that they must go downstairs. She had not thought of a basement flat. But when the luggage was placed in the small, dark hall, Belle led the way, smiling, into a room whose french windows gave on to a balcony. Thea followed her out, and then exclaimed in astonishment and delight. For they looked over roof-tops straight on to the sea, and round the coast the glittering necklace of lights was already shining. Over the dark waters of the harbour gleamed two lighthouses, one emerald green, one red, like the glass jars in a chemist's shop, but throwing their paths of brilliant colour shimmering over the water. Thea cried out again and again, breathless at the beauty spread before her. To the right, the Rocher stood dark against the sky, and the lights which twinkled from it seemed to run up to the stars, while the coast to the left lay thick with fallen stars. "Oh, Mother," she cried, "oh, Mother," and Belle held her close and laughed.

There was a tiny kitchen, which was indeed as dark as one would expect in the basement, and in it they cooked supper, and ate it in the room which was their bedroom and living room, with the french window open to the warm night air. Afterwards they sat on the balcony and talked a little, but were mostly silent. Then Thea went quickly to bed, and lay in contentment, watching her mother brushing and coiling her hair, dressed in the flimsy wrapper with its mad gold dragon falling down the back and flattened slippers which constantly fell off as she moved about the room. Belle looked such a girl in that fantastic dressing gown, with her heavy hair about her face.

There followed for Thea a time of such happiness that she found it hard, then and afterwards, to realise that it was real. She found that her mother was never needed at the hotel in the morning, rarely in the afternoon, but spent most evenings there, entertaining the guests, playing whist with them, performing the duties of a hostess, for which she received a generous salary. So they fell into a routine which would have seemed outrageous in Abbot's Green and whose very strangeness contributed to the unreality of her life. In the morning she and Belle could be together, after a late breakfast of bread, strawberry jam and coffee. They had a fat and delightful woman, half Italian, called Marie, a *bonne à tout faire*, who came in each morning and cleaned the flat, bringing with her provisions from the market. She always carried a huge shiny black bag, from which she drew bread, butter, milk, meat, vegetables, fruit, or anything else they might want, and she spoke very fast so that Thea never, in all the time she was in Monte Carlo, understood a complete sentence. She invariably called Thea, 'ma petite', and Thea liked to attempt a conversation with her, aware that Marie understood as little of her halting French, as she did of Marie's Italian-French. Marie would usually cook them their midday meal. Her cooking was rich, highly-flavoured and very different from the wholesome, 'good, plain' meals which Emily was wont to serve. In the afternoon they would walk, or shop together, if Belle was not needed at the hotel, or Thea would explore the town by herself, or sit on the rocks with a book. Thea would go to bed early, and be awakened in the early morning by her mother's return. Then they would have coffee together, and a late supper, or early breakfast, and Belle would give an account of her evening, with scandalous gossip about the inmates of the hotel and the local celebrities. Then to bed again, until the late reawakening, with brilliant sunshine outside and the sea dancing blue and silver below.

Thea rarely met any of Belle's friends, though she knew her mother had a great many. She went once or twice to have an apéritif with some of them, and their attitude towards Belle annoyed her. It was familiar and a little amused. They treated her like a pretty, spoilt child. Thea resented this, resented the loss of a precious morning with her mother, resented her own youth and inexperience, and became sulky and silent because of all this. She would sit under the garish striped umbrella in the midst of the chattering little group, and sip her non-alcoholic drink, and answer in monosyllables, her face, which could glow so eagerly, pale and blank, her eyes wide and expressionless. Mrs Van Dutyens, a stout American woman, who seemed to look upon Belle in the light of a favourite daughter, tried hard to 'draw Thea out'. She smiled widely at their first meeting, showing numerous glints of gold, and exclaimed, "Sa-ay, Belle, if your little Thea ain't goin' ter be a reg'lar beauty, jest like her ma!"

"Hush, Sadie," said Belle smiling. "You'll put ideas into her head." But Mrs Van Dutyens patted Thea's hand with an impish gaiety which sat ill upon her twelve stones of weight, crying, "Oh, she'll have all the men mad about her." Much offended, Thea withdrew her hand, and, when the general attention was diverted to the choosing and ordering of drinks, she examined Mrs Van Dutyens, her round face sagging under its make-up, her pink cheeks, her bright gold curls and her faded blue eyes. All her clothes looked strained to bursting point, and she wore many jewels strung about her person, which looked oddly out of place in the sunshine. She talked constantly of 'redoocin' but never acted upon her own advice, and Thea was repelled by the overpowering scent of perfume and alcohol which hung over her. She later repossessed herself of Thea's hand, and confidentially advised her to "Marry money, my dear, that's the only thing you can hang on to." Thea, anxious to get her hand back into her own custody, made no reply, but Mrs Van Dutyens continued, still with the confidential air which was belied by her loud voice, "I married twice, my dear, but lost 'em both, lost 'em both." Thea never could decide whether she meant that she had been twice widowed, or whether she had mislaid her helpmeets in some bar. She suspected the latter. Thea was accustomed to the suburban idea of marriage – that it was something fine and eternal, contracted in white satin and maintained until death. She had no heart for the marriage of convenience, crying rather, with the foolish Jane Austen character, "Never let it be said that I made a suitable match!" She withdrew her hand at last and edged her chair away from the matrimonial adviser, and occupied herself with counting the buttons upon Mrs Van Dutyens's dress and trying to decide which would first abandon its arduous post under the strain to which they were subjected.

A few days after her arrival, Thea went upon a solitary journey of exploration. The glorious sunshine still persisted, rather to her surprise. She found it hard to believe that there was a country where one awoke each morning in the certainty of fine weather, instead of peering cautiously out of the window before wearing summer dress, as in England. As she climbed the ramp which led towards La Turbie, she glanced backwards frequently to admire the dazzling brightness of the sea. In the harbour lay two French warships, their flags limp in the heat. At eight o'clock each morning, the bugles sounded on board and thereafter played the 'Marseillaise', which Thea found unfailingly amusing.

She left the ramp, those long, shallow steps upon which one can mount for a considerable time without fatigue, and struck into a narrow street. As she walked along the cobbles, an ancient woman stepped suddenly out of a doorway and accosted her with a stream of unintelligible patois. Thea shook her head regretfully, whereupon the ancient shook a crooked stick in the air, and shouted what was obviously abuse, in a high, cracked voice. Despite the heat, she was dressed in a black woollen dress and her hooked nose and toothless mouth reminded Thea of witches and the Evil Eye of the Middle Ages. Thea stepped aside, murmuring soothing words, and then, as the old woman began to pursue her down the narrow, dark, deserted street, she caught up her dress and ran, the vicious cursing following her. She stopped at the end of the street, breathless and shaken, and glanced back. The old woman was not to be seen. Presumably she had retired to her doorstep, preparing to ask alms of the next visitor, in her own inimitable manner. Thea smiled a little, but her fright had not quite subsided, and she thought how strangely super-stition survives. She did not believe in witches any more than any of her generation, yet she determined to find some other path for her return than that dark alley.

After walking on for some time, she came out on to a path upon the hillside, flanked with olive trees. Not far away, a small boy, scantily clad, was engaged in staking three goats out in a small patch of grass. She paused to watch him, but he stopped in his task and regarded her resentfully. Discon-certed, she said, "*Bonjour.*" The small boy made no reply. Thea hesitated, then, "*Comment vous appelez-vous?*" she asked. The small boy stared at her intimidatingly. At last he replied in tones of acute dislike, "Jean."

"*Vraiment?*" said Thea, and felt proud of the comment. Jean, evidently thinking her not worth his notice, busied himself once more about the goats.

"*Comment s'appellent les . . . ?*" began Thea, and could not remember the French for goats.

Jean ignored her. He never answered unfinished questions. Somewhat abashed, Thea also fell silent, but her curiosity soon overcame her shame. "*Pourquoi,*" she began, "*pourquoi*

vous ne les attachez pas au même, au même . . ." What was
'stake' in French? Jean had paused to learn what new im-
becility the foreign *jeune fille* would enquire. He deigned to
reply this time, speaking very fast. Thea blinked, but gathered
from the agonised gestures of his small hands that the goats
entangled their ropes if they were attached to the same stake.

   "*Ah, bon,*" she said, and congratulated herself once more.
Her chief strength, in speaking the French language, lay in her
ejaculations. Would someone else converse, she was well able
to fill in the gaps. With a look of supreme contempt, Jean
departed. Thea called out, "*Au revoir,*" but he made no sign of
having heard her. His bare feet pattered on the dusty path,
and Thea, smiling, sat down on the grass to rest.

   Beneath her hand, growing in the dry grass, she found a
celandine, and she was surprised at the pang with with she
looked at it. She had seen so many growing in the fields and
hedgerows around Enfield, and England, in that moment,
seemed very far away, and very dear. She, who had seen the
white cliffs of Dover only once, as she sailed away from them
for the first time, found herself comprehending something of
the wistful longing with which those staunch and lovely
buttresses are remembered by Englishmen far from home.
What was it about England, she wondered, that made her
children so faithful and so tender? It was perhaps, above all,
her gentleness, her mild rain, her moderate sunshine, the
pastel shades of her countryside. Thinking of the brilliant,
tropical beauty of the famous Casino Gardens, Thea knew
that she would rather see a clump of primroses, lifting their
pale and fragile faces from beneath the trees of Epping Forest.
At the prospect of living for the rest of her life in the
Principality, Thea was conscious of a faint disquiet. Her
mother, she knew, was happy there, and where her mother
liked to be, so did Thea, and yet . . . and yet she looked
wistfully back to the days of her childhood, to the thrush
singing on the laburnum tree, to her little house in the laurel
bushes, to the time when she and her mother and Nan lived

the quiet life of suburban London together, and seemed contented. But she only indulged in this nostalgia for a moment. Soon her mother would be returning to the flat for tea before changing for the evening. Thea must buy the patisseries and put the kettle on the gas-ring, and her mother would give a laughing account of her afternoon, and Thea would tell her about the terrifying old witch and the hostile small boy called Jean.

Soon the lights would be dancing round the coast, on the Rocher, and high up on the Tête de Chien, which in the daytime crouched like a waiting animal, but at night was daisy-starred with lamps so that the highest always became confused with the night sky. Was it a light, or was it a star? Thea never could decide. The harbour lighthouses would be throwing out their magic beams, and the sea would ripple black and silver, red and green, in irridescent beauty. Oh land of enchantment, thought Thea, angry with herself, how can I long for my pitiful, rainswept, fog-bound England, when I am under the spell of your beauty? How can I seek for days gone by, when these days are so happy? She rose and ran down the path, over cobbles, and, light-footed, down the ramp towards Monte Carlo.

Ten

B elle was anxious that Thea should see something of the surrounding country, so they went on several expeditions together, sometimes on foot within the Principality, sometimes into France, on the railway or by carriage. They visited Laguet, sacred to the Virgin Mary, and went to Roquebrune with its ancient castle, and to St Agnes. On another occasion they drove along the coast and then turned inland, stopping at a beautiful little village, set high among pine woods, with narrow, winding cobbled streets, protected by stone walls from the deep gorge which fell away below. The curé, a little, white-haired, gentle creature showed them his diminutive church with simple pride and then his second treasure, a captive eagle. He smiled at them, his shoulders stooping a little from age, his soutane shabby with long use, while the eagle, attached by a short chain, perched on the wall, blinking in the sunlight. Thea could not forget the eagle, his wise, cruel old eyes, amber-coloured under the cold lids, his air of patient suffering, not of resignation but of hopelessness. She wondered if he remembered spreading his wide wings and hovering over the gorge, if he remembered the feeling of the wind beneath him, of power and strength and freedom.

"He is never tamed," said the curé, affably smiling at his captive. "Always he is a savage, that one."

Belle made suitable replies, and thanked the priest for his kindness, leaving a little money in his box for the poor, by way of recompense. Afterwards they sat in the pine wood and ate their picnic, but Thea still could not forget the eagle.

"Mother," she said at last," wouldn't you think that the priest, being a good man, would let that eagle go?"

"I never try to decide what other people should do," Belle replied, lazily. "It's bad enough trying to decide what one should do oneself."

"But it can't be good to keep that beautiful bird chained up."

"Beautiful, but cruel," remarked Belle. "Did you see its beak, and those talons?"

"It doesn't seem right."

"Lots of things don't seem right," answered Belle. "If you can't do anything about it, it's best not to worry."

"But he was a priest," Thea said, unsatisfied. "I don't see how anyone can believe in God when so many people are unhappy, and things go wrong so much."

Belle, who had been reclining and admiring the blue sky, sat up and regarded her daughter with some apprehension.

"Thea," she begged, "don't become an atheist. Atheists are always so pleased with themselves, as though it's clever not to believe in God, just because most people *do* believe in Him."

Thea smiled unwillingly, but answered soberly enough, "I don't think I do believe in Him."

"I didn't," said Belle, "until I was really in trouble, and then I found that I had to."

"There!" cried Thea, triumphantly, if rather obscurely. "That just shows!"

"It just shows that until we need Him badly, we don't look for Him very seriously," said Belle. "I know I didn't. I just thought of Him as a rather tiresome old gentleman who didn't like me to waltz, and who enjoyed places which smelled rather musty."

Thea, although she was quite sure she didn't believe in God, was faintly shocked by this rather irreverent description, but Belle was absently and inaccurately shying pine cones at their picnic basket. "It isn't until you're utterly alone and desperately unhappy that you begin to look for Him with all your heart," she continued thoughtfully," and then it's surprising how quickly you find Him. It's rather like opening the door to call someone, and finding they've been listening outside." She smiled, sadly and with a little bitterness. "You may forget Him afterwards," she said, "or you may never look for Him again, but if you've known Him for that one time, you must believe in Him for the rest of your life."

"Was that after Father died?" asked Thea, awed.

Belle started, and turned to look at her again. "Your father . . .? I suppose Nan told you that." She was silent for a moment, and then added casually, "He didn't die, you know. He left me."

"Mother!" cried Thea. "Oh, Mother, he couldn't!"

"Couldn't he?" asked Belle.

"But – for good?"

"Oh, I think so," said Belle, with a lightness which Thea felt was not very convincing. "I hardly expect him to come back again now."

"But *why*, Mother?"

"Well . . ." She turned over, and lay with her chin resting on her hands, staring at the distant mountains. "Tom never liked to be tied," she said, almost as though to herself. "Most selfish people put it that way. I don't like to be tied myself." Thea made a quick gesture of protest, but Belle, her eyes on the misty peaks, went on. "I thought perhaps after we were married, he might pull himself together and stay out of debt, but I suppose he didn't love me enough, or maybe it simply wasn't in him. I don't know."

Belle was silent, the little frown between her eyes, the old question in her mind. Did he love her? For how long did he love her? She plucked a blade of grass and began to tear it into fragments, while Thea waited patiently. "I never thought much about how we'd live after we were married. I thought people managed somehow. And Tom always had enough money to bring me flowers and chocolates and to take me out. And he was always cheerful and amusing, and I thought that even if we were poor we would laugh a lot." Thea remembered Nan's voice, with that hint of bitterness, "Your mother likes to laugh."

"He was very handsome, wasn't he?" she asked diffidently. Belle smiled, with a light in her eyes, and a tenderness. "Oh, he was very handsome," she answered, "and he danced divinely. And he paid the prettiest compliments of any man I've ever known."

"And you met him at a dance?" prompted Thea.

"Yes, I met him at a dance. I was wearing that blue silk dress of Nan's, which suited me so badly. I was dancing with Arthur Jervis, who was being very tiresome, and he had trodden on my toes a dozen times and said, 'Oh, I do beg your pardon. Did I hurt you?' and that always annoys me, because you have to say 'No' when it obviously hurts abominably. I'd just said that I was tired, and would sit the next one out, having promised it to him, when suddenly a completely strange man came up to us and asked me for the next dance." She laughed, but Thea saw tears in her eyes. That first sight of Tom, with his dark hair and dark moustache, his hazel eyes dancing with devilment! And poor Arthur, so sandy-haired, with sandy eyelashes. "Tom was tall and very slim, and looked rather like a buccaneer, with brown cheeks and thin arched black eyebrows. He didn't look at all . . . at all . . ." she chuckled wickedly, "not at all respectable. Poor Arthur said that I was tired, very stiffly, and that I had promised the next dance to him. He was so possessive, and so *dull* that it put the devil into me. I picked up my card and crossed out Arthur's name and . . . and then I didn't know what to put instead. So then Tom said to Arthur, as though shocked at his bad manners, 'My dear fellow, introduce us, won't you?' "

"But did Arthur Jervis know him?"

"No, of course he didn't," replied Belle, laughing again, "and he said so, more stiffly than ever. So Tom seized him by the hand and said, 'How stupid of me. So glad to know you.

100

My name's Lawrence, what's yours?' He didn't wait to hear, though, and before I knew what was happening, I was dancing with him, with Arther glowering like a dowager duchess on the edge of the floor. Tom said, 'Such a nice fellow, charming! Rather like a rich uncle,' and after that I knew that . . . that it was Tom." It had to be Tom Lawrence, with his sweet smile, the unexpected dimple in his cheek, with the way he had of looking down from under his lashes, with an amused glint in his eyes. It had to be Tom that she loved.

"And so you married him," said Thea.

"And so I married him. And for a little while, it was like heaven, and we laughed a lot, and we were very much in love. And then, we began to be short of money – more than usual, I mean. Tom was desperately extravagant. He had no idea of economy at all, and never minded being in debt. I tried to make him cut down expenses a little, and we quarrelled over it. I've got a beast of a temper, you know, and his was violent too. When we'd had a quarrel, he used to brood over it, and sometimes he'd look at me as though he hated me, and it used to frighten me, because we hadn't anything except being in love, and liking to be together, and to laugh. When I told him that I was going to have a baby, he went very quiet for a moment, and then he seemed pleased, but after that, we were never so close again. He went out more and, after I couldn't go about with him, I used to be alone a lot, and even when he was home, he used to suddenly go quiet and I didn't know what he was thinking."

Thea clasped her hands tightly in her lap. Belle went on speaking in the same gentle voice. "We were in lodgings by this time, and cheap ones at that. One night, after I'd been sleeping badly, Tom insisted on my taking a sleeping tablet. I slept all night, and woke up feeling drowsy and happy, and stretched out a hand to wake Tom, because it felt late, and he wasn't there. So then I thought it must be very late, but I'd parted with my watch long before that, and I couldn't tell the time. I saw that his brushes were gone from the dressing table, and his dressing gown from off the door, and I think I knew then. He never even . . ." her voice faltered, but she went on, "he never even left a note."

"Oh, Mother, how could he!"

"It was like Tom. You were born two days later. I suppose the thought of the added responsibility was too much for him."

"Then it was my fault."

"No. No, it was bound to happen, sooner or later. He had been restless for some time. I sometimes cheat myself into thinking that Tom left then because it was best for both of us, because we would have worn each other down with quarrels and disagreements until we both hated each other, and it was best to break cleanly, while we . . . while I still loved him. But I know really that he left then because he wanted to, just as he came and asked me to dance because he wanted to."

She stopped speaking and, in her face, gazing unseeing into the distance, was a look of desolation and weariness.

They were both silent for a while, and then Thea said with a quiet violence, "You can't believe in a God who lets things like that happen."

Belle sat up and settled herself against a pine tree, saying briskly, "You can't blame God for my marrying Tom Lawrence. I knew from the beginning that I shouldn't."

"But, if you loved him . . ."

"Oh, *love*," cried Belle, scornfully. "Yes, I loved him, but that didn't make it right for me to marry him."

Thea opened her eyes wide in wonder, and Belle, seeing her expression, threw her head back and laughed. "My darling," she said, "life isn't a fairy story, and fairy story morals don't always work out. If Tom had been as rich as Arthur Jervis, there would have been some excuse for my marrying him, because then Nan could have stopped her dressmaking, or at least not had to work so hard at it. It isn't always the rich man who's bad, and the poor man who's good. Arthur was good and kind and dependable, and very fond of Nan. Tom was feckless and irresponsible and thoroughly selfish, but I married him because I wanted to, although I knew in my heart that I shouldn't, and that it would be disastrous."

"So God punished you."

"No more than a mother punishes a child that plays with a sharp knife after being told not to. The child hurts itself."

"But God seems to leave a lot of knives lying about where people find them."

"We aren't children," said Belle, soberly. "We know what we should do. And very often the knives hurt other people. I knew I shouldn't come out here, and leave Nan alone to look after you and go on slaving at that dressmaking, but I did. We always know what we should do."

"But things don't always happen because of what we do," protested Thea. "Why was Andrew killed, and why did Aunt Ruth die?"

"I don't know," Belle said simply. "But there has to be a reason. You *have* to believe that, or you couldn't bear it. You must believe that they died when it was best for them, that they would have been unhappy later, or made others unhappy."

"Then why should they be born at all?"

"Why is anyone born?" asked Belle, smiling. "We must make some impression on the minds about us. Andrew's family haven't forgotten him, and Ruth brought a son into the world. We see the pieces of the jigsaw. Somewhere there's a complete picture – only we've lost the lid of the box, as so often happens in the nursery."

"I don't understand it," said Thea, frowning.

"Well, nobody does, really." Belle lay down again on her back, staring up at the sky, no bluer than her own eyes. "All we can do is to be as kind to other people as we can, and do what we know we should as often as we can, and go to church and say our prayers, which I don't do, although I know I ought to. Sometimes I think I will, and then it seems so silly to go to church and say my prayers, when I'm leading a perfectly

selfish and frivolous life, and have no intention of changing. If
I went to church, I should end up having to go home and help
Nan, and I just couldn't bear it, or rather I don't want to bear
it. I am selfish, but at least I'm not a hypocrite as I should be if
I said the General Confession once a week, without meaning a
word of it."

"Then I don't see what good church is," said Thea.

"No good at all," Belle agreed, "unless going helps you to
live a better life. Though I believe you're supposed to go to
praise God, but I don't see what good that is by itself without
doing something as well. Still, I imagine it's better than
nothing." She closed her eyes, but Thea still sat straight
and unyielding, with the frown on her face. Belle opened lazy
lashes to look at her, and smiled, saying gently, "I shouldn't
worry about it, darling. Things become clear in time, more or
less."

"I don't like things more or less," replied Thea, with a
shade of irritation. "I like to *know*."

Belle closed her eyes again and went comfortably to sleep,
clearly feeling that she had done her best to explain the
Almighty to her daughter and that further elucidation might
be left to a Higher Authority. But Thea, frowning down into
the valley, was thinking of her father. Why had she not been
told? Why had she been allowed to weave that dear dream, to
love that false idol? She remembered him as she had seen him
so often in the hall at Sunnyside, his hazel eyes, his cleft chin,
and heard his deep, kind voice. She shivered, as with sudden
cold, but the chill was not a physical one. Was there nothing in
the world that was staunch and unassailable? She had thought
of her mother as unfailing, yet she had deserted her. The
Enfield family had seemed protected, yet had proved vulnerable. Aunt Ruth's commonplace little world had overturned
into tragedy. Nan, arbitress of her childhood, was lonely and
vulnerable. And now her father, who had remained for so
many years a steady influence in her life, real if intangible, was
in a moment utterly destroyed, as a sandcastle, pinnacled and

secure, is demolished by the first overwhelming wave. He had never existed as she knew him, he had never been her father, he had never even seen her. She flinched under the cruelty of that thought, and, without reason, remembered a second afterwards the weary, blinking patience of the imprisoned eagle. There was so much cruelty in a world so beautifully fashioned.

Thea turned to look at her mother, sleeping so peacefully, looking as she must have looked on that early morning, when Tom Lawrence crept like a thief away from his wife and his unborn child. She found in her mind the old question which had tormented Belle for so long. Did he love her? For how long did he love her? She remembered the glow on her mother's face when she spoke of that first meeting at the dance, of their love and the early days of their marriage. Why must things change, and always for the worse? She thought of James, and he was strangely confused in her mind with Tom Lawrence. For a moment she did not see James as the generous, kind-hearted, affectionate boy she remembered, but as the selfish man who had been her father, who acted to please himself, who hated to be tied. She flung the conception away from her, wishing passionately that she could have no memory of James except as she had seen him on her first visit to Enfield, that he need never have grown up, nor learnt to wear that sulkiness about his mouth. But, she thought, Andrew is the only one who is unchanged for me. She remembered what her mother had said about Andrew's death, but rebelled against it. Ah no, she thought, I will not believe that the only safety lies in death, that only in dying can we achieve perfection. Yet, what reason is there in life? We are born, we grow from childhood, we grow old, we die. What happens to us in between? Why is the ant born, to run swiftly amongst the grass and then to perish? Why was the eagle reared, to fly for a spell and then to blink its life out on the end of a short chain? What, after all, is life, this brief span of breathing, laughing, crying and then silence?

Belle stirred and opened her eyes and stretched. "I had a beautiful sleep," she said. "I suppose we should make our way back now." Thea nodded, and then, guiltily conscious of her moment of peevishness, smiled and helped to pack the picnic basket. She put in it a pine cone, having always a tendency to carry with her tokens and souvenirs of moments in her life. In her room at home was her mother's handkerchief, set apart, the kite from Enfield, a shilling given her by Uncle Robert and never spent, a cheap little ring out of a cracker which Aunt Ruth had given to her, having come upon it while Thea was at the house. She knew that by touching these inanimate objects it was possible to retrace her life, however briefly, as though they guided the memory into a short, clear groove which might otherwise lie forgotten. She did not want to forget this village, or the little pine wood where she had watched her mother sleep.

As they walked slowly back to the village, the sun hot at their back, Thea saw a little path which ran off to the left and a noticeboard which stood at its commencement. She went to read it, expecting it to be a signpost, and stopped in front of it in bewilderment.

"Mother, what does this mean?"

"What does it say?" asked Belle, too lazy to leave the path and see.

"It says, '*Prenez garde au Loup*'."

"That's right."

"But – 'Beware of the wolf'?"

"That's what it means."

Thea fled down to her mother's side in sudden panic. "Wolves!" she gasped. "Fancy meeting a wolf!"

Belle laughed. "I don't expect one meets them very often," she said. "Still, it's rather fun to think that you might. How much pleasanter Abbot's Green would be with a notice like that on the station."

Thea was amused at the suggestion. "Miss Luke would say that it was *too* romantic," she remarked.

106

"Would she?" said Belle. "Yes, I suppose she would." She looked at Thea curiously. "You're interested in people, aren't you?"

"Yes," said Thea, flattered. "I think I am."

"And rather critical of them?" suggested Belle.

Thea was less pleased. "Am I?" she asked. "I don't think I am. I just like to see what they're like."

"What do you think of Mrs Van Dutyens?" enquired Belle, with an air of beginning a new subject. Thea hesitated, afraid of seeming too critical. "Well, she's rather . . . I mean, she doesn't seem to be very fond of her husbands."

"No," said Belle. "She doesn't think much of men, altogether. She worked in a restaurant for some years, and it gave her a poor opinion of men."

"I wonder why," said Thea. Belle looked at her sideways, but offered no suggestion. "It's a pity she's so fat," Thea remarked.

"Poor Sadie," laughed Belle. "She always means to get thin, but it's always a celebration, or she needs cheering up, or someone else does. Bless her, I like her fat. She wouldn't be Sadie if she were thin."

Thea longed to ask why her mother liked Mrs Van Dutyens, fat or thin, but mindful of her recent gentle rebuke, kept silence. She thought of the gross bulk, the sagging cheeks and false yellow curls and was puzzled.

Eleven

A few days later, as Thea and her mother were strolling down towards La Condamine to do a little shopping, they were met by a tall thin Englishman who was among Belle's friends. Everyone called him Ambrose, and Thea never remembered his surname. He talked to Belle for a few minutes, and then persuaded her to turn back with him and join a small party for an aperitif on the terrace of the Café de Paris. He always spoke to Belle as though she were alone, and Thea, furiously angry that he should intrude upon their morning, further resented his calm ignoring of her presence. She walked along beside her mother, pouting and dumb, while Ambrose talked in his lazy drawl of the latest gossip or the international situation and Belle laughed at him, secure in the consciousness that she was beautiful and that he appreciated her beauty.

On the terrace, they found Mrs Van Dutyens with a friend of hers called Fanny, and a handsome old gentleman named Colonel Morris. They greeted Belle warmly, and Mrs Van Dutyens called out, "Here's my little Thea," with the air of one gallantly refusing to admit defeat. Her little Thea sat firmly down beside her mother, ignoring the chair indicated by the irrepressible Sadie, and viewed the assembly with chill dislike. Belle, annoyed and disconcerted by her behaviour, was remembering the brooding coldness which she had discovered long ago in another pair of hazel eyes.

"My dear Fanny," said Ambrose, plaintively, "it is quite clear that you must move to the next chair, or how can I sit next to Mrs Lawrence and to you at the same time?"

Fanny laughed and moved to the next seat, and Thea thought how clever this man was, who made people laugh at him, and always got what he wanted. By adopting the position of Court Jester, he was permitted to say what he liked and to use familiarities which would have been indignantly denied to a more serious suitor, and yet he had become indispensable to any entertainment which was given. Having settled himself in the place he desired, he edged his chair nearer to Belle's and watched her with pale blue eyes.

While the drinks were being ordered, Thea turned her attention to the other lady of the party, a bony woman with thick red lips, enormous eyes and, it seemed to Thea, far too many teeth. Not only were they very large, but she seemed to have more than her fair share, and she smiled constantly, as though thrusting them forward for inspection. When she raised her small glass to her mouth, she looked like an alligator attempting to drink out of a thimble, and she wore two rows of metallic beads and four bracelets, which rattled, thought Thea, like the clatter of innumerable teeth. With a flood of absurd amusement bubbling up beneath her ill-humour, Thea was waiting for that delicious moment when the glass should vanish suddenly into that toothy cavern, never to reappear.

"Fanny," said Mrs Van Dutyens, "where's that husband o' yours?"

"Oh, don't talk to me about Bertie," replied Fanny, with much rolling of her eyes, "I had such a quarrel with him this morning."

"I thought you two never quarrelled," said Belle, smiling.

"Never quarrel with yer husband," cried Mrs Van Dutyens. "When he makes you mad, jest go out an' buy yerself a nice mink coat, or a diamond brooch. It sweetens yer temper, an' then you got the goods afterwards."

"Yes, but supposing he won't pay for them," protested Fanny, seriously considering the problem.

"Whaddoyou care?" said Mrs Van Dutyens. "You got the

110

goods, ain't yer? Get yer hands on portable property, girls. That's always been my motter."

Thea shuddered, almost visibly, and Ambrose removed his gaze from Belle's face long enough to say, "If Bertie were here, he'd be getting worried about his bank balance."

"I don't think he's got one any more," sighed Fanny, "after last night."

Then they all began talking about the Casino, and systems, while Thea sipped her drink and watched Ambrose's grey-gloved hand upon the arm of her mother's chair.

"Ambrose," said Mrs Van Dutyens suddenly, "what're you wearin' to the Fancy Dress Ball?"

"Ambrose should go as Don Juan," suggested Fanny slyly.

"Every man should realise," pronounced Ambrose, "that what he wears to a Fancy Dress Ball is of no interest to anyone but himself." There was an exclamation of protest.

"I am going as a pirate," Colonel Morris announced, impressively.

"That should be a novel costume," said Ambrose, gravely and politely, and Thea saw her mother's elbow move ever so slightly to nudge his arm, though her face remained serious.

"We-ell," began Mrs Van Dutyens, "I thought I'd go as Minerva."

"Enchanting," murmured Ambrose.

"But, an owl," cried Belle. "You must have an owl on your shoulder."

"Don't I know it!" agreed Mrs Van Dutyens. "I heard that a woman had a stuffed owl, a concierge jest roun' the corner."

"A stuffed owl as concierge?" enquired Ambrose, thoughtfully. "As useful as most concierges, probably."

"So I went roun' to try to get her to lend it me. Well, she brought me everything she possessed, I guess. 'No,' I says, 'No, *oin oiseau*,' – not rememberin' the French for owl. So then she brings me a canary. 'No', I says, '*oin grand oiseau, comprenez?*' So she says, yes, she comprennes, and brings me a hat with a feather in it, an ostrich feather. I suppose an ostrich

111

is a big bird." Mrs Van Dutyens joined in the laugh against herself, adding, "Every time I say 'oin oiseau' it sounds sillier than the last time."

"I'm going as Red Riding Hood," said Fanny, proudly.

Grandmother, quoted Thea to herself, what big teeth you've got.

Ambrose apparently had the same idea, for he said languidly, "I suppose that Bertie will be going disguised as a wolf?"

"Oh, Bertie!" cried Fanny, "he'd better go as a bear – a bear with a sore head!"

In the babble of laughter and jokes which followed this witticism, Ambrose said softly to Belle, "I couldn't decide whether to be a pirate or a pierrot. Now, I shall certainly be a pierrot," with a meaningful glance at the self-satisfied countenance of Colonel Morris.

Belle smiled, and Thea was once more torn with jealousy at the intimacy of a shared private amusement which she saw between her mother and this man.

"How dull," said Belle, reprovingly. "Can't you think of a more –" her voice quivered – "a more novel costume?"

"When I am dancing with you, no one will be looking at me," said Ambrose, lightly.

"Oh, indeed, and supposing you are not dancing with me at all?"

"Then I shall be too miserable to mind whether other people look at me or not." They smiled at each other again.

"Now then, you two," came the coarse, loud voice of Mrs Van Dutyens, "no whispering. Belle, what are you wearin'?"

"I haven't decided yet," replied Belle.

"Go as Joan of Arc," suggested Colonel Morris, with a look of surprise at finding himself so imaginative. The others applauded the idea, but Belle shook her head, saying, "I don't really know what she would wear."

"Go as Venus," recommended Ambrose, still drawling, but with meaning in his voice.

There arose in Belle that spark of devilment which had made her turn readily to the daring unconvention of Tom Lawrence.

"I'm not at all sure that *she* would wear anything at all!" she said, laughing, and the people at neighbouring tables turned to stare at the shout of amusement which rose from the group, with beautiful Mrs Lawrence tossing her auburn head, and only the small, pale young girl sober and impassive beside her.

Back in the flat, Thea remarked that she did not like the Englishman, Ambrose. "He's so . . . so familiar," she explained.

Belle stopped ironing her muslin dress and looked at her. "Now, Thea," she said, flushing, and with a voice that Thea had never heard before, "if all you can do is criticise my friends, you'd better go back to England, for I won't have it. You sit about, with a face that would turn milk sour, and make no effort to be pleasant, and make everyone feel uncomfortable. If you don't like it here, for goodness sake go home. But don't spoil everyone else's pleasure."

Thea stood quite still for a moment with a wild look in her eyes, and then turned and fled. Sitting on the rocks, watching the sea churning and frothing below, she had the same feeling of dismayed betrayal as when she found her mother gone to Monaco, all those years before. It reminded her of a dream she had often had, when she was climbing up a long hill with no foothold and suddenly found herself slipping, falling, with the blood beating in her head and her breath coming fast. She thought of what she had said with a hot sense of discomfort, and knew that her mother's annoyance was justified, and yet felt no less betrayed, because her mother had never spoken to her except gently, and she had thought that to her at least she could say exactly what she liked. She remembered her bad behaviour on the terrace and blushed and sighed, and her mother's angry words thudded fiercely in her brain, and she felt that she had nothing left to live for. It was at moments such as this, she thought, that people killed themselves. She heard a footstep behind her, but did not turn her head, because the tears were beginning to flow, and in a moment, Belle had knelt beside her, her cheek to Thea's, her arms about her, saying, half-laughing, half-crying, "My darling, I couldn't find you. I'm so sorry. I didn't mean it, you know I didn't." They clung to each other, and laughed, wet-eyed, and Thea felt an ecstasy of happiness, because, after all, her mother's love was safe and their relationship even more secure for the brief disturbance.

"Ambrose isn't too bad," said Belle, persuasively. "He makes me laugh, and he's a beautiful dancer. I'm sorry for him, too." Thea looked a question, and Belle explained, "He and his wife don't get on well together."

"He's married?" said Thea in surprise.

"Yes, he's married to Fanny's sister-in-law – Bertie's sister."

"Fanny doesn't like Bertie very much, does she?" asked Thea.

"Oh, I think they're quite happy. But Fanny says that Ambrose's wife is dreadfully bad-tempered. He married her while he was still at Oxford, and they were never happy together. But unfortunately she's a Roman Catholic, so she won't give him a divorce."

Thea remembered Janey saying, "Our sort of people don't get divorced."

"Have you met his wife?" she asked.

"No, she's in England," Belle replied. "They're separated."

"What a shame," said Thea, with as much feeling as she could manage.

"Yes, it is, isn't it?" cried Belle, catching at her words gratefully. "He's so easy-going and good-tempered that it seems hard that he can't marry again. Everyone likes him."

They were strolling homewards now, and Thea could not help feeling a certain relief on finding that Ambrose was married. She had wondered for a while whether . . . And she did not want another father. More especially, she did not want Ambrose as her father. But, if he was married, however unhappily, then there was no danger, and he and her mother were just friends, as she should have known. She pressed Belle's arm, contritely, whispering, "I'm sorry I was so silly."

"My darling, that's all right. I'm sorry I was cross. We have the whole afternoon to ourselves. Marie is cooking us a ragôut for lunch, and then we'll walk up on to the Rocher and have a nice peaceful time, just the two of us."

"Oh, wonderful!" breathed Thea, with such awed delight that Belle was torn once more between amusement and pain.

"I wonder," said Thea, thoughtfully, "how often in our lives we're allowed to be perfectly happy."

Belle was watching her with the tender, smiling face she usually had when her daughter became philosophical.

"Not very often," she replied. "But there are a lot of times when we are not perfectly happy, and yet are contented enough, when small pleasures are enough for us, and life is good, if not wonderful."

"Do you think that makes up for the times when we're miserable?" asked Thea.

Belle was silent. She saw a bare, ugly room, linoleum of a sickly hue on the floor, pale brown curtains at the one small window. She saw the empty hook on the door, watched the damp stain on the wall which was the shape of a man's head. She felt on her arm the warm, light little body which had so newly ventured into an unfriendly world. "My little Thea, Dorothea, the gift of God." For herself, she had only one desire, to die, to be released from this pain and humiliation and loneliness. But, for the child, his child, the fragile little creature he had not waited to see . . . What should she ask for a child born in such an unhappy moment? A distant echo caught at her mind, eluded her, came to rest again.

"*You were born in a merry hour.*"

"*No, sure, my lord, my mother cried. But then there was a star danced, and under that was I born.*"

115

Belle, sitting in the sunshine, with the Mediterranean Sea dancing below, remembered how she had turned weary eyes towards the cold square of sky, lying in that springless bed above a dirty London street.

"Oh, God," she had prayed aloud, "it doesn't matter what happens to me. My life is over. Only, let my Thea be happy. Let a star dance for her, Lord. Let her be happy."

Her voice had broken into weak sobs. In the pale November sky, whipped clear by icy winds, a single star had shone suddenly, like the star once poised over Bethlehem. Through the tears which filled her eyes, it had seemed to dance.

She turned, and found Thea still waiting for an answer.

"I think," she said slowly, "that there are times of unhappiness for which no joy could ever compensate, except perhaps in Heaven."

Thea nodded, and, at the understanding in her face, Belle felt a horror and shame, that she could so have hurt her daughter, even as Tom had once hurt her.

"The worst part is that no one else can ever know how you feel," said Thea. "And when you're unhappy, it makes you lonely."

"God knows," Belle put in, casually, and Thea frowned. How could God, even if He existed, know about childish misery, living in His heaven, with cherubim and seraphim casting golden crowns upon the glassy sea? How could it be any comfort to know that, immeasurably far away, existed a being, incomprehensibly great, called God, who looked down upon human affairs with the calm understanding of a naturalist watching beetles?

"No," continued Belle, "the worst sort of unhappiness is when you don't want anyone to know. That's how it was with me after Tom went. I didn't let Nan know, I didn't even tell her where I was. She hadn't my address. I felt that I couldn't bear any sympathy, that if anyone touched me I would scream. So I just lay and waited to die." She laughed at herself, but shivered in the sunlight. "In the end, Robert heard

where I was – I never discovered how – and he and Mary came
and took us home."

"Uncle Robert?" asked Thea, wonderingly.

"That's right." Belle was remembering Mary's gentle, calm
voice saying, without emotion, "We have come to take you
home." She remembered Robert, how his tall, square-shouldered figure seemed to fill the bare room, how his arms were
strong about her, how tenderly Mary had carried the baby
down the narrow staircase, away from that house of despair.

Thea said with sudden vehemence, "I hate that you should
have been so unhappy. I just hate it!"

"My darling, it was so long ago."

"But you haven't forgotten it."

"No, one doesn't forget. But it stops hurting, nearly. I
sometimes think that, apart from the fact that we usually
bring unhappiness on ourselves, it's something of a compliment to have troubles. Some people seem to go so easily
through life, but they don't have the qualities of sympathy and
understanding which only grow by being unhappy. Look at
Nan. She's had more grief than anyone I know, but she's
never lost her faith or her courage, or her sense of humour.
Then, people who've had real troubles, seem to be immunised
against the small worries of life, they're usually more contented than those who don't know what despair can be." Belle
looked at Thea, and felt a sudden urgency, as though she must
make her understand this vague creed of hers. "Don't you see,
darling, there must be some reason for the things that happen
to us. I think that usually there are many reasons. First,
they're sometimes our own fault. Or they may be right and
best for us. Or it may be that we are too confident and too
selfish. We need to be shaken up, to learn that we can't run
our lives as we thought we could. And, beyond all the rest,
when we look back upon unhappiness, it fades and lessens,
until sometimes we find ourselves remembering with nostalgia
our early troubles, because of the people we shared them with
and the way we faced them."

117

"But we may be unhappy all our lives, and then die and go to Hell."

"I don't believe it," cried Belle, "and I won't believe it. I think we make our own hell on earth, when we are far away from God, and won't ask for His comfort. I won't believe that we can suffer so on earth because we are stupid and headstrong, like children, and then, for that same childish folly and wilfulness, go into everlasting torment!" She smiled a little, after her earnestness, and said, "When I die, I shall go straight to the gates of Heaven, and I shall say, 'Remember me, Belle, who was so fond of dancing and pretty clothes, who was so naughty and selfish? Remember that house in Dray Street, in London? Wasn't that my hell, and may I not come into Heaven now, to find peace and comfort with the other foolish children?' Then God will shake his head at me, and say, 'You don't deserve it, Belle, my dear, but come in. St Peter and all sinners are waiting for you. Only don't let St Paul see that I'm letting you in.' Then God will open the gate and spread his sleeve out so that St Paul and all the good men can't see me, and I shall slip quietly into Heaven." She smiled still, but turned her face away, as though looking for Corsica, so that Thea should not see the tears in her eyes.

Twelve

For Thea and her mother, the enchanted moments fled swiftly by in the little Principality, with the ancient cannons guarding it up on the Rocher, and toy soldiers strutting to and fro with self-importance in their gay, musical-comedy uniforms. Silvery dawns followed starry nights, glaring noon gave way to mimosa-scented dusk. The days slipped away like the falling petals of a rose.

Thea awoke one morning to find Belle returned from a dance at the hotel, already in her dressing gown and taking her hair-pins out before the mirror.

"Did you have a nice time?" asked Thea, still half asleep.

"Lovely," replied Belle, and Thea could see in the mirror the colour in her cheeks, and her eyes sparkling. She sat up in bed, rubbing her eyes and trying to rouse herself.

"I'll make the coffee," she said.

"No, don't you get up," answered Belle, standing up with her hair down her back. She did a few dancing steps across the room, her flimsy dressing gown swirling out behind her, dropped a kiss on Thea's cheek as she passed, and went into the kitchen. Thea could hear her humming a tune as she lit the gas-ring and rattled the coffee-tin.

Thea got out of bed after a few minutes, struggled into her dressing gown and slippers and shuffled, yawning, towards the kitchen. Then Belle screamed, and Thea's sleepiness fell from her like a garment. She ran to the doorway. The fantastic dragon was madder than ever, writhing in the midst of licking flames. The bright glow of Belle's hair was drowned in a yet

119

brighter light, its red-gold matched by the blazing fire. The gas still bubbled innocently and unambitiously, with its tiny ring of flames. But beside it stood Belle, still screaming, with her hands up to her face.

"No!" cried Thea, "Oh, Mother, no!" But in her mind was a dreadful sense of satisfied apprehension, as though this was what she had been expecting and waiting for.

Thea dragged the bedspread from the next room, and somehow the flames were at last extinguished, and Belle was lying still and silent on the floor. Thea stood for a moment looking wildly round the room, as though waiting for someone to come and help her. Then she ran outside and stood on the landing outside the flat, calling for the concierge in a high, hysterical voice. She came at last, a very stout woman in a checked dressing gown, with her grey hair in curlers.

"*Un médecin,*" said Thea, like a child repeating an uncomprehended lesson, and Madame called to her husband one brief sentence, before following Thea into the flat.

The doctor was a brisk, fat little man with pince-nez. He was not exactly kind, but dependable. Thea felt that she could trust him. He came to where she was sitting in the kitchen, and said, "She is not well." Thea looked dumbly up at him and nodded. "You are alone?" he asked, and she nodded again. He pursed his lips, and said in his bad English. "I will send a sister." He lingered, doubtfully, and then asked, "You desire that I shall send for a priest?"

"Oh, no!" cried Thea, emphatically, all her narrow, suburban superstition rising up with the realization that this was a Roman Catholic country. "We're . . ." she hesitated, "we're *Protestant*," she finished. The doctor looked down at her oddly, but made no reply. He turned towards the door, repeating only, "I will send you a sister, Mademoiselle." Thea saw him speaking to the concierge in the hall and shrugging his shoulders. It did not occur to her until long afterwards that by 'priest' he meant a minister of religion – any religion.

Shortly after the doctor's departure, there was a knock at the door and Thea went to answer it, thinking what a relief it would be to have a calm, efficient hospital nurse. The concierge, like a fat, female Good Samaritan, was sitting with Belle. Waiting outside the door, Thea found two shadowy figures, in black robes, with pale faces glimmering in white frames. The doctor had sent not one sister, but two.

All through that grey morning, the two nuns nursed Belle with devoted tenderness. Madame la concierge retired to dress and take out her curlers, of which she had been rather conscious. Thea wandered restlessly about in the kitchen and the hall. The coffee-pot lay on the floor. Thea stood and looked at the gas-ring in horror and disgust and covered her eyes with desperate fingers, as though she could thus wipe away what she had seen.

At last, one of the sisters opened the bedroom door and beckoned Thea inside. Belle was unconscious, but moaning and murmuring Thea's name. Thea sat down beside her and spoke to her in a small, cool voice, and saw that it made her quieter. The two motionless black figures on the other side of the bed might have been statues, with their waxen, expressionless faces and their imperceptible breathing. The room was very still and quiet. Belle's dress lay where she had flung it over a chair, and her dancing slippers nearby, one on its side, as she had kicked it off. On the dressing table was a spray of white roses, fading for lack of water. Thea remembered those other white roses which Arthur Jervis had given her mother on the night she first met Tom Lawrence. She guessed that Ambrose had given these, matching them to her white and silver ball-dress. The small clock on the dressing table ticked away the vigil and no breath of wind stirred the long curtains which hid the harbour lights.

After a time, Belle moved and awoke, saying, "Thea."

121

"Yes, Mother," replied Thea, leaning forward, and speaking in a calm, controlled voice.

"If I . . . if I don't come through, don't mind too much." Thea could not answer, and Belle added, with a great urgency in her weak voice, "I want you to be happy, darling."

"Yes, Mother," said Thea, thinking only of stilling the anxious movement of those bandaged hands. Belle closed her eyes and drifted away into unconsciousness again. A little later she said, as though continuing without any interval, "Tell Nan . . ."

"Yes, Mother, tell Nan . . . ?"

"Tell Nan, I'm sorry," she finished, and sighed. Thea slid on to her knees, to be nearer to the tired voice. She could see only her mother's eyes and mouth, all else being covered with thick bandages. It seemed for a moment that Belle was sinking silently, but presently she whispered, with greater difficulty, "You've got Tom's eyes." One of the nuns made a movement towards the bed, but the other checked her with a hand upon her sleeve. Belle spoke again, with the old chuckle in her voice, the spark of devilment in her eyes. "They wanted me to go to the Fancy Dress Ball as Joan of Arc," she said. "There's nothing like living the part!" Thea smiled, and saw Belle's mouth quirk a little. In after years, she was glad that her mother, who had always made her laugh, should have made her laugh with her last breath. For it was her last. The smile ended in a moan, she sighed sharply, and between her bandaged face and Thea came a black, impenetrable shadow, as one of the sisters came silently round to bend over her. Thea thought that it was a symbol of the darkness that must always be, from then on, between her and her mother.

The nuns were very kind to Thea. One of them, Sister Marie-Thérèse, called her *ma chère*, and the endearment came strangely from her pale lips, like an unfamiliar language. With the help of Madame la concierge, they made up a bed for Thea in the kitchen, the gas-ring now black and harmless. Sister Marie-Thérèse leant over her to tuck in the sheet, and her big black wooden cross swung close to Thea's face.

That isn't my god, thought Thea, with fierce hatred, the god of pain and ugliness and suffering. My god is laughing and happy, like the ancient Pan. He is the god of dappled, leafy shadows, of sunny hilltops, and a high, sweet fluting beside a stream.

She lay in the dark, listening to the sounds of movement from the bedroom and the murmur of soft French voices. Every time she closed her eyes, two pictures forced themselves upon her, Belle screaming in the midst of the flames, or Belle masked in bandages moaning on the bed. Somewhere a clock struck four, and Thea remembered that the same clock had struck one as she had watched her mother taking down her hair before the mirror. At that thought, a desperation seized her. She crept out of bed and hesitated, looking down at her nightdress. Her clothes were all in the bedroom. She pulled on her dressing gown and slippers and went silently out of the flat and up the stairs to the street. Once outside, she began to run, and did not stop until she was clutching the great door-handle, like a prisoner reaching sanctuary.

The door yielded, and the close, musty smell inside welcomed her. The first dim light of dawn showed the empty seats, the aisle, and the bare altar. She ran up the aisle in her slippered feet and fell down upon the altar-steps. She beat with her clenched fists on the carpeted ground, and cried out loud, "Oh, God! Oh, Mother! God, help me!" Her voice echoed in the empty building, and was followed by a great silence. There was no one there but her. The figure on the cross remained twisted and motionless. She hammered on the brass rail, as though she would batter at the very gates of Heaven. No answer came. No voice replied. Desolation closed in upon her, and she put her head down on the smooth carpet.

"Oh, God," she whispered, humbly, "I can't bear it alone."

As Thea crept back into the flat, the clock was striking five.

No one heard her as she closed the door softly behind her and lay down again in the kitchen. With an odd comfort close about her heart, she closed her eyes, and fell asleep at once, like a child safe in its mother's arms.

Thirteen

Thea awoke next morning to find Mrs Van Dutyens standing beside her, holding a tray. She was unfamiliar in a plain black dress, in which she looked like an elderly waitress. Gone were all her jewels. There hung about her no scent of perfume, or of alcohol. She said, in a matter-of-fact way, "Here y'are, dear, here's a nice cup a coffee." Thea sat up, dazed and uncomprehending, and Mrs Van Dutyens put down the tray.

"You'll find the coffee's all right," she said. "I useter make it fer my livin', and I ain't quite fergotten how." She put the dressing gown around Thea's shoulders. "Now you jest have a drink of that. Have a bite of roll, too. It'll do you good."

Thea leant back against the pillow and drank the coffee, trying to realise that all that had happened early that morning was true. As a child, she had once dreamed that her mother was dead, and had awoken in the morning with tears pouring down her cheeks. How blessed had been the relief to find that it had been only a dream and to hear her mother's voice from the next room! And now she must realise that the nightmare had been no nightmare but cold truth, that her mother was dead in fact, that she would never see her again. Her mind slid constantly away on to trivial matters, wondering whether Mrs Van Dutyens had found any coffee in the coffee-pot, whether anyone had put the roses in water, where they had put the charred bedspread, but behind all trivialities lay the one important fact, which she could not escape. Her mother was dead.

"Have a drop more coffee," said Mrs Van Dutyens, and poured out another cupful.

"It's very good," said Thea, grateful for no mention of Belle.

"I useter be in the resterant business, until I married my second. People useter come from miles away for my coffee."

"Mrs Van Dutyens . . ." began Thea, but was interrupted.

"Now, you just call me Sadie. It's easier than all that long name. You don't have to talk unless you want to. I thought mebbe you'd come to my hotel for a day or two, jest until we can arrange things, an' fix up yer passage home."

"Oh yes," said Thea.

"I'll let yer granny know that you're comin' home, an' she'll be there t'meet you." She stood up and picked up the tray in a practised way, holding it on her hip as she paused and looked down on Thea. "You jest take it easy for a while an' get up when you feel like it. Was there anythin' else you was wantin'?"

"It was just . . ." began Thea. The big face above her was empty of all expression, all sympathy, calm and attentive as that of a good waitress. It gave Thea reassurance. "My clothes are in the other room," she said. She could not explain that she did not want to go into the familiar room, made strange by the figure which was her mother's, yet which bore no resemblance to her, still and silent instead of warm and colourful and full of movement.

"I put yer clothes here on the chair," said Sadie. "I'll pack up yer other things and bring them to the hotel." She put the tray down by the sink, and turned back to Thea. "If you want me for anythin', jest call," she said, and went out with her steady, flat-footed gait. Something in her unemotional way of speaking, her unobtrusive assumption of authority, reminded Thea of Nurse. She was conscious, behind her grief and despair, of a faint sensation of relief at the knowledge that Mrs Van Dutyens had come to assume the responsibilities she dreaded, that she would give orders and Thea had only to obey them.

"There's just one thing, Thea," said Mrs Van Dutyens turning in the doorway, "I got to say to you. You'll be wanting somethin' black to wear. Shall I get it made for you?"

"No," said Thea. "Mother didn't want me to wear black."

"You don't think mebbe yer Granny w'd like you to wear it?" Thea tried to remember what her mother had said. "Unless Nan were still alive . . ." She looked up at Mrs Van Dutyens. "She would want to be buried here, I think. I won't wear black for the funeral. But I ought to have some black clothes to wear when I go home. Nan would like it."

"Very well. I'll see you have that."

There was no tremor in Thea's voice when she spoke of the funeral or mentioned her mother. She moved and talked mechanically. She showed no warmth of gratitude or affection to Mrs Van Dutyens, and none seemed to be expected. She did what she was told, docilely, she asked no questions and never made any suggestions. Only on one point had she stood firm. She would not wear black at the funeral, nor would she put anything on the grave but roses.

They stood under the same brilliant sunshine and blue sky to which Thea had become accustomed. Mrs Van Dutyens was in deep mourning, and Fanny was there, no longer comic or foolish but plain and silent and rather pathetic. Ambrose and Colonel Morris and Fanny's husband had come, with other friends of Belle's. Thea alone was dressed in her best Sunday frock and hat. She did not notice the other mourners, nor was she offended by the tears of Fanny and Sadie. She saw that Fanny had brought a huge wreath of lilies, and felt that she should be amused by it, that Belle would have laughed at it, but found that she could not even smile. Perhaps my sense of humour has died with Mother, she thought. Perhaps it was so much a part of her that it is buried in this grave. She looked at the grave for a moment, with her bunch of white roses and the great wreath of lilies showing clearly among the many other flowers. Then she turned away. She was certain of only one thing in the turmoil of her mind. The resurrection of the body was a fantastic belief, but far more incredible would it be to believe that this wooden box, this hole in the rock could be the end of Belle Lawrence, with her warmth and laughter, her selfishness and repentance, her gaiety and tolerance and love.

This is not the end, thought Thea, walking back to the hotel with Mrs Van Dutyens. Groping and frightened, she held on to that one steadying certainty, "This is not the end."

With the funeral over and her clothes and Belle's packed for her return to England, Thea began to dread the long journey alone across France, the ordeal of engaging and paying porters, of finding her way across Paris and on to the Channel steamer. The day after the funeral Mrs Van Dutyens remarked casually, "I booked yer passage. As I got some business in Paris, I thought you wouldn't mind if I was to come with you as far as Calais. Yer granny'll meet you at Dover, an' maybe you wouldn't be sorry to have the crossing by yerself."

Thea looked at her, and for a moment she felt like putting her head down on Sadie's shoulder and sobbing out her gratitude and relief. But she was afraid that if she started to cry, she might not be able to stop. There was something shameful, she thought, in opening to strangers the secrets of your emotions. A middle-class convention of reticence and dignity had upheld her through the anguish of the days since her mother's death, and she dared not relinquish it. She felt that it was the only strength she possessed.

"Thank you," she answered. "I'm glad you're coming." Mrs Van Dutyens nodded and seemed satisfied.

On the way to the station, Thea suddenly said, "I want to go past the flat." Mrs Van Dutyens hesitated, and then gave the order to the driver. Thea leant forward to look at the dark doorway, and for a moment it seemed ridiculous that she should be driving away from it with Mrs Van Dutyens.

It seemed that Belle must be in the flat, doing some mending or writing to Nan; as though Thea's conscious, reasoning mind accepted Belle's death, but a faint, rebellious voice behind refused to believe it. It was as though the big, light room, looking out over the Mediterranean was waiting for her, with her mother sitting on the balcony, the sun burnishing the lights of her hair, throwing a glow of health on her cheeks. It was as though the room would never change, never be occupied by other tenants, but would wait for her thus for ever.

The palm tree on the station platform was there to mock her, and every landmark which she remembered from her former journey struck at her like a physical blow. She sat quite still in her corner of the carriage, with her face calm and quiet, her hands loosely clasped in her lap. Only in her eyes, staring out of the window, did the pain and loneliness lie open and undisguised. Mrs Van Dutyens did not watch her, nor attempt to make her talk. She looked comfortable and homely in her loose black dress, and she made casual remarks at intervals, as though to remind Thea that she was not quite alone. She fed her too, in the same impersonal way, as though she had been one of her customers. When night came down, and Thea dreaded the long, dark hours, Mrs Van Dutyens supplied her with magazines and dozed herself in the lighted carriage. The next day, she talked a little, of her own life, of Joe Marchant, who kept the 'Now or Never', an eating-house, which catered for highway traffic and miners from a nearby quarry in Wyoming. He had married Sadie, his head waitress, because her coffee was "way ahead" of anyone else's. When Joe died, "of overeatin' chiefly, I guess," Sadie had taken charge of the restaurant, until Mr Van Dutyens had driven by in his millionaire fashion, stopped for a cup of her now-famous coffee, and lost his golden heart to her yellow curls.

"I kinda hated t'leave the 'Now or Never', though," said Sadie. "A'course, you don't see the best side of men when they're thinkin' of nothin' but grabbin' a meal in the quickest time they can, but they shore liked my cookin'. I felt I was doin' a good job a work."

"When did Mr Van Dutyens die?" asked Thea, trying to forget how the cockatoo in the flat above had screeched its monotonous, lonely cry while she was waiting in the kitchen, and how the gas-ring had twinkled slyly at her, like a live creature.

"Oh, a coupla years ago. He wasn't too bad, for a Dutchy. When he was sober, he was that mean, he wouldn't give you an old boot-button. But when he'd had a drink or two, he'd start handin' round dollar bills like they was tickets to a no-good variety show." Thea nodded, and tried to smile. "When you git married, Thea," said Mrs Van Dutyens, suddenly, "you want to marry a man who's a few years older'n you are."

Thea remembered Tom Lawrence. I'll never get married, she thought. It's too dangerous. I don't want to run that risk.

"Not too old," Mrs Van Dutyens continued, "about five or six years older w'd do. But you want someone who'll take care of you."

No, thought Thea, never again. I'll never again be dependent upon one person for my happiness. I will never love anyone as I have loved Mother. It isn't safe.

At last the journey was over, and Thea, with her luggage, was settled on the boat in Calais harbour. Mrs Van Dutyens prepared to go ashore, and the moment which Thea had dreaded was arrived. Somehow she must thank Mrs Van Dutyens for all she had done, without breaking into the wild storm of tears which would flood away all her precarious defences.

"Sadie," she began, "I—"

"Now, don't you say a word, honey," Sadie interrupted, "not one word."

"I'll never forget what you've done for me," said Thea, trembling. With unexpected firmness, Mrs Van Dutyens replied, putting a hand on her arm. "I want you *should* forget it," she said. "I want you should forget *all* of it, 'cep' the time that went before. An' if you sh'd ever want any help, either money'r anythin' else, jest write straight t'me. Here's my address in the States, 'cause that'll allus find me." She stood before Thea like a great rock, in the black coat and dress, with the plain black hat dragged down over the incongruous yellow curls. Her faded blue eyes were suddenly very wise and kind. "Jes' remember you've allus got a friend, if you want one," she said, "but don't bother't'write unless you want some help.

Ef I hear from you, I'll know you want some help, an' I'll do anythin' you want."

She bent and kissed Thea quickly, without putting her arms about her, turned and was gone. She did not wait on the quayside. She had known and forestalled all Thea's wishes, from that first morning when she laid her clothes ready beside the bed. She knew now that Thea wanted to be alone on the boat, to prepare for the meeting with Nan.

Thea never did write to her. As Sadie had foreseen, she was reluctant to keep open any link with Monte Carlo. When the bulky figure passed behind a group of passengers, out of sight, she passed also out of Thea's life, without any sign of emotion, or any word of farewell. She had done her duty to her dead friend, calmly and efficiently, as she had once run the 'Now or Never' eating-house. Because, behind the curls, the jewels, the perfume and alcohol, she was plain Sadie Marchant, daughter of the foreman at a quarry in Wyoming. She had seen that Thea wanted care, but not petting, and her affection for Belle Lawrence showed itself in the practical form of showing no emotion to her daughter. Thea meant to write to her, to thank her, but it was as though the Mrs Van Dutyens she had known in Monte Carlo had no connection with her companion of those last few days. It was as though Sadie Marchant was a messenger sent from God to guide her through the nightmare, who had vanished on the quayside when her work was finished. It was only Belle Lawrence who had seen in fat, rich, vulgar Mrs Van Dutyens that one redeeming quality which made her fit to be a messenger from God – her understanding heart.

As France slid quietly away behind her, Thea was trying to face and overcome the fact that she did not want to meet Nan. She understood now why Belle had not written to her mother after she was deserted by Tom Lawrence. Nan was too loving, too sympathetic, and her own grief would be nearly as great as Thea's. She would look at Thea with anxious eyes and by her desire to comfort would force her out of the protective calm in which she was sheltering. If only, thought Thea, I could be alone for a while, perhaps I could make myself understand that Mother is dead and try to build a new way of life for myself, without her as its foundation. She thought longingly of the peace she had found in the church on the morning of her mother's death. Lying on the altar-steps, she had been so sure that she was not alone, that the God who was suddenly *her* God was beside her. She had stayed quite still for a long time, while the peace and comfort crept about her heart and left her calm. Later she had knelt and looked up at the Cross and smiled with a strange exultation.

"This *is* my God," she had cried, "who has known pain and loneliness and despair. He is not the irresponsible, laughing god I wanted, like Pan, but he brings comfort and kindliness and understanding. I will never be alone again."

But the late awakening had brought its chill and desolation, and in the days that followed, she had not even sought for comfort. She remembered what her mother had said, lying in the little pine wood above the village. "If you've known Him for that one time, you must believe in Him for the rest of your life." I do believe in Him, thought Thea, watching the grey sea rushing under the ship. I believe that He is here, beside me, now. But it is not enough. If I were a saint, it would be enough, but I am weak and frightened and lonely. I cannot live with divine companionship alone. I want a loving arm about me and a dear voice to tease me and talk to me. I would give all Heaven, for my mother's life. But, perhaps I had, in the church in Monte Carlo, a foretaste of what Heaven is. Perhaps I might know that peace and comfort when I die, that feeling of infinite safety. Perhaps Mother knows it now.

She thought of Belle slipping like a naughty child into Heaven, beneath God's protecting arm, and, at the thought, the ice in her heart began to thaw. When a far white curve showed that she was near to England, Thea turned with a soft light in her eyes towards the gangway, to catch the first sight of Nan, waiting for her so patiently.

Fourteen

It was growing dark as Nan and Thea arrived at Sunnyside. A drizzle of rain had turned the crisp fallen leaves into a slimy, sodden mass, which clung to the pavement, to their shoes and to the bottom of the gate. As Nan opened the door with her latchkey and stepped into the hall, Thea hung back for a moment, feeling that when she entered the house and closed the door behind her, she would make Belle's death final and irrevocable. She lifted her face to the sky, dark with menacing storm-clouds, and felt on her cheeks the soft, light rain. Nan's voice, infinitely removed, called, "Emily!" and from behind the closed kitchen door came the sound of Emily's heavy movements. Still Thea hesitated in the shadows, outside the square of light which had fallen out of the open door and holding her breath as though she could thus persuade Time itself to pause. Then the driver came up the path with the first of the trunks, and Thea stepped inside, out of his way. Her trunk and Belle's had been carried into the house, and Nan had fumbled in her bag and paid the man, before Thea realised that she was standing in the sitting room, where the red plush curtains were unchanged and the red tablecloth reached nearly to the floor.

"Well, Miss Thea," said Emily, "I expect you'd like a nice cup of tea." She stood in the doorway, like a respectable monument, and Thea was surprised to find how clearly she remembered Emily's features, the lines on her face, her brown eyes and the mole on her left cheek. It was like revisiting a town, well-known in childhood, forgotten in the years be-

133

tween, yet cherished in the silent memory. Her tone, too, struck upon Thea's ears with a familiarity, and yet difference, which puzzled her until she realised that Emily was speaking to her in the tone she used to use to Belle, quite different from the hectoring way in which she always addressed Nan. Thea moved to kiss the rough, red cheek, and saw a convulsive movement break the granite stillness of Emily's features. Then she said gruffly, "I got the kettle on," and retreated to the kitchen, whence sounds of banging and rattling indicated that she was overcoming her emotions in her usual manner.

After tea, Thea went slowly upstairs and into her bedroom. She closed the door and leant against it. She drew off her hat, as though trying to hold back a moment which must come, and even turned to light the gas. But all the time, her grief, like a crushing physical force, pressed down upon her, and at last she surrendered to it and fell on her knees beside her bed, in the dark, silent little room, burying her face in the coverlet to smother her sobs.

When she raised her head, it was to see the old street-lamps dancing and glimmering in the rain, and she remembered the tears of her childhood, so bitter, but so brief and, as it seemed now, having in them more of pleasure than anguish. Her eyes and throat ached unbearably, unrelieved by the fit of crying, but as she knelt and looked out of the window, the sharp pain slipped out of her mind, leaving it still and frozen and empty. It was as though she had passed a great danger, and the path before her was dreary indeed, but not impassable.

Thea settled into the life of Abbot's Green more easily than she had expected. Of great assistance was the fact that her mother had been in Monte Carlo for a number of years. Thea and Nan had built up, in that time, a life together, and memories, in which Belle had no part, and if they spoke cautiously, if they watched each other warily, if their speech had a brightness about it that was painfully forced, yet the routine commonplace of their daily occupations was a relief to Thea. She went shopping with Nan and helped her with the dressmaking. She took cooking lessons from Emily – lessons which were of little use to her, since Emily calculated her quantities and ingredients 'by instinct', an instinct which was sometimes helpful, but frequently disastrous. She noticed with pleasure how quickly the days were passing, until the thought came to her with a sudden shock that it did not matter whether the days passed quickly or slowly, for she had nothing now to look forward to. Then the old pain caught her by the throat, but it was only for a moment, and such attacks of acute agony grew more rare and passed more swiftly, until they hardly came upon her at all, and she was left only with an enduring sadness of which she was barely conscious.

A few days after her return, Thea met Elsie Winter. They greeted each other warmly, and then found themselves dumb and awkward. Thea knew that, to Elsie, death was something exciting, indecent, something to be spoken of in whispers. She heard two childish voices, one eager and awed, the other smugly superior.

"*Will there be plumes on the horses' heads?*"

"*I expect so.*"

She was suddenly conscious of her black clothes, as she had once been embarrassed by her mourning band.

"You must come to tea one day," said Elsie, glancing slyly over Thea's shoulder, like a cat. Her yellow hair was elaborately dressed under a hat that was too fashionable for a girl of eighteen. Her blue eyes wandered restlessly while she spoke. Thea suddenly found her dreadfully vulgar and, to cover the discovery, answered with disproportionate warmth.

"Oh yes, I'd love to."

They looked at each other. The silence fell once more. Elsie giggled unexpectedly and said, "Oh dear, I must hurry. There's that silly boy Ronnie Steadman and I expect he's coming to ask me out again." She giggled again as Thea glanced round to see a tall young man strolling down the road, swinging his cane, and added, "Oh, don't let him see you looking. Goodbye, I must run." She paused another minute, however, until the young man was within a hundred yards of her, and then set off at a mincing walk which looked faster than it was. The thin young man quickened his pace, passing Thea at a brisk trot. His hurrying footsteps thudded behind Elsie's superbly unconscious figure. He drew abreast of her, and took off his hat, and she started, stopped, looking shyly up at him.

With a feeling of violent repulsion Thea turned and went inside the house, hating Elsie Winter, hating Ronnie Steadman, hating herself for having taken part in the comedy. Love and young men was for servant-girls, and then was not to be encouraged. She was infuriated to find within her contempt for Elsie Winter, some faint envy, envy not for Ronnie Steadman and the transparent subterfuges practised in the street, but envy for the blush, the glow in the stupid blue eyes, the coquettish lightness of step.

Just before Christmas, Aunt Mary came to visit Nan, bringing with her Charlotte and Janey. Thea felt with them, as she had with Elsie Winter, the same reluctance and shrinking. Janey troubled her more than Charlotte, because she was so sympathetic, so anxious not to upset Thea by direct comment, and yet to show consciousness of Thea's loss. Charlotte, as cool and withdrawn as ever, showed no such anxiety.

They talked in the window, the three girls, while Nan and Aunt Mary sat by the fire. The talk spun awkwardly, like a children's top, now staggering dangerously, now coming to rest, now set going again with a hasty turn. Charlotte suddenly went over to the heavy mahogany bookcases, where reposed Grandfather's set of Dickens, his Works of Shakespeare, and other monuments to Victorian solidarity. She studied the books for a moment, and then opened the case and drew one out. It was the book of Morte d'Arthur which had been given to Thea when Aunt Ruth died.

"What a lovely book!" Charlotte remarked, and came to sit

between the other two, the book on her knees. Janey shot a frightened glance at Thea, but kept silent while Charlotte turned the pages with thin, clumsy fingers. She paused at the first picture of Guenevere, saying, "Oh, *that's* the one, is it?" Thea caught her breath at the slim figure, with red hair falling to the waist, but for a moment made no reply. As Charlotte continued to search through the book, Thea said in a low voice, "I think it was mostly the hair. She isn't much like Mother otherwise." She was thinking that there was about Guenevere a lightness, almost a wantonness, which cut her off for ever from Belle Lawrence.

"And this isn't much like James," Charlotte added, "and yet there is a resemblance somewhere." They were looking at Sir Launcelot, magnificent in armour, dark-bearded and with a fierce yet laughing eye.

"Find me," Janey begged, and they all three laughed, comparing the slim, dark Cornishman with his round-faced, rosy-cheeked namesake.

"I've often wondered, Charlotte," said Thea, all awkwardness forgotten, "why you chose Mordred?"

"I think he's more interesting than the others," Charlotte answered. "Like Judas," she added, as though that made all clear.

"Or Satan in *Paradise Lost*," Janey suggested.

"No, because Satan just wanted the throne, like Macbeth or Richard the Third. But Mordred started well, like Judas."

"But, do you like all bad men better than good ones?" asked Thea.

"Oh, bad and good, what are they?" Charlotte shrugged the words away. "If Hamlet had been written from the other point of view, you might have made him the villain. Coriolanus was almost certainly the villain. We're all half villains, only we don't always get the opportunity to show it."

"But then," Janey protested, "men make different uses of the same opportunity. You can't say some men aren't better than others."

"No two men ever do get the same opportunity," replied Charlotte. "At least, it never looks the same to them, because their minds are different, and their will and their desires. Every man stands alone."

There was a faint glow of colour in Charlotte's pale cheek. Thea saw her for a moment, exultant and solitary, self-sufficient in a world of men who clung to their fellow-beings for comfort and support.

"Oh, that's silly!" Janey exclaimed. "Some men will always behave badly, no matter what chances they have."

"Yes," Charlotte agreed, "some men will always do well, and some men will always be hopeless, but there are others who stand in between, who only seem to need some small chance and hazard to turn them to one side or the other. They are the ones who are most interesting."

"But don't you think that everyone is like that?" said Thea. "Halfway between good and bad?"

"Nearly everyone," Charlotte answered. The others looked at her in perplexity. After a moment, she explained, "But then you get the ordinary man, and the great opportunity, for good or bad, and the two together make an interesting character." She began turning the pages again, as though the discussion was ended, and she had made herself quite clear.

"But, I don't see the moral," said Thea slowly.

Charlotte chuckled, so that for a moment the plainness vanished from her face and her grey-blue eyes danced. "There isn't any moral," she replied. "It's just interesting."

"But I don't think it happens like that," Thea persisted. "I think that a man is destined to be great, to be good, to be bad or mean right from the beginning. I wouldn't like to think that it was all haphazard."

"Not haphazard," said Charlotte patiently. "Take a man, any ordinary man. He lives an ordinary life and nothing much happens to him. Then something does happen to him, an accident, or a war, or the chance of a fortune. And immediately that event meets that man's character, it becomes part of him. He can accept it or reject it, or perhaps it's forced upon him, and then he can take it as it comes, or twist it to suit him better. But it lies in his power, and when it has passed, he will be different because of it."

"All you're saying," put in Janey, with sisterly impatience, "is that we can't stop things happening to us, but we can decide how they're going to affect us."

"So there *is* a moral to it," said Thea, laughing, but Charlotte shook her head, and returned to her usual silence and restraint.

James, Aunt Mary disclosed over the tea-table, was in the North of England, working in the office of one of his uncles.

"He seems to be very happy," she added, in her soft, calm voice, "and he finds the climate very bracing." Thea caught herself wondering how he found the girls, and reproved herself for malice. It was strange, she thought, how coolly and objectively she could think of James, as though that last week in Monte Carlo had rubbed from her mind all feelings of tenderness and sensibility. She could not help imagining that Aunt Mary felt some relief at his absence, though she spoke of it with regret. She wondered if Charlotte would include James among her 'ordinary men', and, if so, what opportunities would present themselves to him. Janey had been afraid, she remembered, that he might make a mistake in the books and get himself into trouble. But, ah no! she thought, with a sudden glow of the old warmth, James is meant to be great. Something will happen which will give him a chance, and he will take it. He will laugh, but take it, and we shall all be proud of him.

"And Lydia is very happy, and very pleased with her new house," Aunt Mary continued. "Thea, you will have to go and stay with her one of these days."

"I'd love to," Thea answered, and thought that Charlotte's eyes met hers with a glint of amusement. It never occurred to Aunt Mary that one of her children could be less pleasant company than the others. James was, perhaps, her favourite, but, to her, Lydia, Charlotte and Janey were all equally gifted and delightful.

The room seemed very quiet to Thea when her aunt and cousins had left. Nan's face looked worn and wrinkled in the firelight, and it came to Thea with a sudden pang that Nan was getting old. In that moment of fear when she realised how little she could bear to lose Nan, Monte Carlo was put behind her for ever, and she knew that in this quiet room, in dear, unselfish Nan, who was always there when Thea had need of her, was bound up all her future security and comfort.

"I don't want to go and stay with Lydia," she said suddenly. "I'd much rather stay here with you."

"Just as you like, dear," Nan answered placidly. "Of course, I like to have you."

Thea picked up her sewing with a breath of relief, feeling that this house was a refuge in which she would stay as long as she was allowed to. If she spent the rest of her life in such a quiet haven, she would be satisfied.

The winter passed, the spring and summer followed unobtrusively, and a year had passed since Thea's return, a year which was not, like most years, firm and rounded by new experiences, new events and strengthened friendships, but as empty and frail as a corn-husk which has never known the fruition of the grain. Thea felt that she had been neither happy nor unhappy, and was grateful for it. There was a certain painless numbness which had taken possession of her, and which she had no desire to exchange for painful sensations once more. Meanwhile, she passively underwent the kindness of the neighbours, Miss Luke and her invalid mother, Mr and Mrs Winter, the Vicar, Mr Benson, with whom, like too many ministers of the Church of England, it would have seemed a breach of good manners to discuss religion. Mr Benson was greatly occupied in persuading his parishioners to forget that he wore a dog collar. If he could hear someone say admiringly, "You'd never know he was a parson!" he was delighted. Thea, when she first saw him after her return, had been anxious lest he should offer her the encouragement and consolation of his church. Afterwards she was resentful that he hadn't tried to do so. She maintained an uneasy friendship with Elsie Winter and a more satisfactory one with Mrs Luke. She would sometimes go in and read to the old lady when Miss Luke wanted to go out, and she enjoyed listening to tangled reminiscences of a life which seemed to have contained no fierce currents, no ugly whirlpools, but only a gentle, easy flow, from birth towards death.

The first interruption in Thea's calm was made by an invitation to a Christmas party at Mrs Winter's house, bearing the ominous word, 'Dancing' upon the card.

"I'll refuse it," Thea said, easily. "I've got a cold – very nearly."

"I think you should go," said Nan.

"No, they won't mind. I'll stay indoors for a day or two beforehand."

"But it would be good for you to go," Nan protested.

Thea began to deny it, but met an anxious glance from Nan and wavered.

"I'm quite happy, Nan," she assured her.

"You should get out more," Nan answered firmly. "You should meet more young people. I'd like you to go."

"Well, all right," said Thea, "but I shan't enjoy it."

"I'll go and get that white dress out," said Nan. "I'm sure we can make it over for you. We shall have to buy a pair of white satin slippers to go with it though, your old pair are quite worn out." She hurried from the room, pleased and excited, leaving Thea much regretting that she had agreed to go. In fact, it was Nan who enjoyed the preparations most, and even Emily showed signs of animation when the evening of the party arrived and Nan was pinning one of her own brooches on the bosom of the white dress and trying the effect of a small bow in Thea's hair. Thea herself stood cold and miserable under Nan's ministrations, yet moved by the realisation that Nan felt that she was once more sending a daughter off to a dance. How often must Belle have stood smiling, while Nan fussed about her gown and hair, and Emily admired from the doorway!

But Thea felt more miserable when she arrived at the Winters' house and found a room full of strangers, except for Elsie flirting with Ronnie Steadman. When the dancing began in the drawing room, cleared for the purpose of all furniture, Thea was glad to retreat into a small alcove, where she sat half behind a curtain and tried to look self-possessed, while a dreadful shyness and embarrassment racked her. She knew that her dress was old-fashioned, and was in terror lest her hair should come down, but most of all she felt humiliated at the thought of returning to Nan and Emily with the news that she had been a social failure, that no one had wanted to talk to her or dance with her, and that she had sat alone until it was time to go home. Then she saw Mrs Winter coming towards her, with a sturdy, square-shouldered young man close behind. Oh, go away, Thea prayed. Don't let her come to me. Let her leave me alone. Her prayers were in vain. Mrs Winter, having murmured introductions, left her with the young man, and Thea was forced to leave her sheltered alcove, to smile, stiff-lipped, and say that she would be delighted to dance.

Looking back afterwards, Thea realised that she had enjoyed the party from that moment. The boy, Jimmie Stainforth, was a friendly soul, who talked of his new motorbike, who said she danced divinely, who adjusted her scarf round her shoulders after each dance, and who fetched her ice-cream and trifle in the manner of a knight serving his lady. Thea, flushed and excited, ordered him about with a coquettish imperiousness which would have surprised her cousins, scolded him for not dancing when she had been claimed by another partner, and found in his stolid, protecting admiration an unexpected and exhilarating enchantment. The evening passed like a breath of wind, and before the party ended,

Thea said that she must go home. She gave as her excuse the fact that Nan would worry, but she knew that it was not true. Rather it was that she was afraid to stay longer, lest the magic should vanish. She ran lightly upstairs to put on her mother's velvet evening cloak, leaving Jimmie patiently waiting for her in the hall. In the mirror of Elsie's dressing-table, she paused to look at herself, and saw light hair gleaming over a white forehead, hazel eyes dancing and cheeks flushed like a wild rose. She stood still for a moment, smiling, and then drew the cloak round her and turned to go.

The hall was deserted, except for Jimmie. Thea smiled and held out her hand.

"I'll see you home," Jimmie said, but Thea answered, "Oh no, it's only next door. Goodbye."

Jimmie took her hand, breathing hard, and then took a quick step forwards. He pointed upwards, and Thea glanced up to see a sprig of mistletoe suspended above her, before the boy kissed her full on the mouth. She started back, her eyes wide and astonished. Then she turned and fled through the front door and down the path, leaving him in the dim, gas-lit hall.

Thea had given an account of her evening to Nan, suppressing all mention of the breathless kiss in the hall, and had drunk the cocoa which Emily had left ready for her (Emily who never believed that she got anything to eat anywhere but at home). She had said good-night and gone to her room, but she did not go to sleep. She sat on the edge of her bed, watching the street-lamps and listening to the voices of the departing guests. As she thought of Jimmie Stainforth, her hand went up to her flushed cheek, with a sudden movement of shame and disgust. She remembered how oddly choked his voice had sounded, as he said "Thea!" just before he kissed her, and remembered how warm and soft his lips had been on hers. She shivered with repugnance, as she realised for the first time that love was not just a beautiful speech made by a knight to his lady, but something physical and material: Jimmie

143

Stainforth's square-fingered hand seizing her hand, his heavy, flushed face close to hers. "No," she whispered to herself. "No. I don't want it to be like that. I won't ever be in love." Even as she said the words, she wondered if it would have been different if James had kissed her, James with his lean, brown hands, James with his thin, humorous face, his grey eyes and gentle mouth. Then she stood up in a violent, almost angry movement, as though she had started back from a cliff-edge. She said out loud, "No! No!" with her hands over her eyes, because a dangerous path had opened before her, and she did not want to see it. "I won't fall in love," she told herself, "I won't. It isn't safe," and she picked up her handkerchief and rubbed her lips with it, as though she were wiping away that wet kiss, and with it the awareness and disturbance which it had brought her.

Fifteen

"It is a far, far better thing that I do," read Thea, "than I have ever done; it is a far, far better rest that I go to, than I have ever known." She laid the book down, and looked at Mrs Luke, who was comfortably wiping her eyes. "I don't think we'll have time to start another before Miss Luke and Nan get back," she said.

"Oh, no, my dear," sighed old Mrs Luke, "I wouldn't like anything else after that. It was so beautiful. Mr Luke always liked that the best of all Dickens's books."

Thea glanced furtively at the grim photograph on the dressing table, and tried once more to imagine that stern countenance, with the mutton-chop whiskers and high white collar, animated by enthusiasm for the noble death of Sydney Carton.

"Don't you wait," said Mrs Luke, "if you'd like to be getting home. I shall be quite all right until Ada arrives." For Miss Luke and Nan had gone to a concert together.

"Oh, I like to be here," Thea replied, truthfully enough. She had no desire to return to the empty house, with the rain beating against it and the March wind sighing outside. It was strange, she thought, that it was not the warm summer days which made her think of her mother. Sometimes a branch of almond blossom against a blue sky would remind her of Monte Carlo, but rain on wet windows, puddles on the path, sodden leaves by the gate, all spoke to her of Belle, who loved warmth and brightness.

Mrs Luke leant back against her pillows. "You shouldn't be

145

reading to an old woman at your age," she said, "You should be going out with a nice young man." Thea, embarrassed, murmured that she was quite happy. "Ah, well," continued Mrs Luke, "Mr Right will come along one of these days."

"Mr . . . ?" queried Thea, glancing anxiously at the late Mr Luke.

"Mr Right," repeated the old lady, nodding her head. "You'll see. A pretty girl like you will soon find somebody. We shan't have you here for very long. Quite right too."

"Some women don't marry," said Thea, shyly.

"A woman's place is in her own home," said Mrs Luke, with the air of a discoverer. "Though, of course," she added hastily, "a daughter like Ada may give up all for Duty." She sighed, and Thea realised suddenly that she would rather have had a son-in-law than a dutiful daughter, that a grandson would have meant more to her than a thousand trays willingly carried upstairs, a hundred books meekly read aloud. Mrs Luke closed her eyes, falling into a light doze, and Thea watched her thoughtfully. Her cheeks were still rounded, her white hair was plentiful. She seemed to have changed not at all during the years in which Thea had known her. There was something more permanent in her calm old age than in the vitality of youth, as though she had outlived death, as though she had slipped unobtrusively past the age of dying and reached a dull, but not unpleasant immortality. Thea looked round the bedroom, at the armchair with the lace antimacassar, the picture of a stag at bay, the medicine bottles and the glass with the beaded-net cover draped over it. The room had been just the same when she had been brought in as a child to visit Mrs Luke, bedridden even then. She wondered if the room would be just the same in ten years' time, hot and airless, with the same dusty plants on the table in the window, the same faintly musty smell which one finds in a museum, the same placid figure in the big double bed. She shuddered, as Belle might have done, and thought of Miss Luke, living her life out in this close room, with her mother who was disappointed that she had not married some nice man. She thought of those two figures, Mrs Luke, the invalid, Miss Luke, the spinster, condemned to live thus for ever, like prisoners manacled together, serving and served, each dependent upon the other, with no escape but the death which both dreaded. Was this safety?

The sound of the front door opening below disturbed Thea's meditations and woke Mrs Luke from her sleep. They listened to the rattle of an umbrella in the stand, and Miss Luke's high voice speaking excitedly. Quick steps on the stairs were followed by another shrill laugh as Miss Luke ushered Nan into the room.

"We had such a nice concert, Mother dear," she said, her bright little eyes moving about the room, noticing the closed book, the fire burning low, the medicine glass, the curtains yet undrawn. She drew the curtains and knelt down to repair the fire, talking all the while. "There was a lady sitting in front of us with such a funny hat. I didn't know how to control myself, and then – just think, the conductor dropped his baton! Poor man, I was so sorry for him, but of course we couldn't help laughing." She looked round at her mother and Thea, and her teeth when she laughed were pointed and stuck out slightly, like a mouse's. "But the music was lovely," she added, afraid of sounding too frivolous.

"It was indeed," Nan said. "Thank you very much for taking me."

"It's nice for Ada to get out with young people for a change," said Mrs Luke. "I was telling Thea that she should meet more young folks."

"Yes," Miss Luke agreed, and now the old strain of malice was back in her voice. "Thea's growing up, isn't she? You'll have to find some beau soon, Thea."

"Not just yet," Nan put in, and although she smiled she answered the challenge. "Thea's only eighteen. She has plenty of time for that yet."

Thea moved to put on her coat. "Are you sure you won't stay for tea?" asked Miss Luke hastily.

"Quite sure, but thank you all the same. Emily will have tea ready for us."

"Well, Mother, there's a surprise for you for tea. Mabel has made some of your favourite cakes, and she's made some hot buttered toast."

"How nice," said old Mrs Luke, as her daughter plumped up the pillows and re-tied the ribbons of her bed-jacket. "That *is* nice. We are cosy in here, aren't we? We must pity the poor sailors on a night like this. As soon as it starts to get dark on a windy night, I think of the poor sailors." She leant back again and smiled up at the thin, pallid face, the thin grey hair and sharp features above her. The fire blazed brightly and no errant breezes strayed into the warm stillness of the room. Thea and Nan started downstairs, while Miss Luke closed the door upon old Mrs Luke, lying contentedly in bed, waiting for her tea and hot buttered toast.

"You're late enough," said Emily crossly, as she carried in the tray, "I thought you was never coming."

"I'm sorry, Emily," Nan replied, adding ingratiatingly, "What a lovely tea!"

"Hm," said the uncompromising martinet. "If it isn't spoilt I don't know whose fault it isn't." She retired to her lair, like a boxer who has laid his opponent low and retreats to his corner before he can be hit in turn.

"I wonder," pondered Nan, "whether Emily meant to say, 'I don't know whose fault it is' or 'I know whose fault it isn't'?"

"I'm not sure," began Thea, puzzling over the problem quite seriously, until, struck by its absurdity, she started to laugh.

"Hush," Nan begged, "or she'll hear you," but the attempt to silence her amusement plunged Thea into hopeless giggles, in which she was soon joined by Nan. The ringing of the doorbell and Emily's subdued mutter of protest as she stumped along to answer it, only convulsed them further, but they were startled into solemnity by the sound of a man's voice. They heard the front door close and Emily sidled into the room, closing it behind her with a conspiratorial air.

"It's a gentleman to see Miss Thea," she announced, all her ill-humour astonished out of her.

"What name did he give?" asked Nan, looking troubled.

"I couldn't catch his name," Emily replied, who never did catch names, however neatly thrown to her.

"Well . . ." Nan hesitated. "Well, show him in, Emily."

Thea smoothed her dress and pushed hair-pins in with fingers that trembled. Not Ambrose. Oh, God, don't let it be Ambrose.

Emily sidled out of the door, and then flung it open, evidently feeling that she should make some announcement. "Mr – please walk in," she mumbled, and pulled the door shut so hastily that the visitor glanced round, startled. Thea was conscious only of relief that Ambrose had not returned to trouble her, that this man, who looked vaguely familiar, was not the man whose gloved hand had lain upon her mother's chair on the sunlit terrace.

Paul Bruner said, stammering a little, "I'm afraid you won't remember me."

Thea hesitated, and then remembered the crowded room and chattering guests and the one particular guest who had talked to her when she was left alone, and whom she had unceremoniously abandoned when James came to fetch her.

"Of course I remember," she answered, searching for his name. "It's . . ."

"Paul Bruner," he supplied, and she said again, "Of course." She was smiling in her relief, and the effect was one of delighted recognition. Paul's face was suddenly softened and warmed by pleasure. Thea introduced him to Nan, and he clicked his heels and bowed slightly, very much, thought Thea, like a well-brought-up child. Then, after apologies and protests, he sat down to tea with them, and Thea felt a glow of pride because Nan talked to him so kindly, setting him at ease and asking him about his home.

149

He had just returned from a visit to Germany, he told them, and now expected to be in England for some time.

"Your family must miss you," said Nan.

He laughed. "They are used to my being away," he replied. "My mother does not mind so long as my brother is still at home."

Thea wondered if he spoke with a hint of pain, and Nan enquired, "Is your brother older than you?"

"No, younger. Fritz is only a schoolboy. He will not leave home just yet at least."

"Perhaps he will continue to live at home when he leaves school," Nan suggested.

"Perhaps. Though," he added, smiling, "he says that he wants to be a soldier. But I do not think that my father would allow it."

"I hope not, for your mother's sake," said Nan, smiling also. "It must be bad enough for her having one of you so far away."

There was a brief silence, during which Thea thought that their visitor, frowning into the fire, had let his mind travel into his own country and was worrying about his brother's future. She thought that it was easy to picture him as an elder brother, solicitous and protecting. Then he looked up, and she blushed that he should find her eyes on his face.

"I have just been visiting your uncle," he said. "He and your aunt gave me messages for you, and that is my excuse for calling."

"Next time," Nan put in, gently, "you won't need an excuse." Paul Bruner smiled his sudden, charming smile, which lit up his face and put little crinkles at the corners of his eyes.

"You are very kind to a lonely foreigner," he said. He looked round the small room, with the heavy Victorian furniture saved from more prosperous days, and the hyacinths in bloom on the table. "It is nice to come to a home."

Thea sat very quietly while Nan and Paul Bruner talked

and, while half her attention was upon their conversation – Paul's home in Berlin, Nan's account of a concert at the Crystal Palace, their discussion of the culinary differences between England and Germany – she was at the same time noticing how blue his eyes were, and how his hair waved slightly where it grew back from his forehead, and how his voice was deep and rather slow, with a trace of foreign accent which lay more in hesitation and preciseness than in any faults of pronunciation. She felt warm and comfortable, with a feeling of happy expectancy, such as she used to have as a child when she woke up in the morning and realised that it was her birthday or Christmas Day. No voice of danger warned her, and no shame or self-questioning troubled her. She felt only that she would be contented if she could sit beside the fire for ever, while Nan and Paul Bruner talked.

The clock struck six before Paul started up, saying that he had an appointment, and Thea felt a sick disappointment because the evening was over, and dread lest he should never come again.

"Perhaps you would be still more kind to me," he said, as he took Nan's hand, "and come to a concert with me, if I could get three tickets. There is one next week that I think you might enjoy."

"We should like that very much," Nan replied, "wouldn't we, Thea?"

A great breath of joy seemed to be pressing against Thea's ribs, so that she was surprised to hear herself answering in ordinary tones,

"Yes, very much."

Then Paul had taken her hand in his for a moment, and turned away quickly, as though afraid to look at her for long, and he had gone, into the hall and through the front door. Thea listened for the click of the front gate, and lifted the corner of the curtain to watch him go. She could just see his hat above the privet hedge, in the closing dusk. She let the curtain fall quickly, as a familiar clatter came to her ears, approaching, and punctuated by shrill poops on a horn. It was Jimmy Stainforth, playing her a nightly serenade on his motorcycle, and she stood by the window, sheltered by the thick red plush, laughing softly to herself. The spring of humour, which had dried up on that dim morning in Monte Carlo, was warm and free inside her. She imagined Jimmie, like an aimable frog in his motoring goggles, bent low over the handlebars, and the squeak of his horn was suddenly the funniest noise she had ever heard. The engine spluttered and died as he reached the end of the road, and she heard him scraping his feet on the ground as he turned painfully round, and then coughs and explosions as he cranked it again. Then followed a triumphant roar as he swept by in the opposite direction, the 'poop-poop' growing fainter in the distance.

Thea drew the curtain aside once more and looked out at the friendly and familiar scene. The rain had stopped. Already the daffodils were blooming, and soon the summer would be here, with roses and warmth and sunshine. Always life, like the earth, was pregnant with good things. They stirred in the darkness, like the unborn child, faint heartbeats of hope and promise. Life was never barren, and the time of waiting for the birth had a peace and sweetness of its own. She smiled as she looked out of the window, with a light in her eyes, like a child seeing for the first time the mystery of falling snow or the wonder of the moon's path over the sea.

Nan returned to the room, and it seemed to Thea that her step was lighter and she carried her head a little higher. For the first time Thea wondered how much it had grieved Nan to lose her house in the pleasant residential part of Putney Hill, how much she missed her cook and parlourmaid, and her At Home day once a week. But just now Nan was smiling, and she patted a strand of hair into place with a gesture that reminded Thea faintly of Belle.

"What a charming man!" she exclaimed. "And how nice of him to ask us to the concert. I suppose Aunt Mary knew that he was living near here and so gave him our address." She

152

came to stand by the fire, and for once she did not take up her sewing, but stood in thoughtful idleness. "I've always liked Germans," she remarked. "They are so civilised. I always think that they're more like us than any other nation. They like music, and their manners are good without being ostentatious."

Thea nodded, but kept silent, with a ridiculous feeling of pride, as though Nan was praising her.

"I remember being very fond of a German just before I met Grandfather," Nan continued. "But, poor fellow, he hadn't a penny, and Father – that's your great-grandfather – told him that it was time he went away and made some money before he started unsettling young girls' affections." Nan's grey eyes were full of laughter. "So poor Heinrich went back to Germany and made quite a fortune in an ironworks, but of course by that time I had married Grandfather."

"Why, Nan, you never told me this," cried Thea in amazement.

"I'd hardly remembered it myself," Nan answered. "I gave him a lock of hair, and promised to write to him, but I never did. Father wouldn't have allowed it, because one didn't write to a man unless one was engaged to him."

"But, good gracious, Nan, we might have been German citizens if he'd made his money before you met Grandfather."

"I doubt it," Nan answered, smiling. "Father didn't like foreigners. He always said that they were financially unsound. Besides, I wasn't all *that* fond of Heinrich. I haven't thought of him for years. It was just that Paul Bruner reminded me of him. His voice and little tricks of speech, and the way he bowed." She looked reminiscently into the fire, and Thea thought again how often the lives of ordinary people were like old-fashioned romances. A few years in an ironworks had stood between Nan and Germany. And the 'financially sound' man of her father's choice had left her poverty-stricken, while the penniless foreigner was rich. But then if Nan had married Heinrich, there would have been no Belle, no Aunt Ruth. Tom

Lawrence would have married someone else (and probably left her too) and Thea herself would never have been born. Belle would not have been burnt to death in Monte Carlo, but neither would she have existed at all. Mrs Van Dutyens, Fanny and Ambrose would have sat round that table on the terrace, talking nonsense and laughing, yet never looking for Mrs Lawrence to complete their circle. How strangely, thought Thea, how fantastically were woven the threads of destiny. Because Heinrich was penniless, Paul Bruner came to a little house in Abbot's Green to meet Thea Lawrence, who otherwise would never have been born. For a moment, all her life seemed to tremble by a whirlpool of hazard and might-have-been. Then Nan's voice reached out and placed it once more firmly upon dry ground.

"Anyway, I could never have married Heinrich," she said. "He had such bad teeth."

Sixteen

W ithin the sitting room was a noise such as if Handel's *Largo* had been performed on an organ, in a bathing-hut. With one hand resting on the piano, the other clenched upon her massive bosom, Mrs Winter was singing a song whose pathos depended upon tone of voice and expression, since not one word was distinguishable. Paul Bruner played the accompaniment with a tact which necessitated frequent changes of tempo, to keep pace with the flow of Mrs Winter's breath and emotion, and even an occasional change of key. The audience consisted of Elsie Winter and Ronnie Steadman, Nan and Thea, and Mr Winter, who clearly wished himself elsewhere. In the kitchen, Emily criticised the performance freely, as she prepared the refreshments. "Lot of caterwauling!" she remarked to herself, and, as Mrs Winter's powerful contralto voice hovered between two notes, and finally pitched upon a third, " 'Grief' indeed!' " This, as Mrs Winter enunciated the word with unexpected clarity. "The grief's for them as has to listen to her."

But, as Mrs Winter ended her song, with evidence of strong distress, there was no discordant voice among the congratulations.

"I fear I did not play very well," Paul apologised. "I do not know the music of that song."

"Oh, not at all, Herr Bruner," replied the prima donna, graciously. "You played very nicely. Practice makes perfect, you know."

"Perhaps you would sing us another," Paul suggested.

155

"No, no, not just now," sighed Mrs Winter, as one who should say, *We artists exhaust ourselves.* "Perhaps Thea will oblige."

"I'm afraid I don't sing," Thea answered. "But, I know Elsie does."

There was a brief passage of mutual encouragement between Elsie and Ronnie, now an engaged couple, before Elsie was prevailed upon to wish for the wings of the dove, in a voice more remeniscent of an ambitious grasshopper.

Thea could see Nan wondering, as Elsie quavered to rest, whether she had better ask Mr Winter for a flute solo next, or whether Ronnie had better sing. She looked from one to the other anxiously, but both maintained a front of perfect indifference. Her doubts were resolved by Mrs Winter, however, who whispered to her husband, "Better get your flute, Albert, in case it's wanted." So Mr Winter was duly persuaded to play, while Mrs Winter accompanied him upon the piano. Paul, released from his duties, sat down next to Thea, and tried not to see Elsie, who fixed her eyes on his face with determination, removing them with a start and a blush whenever he looked up. She had confided to Ronnie that Herr Bruner, she was afraid, rather admired her, and this by-play was intended to lend colour to the supposition. Ronnie viewed his unconscious rival with gloom. Nan, happy to think that she was once more holding A Musical Evening, was only troubled lest Emily should kick the door open when she brought in the refreshments, and lest her sense of economy should lead her to remove half the sandwiches from the plates before bringing them in. Emily tended to calculate the capacity of each guest, with embarrassing results. "One of each all round, and one over, is quite enough," she had been known to say, when chided for this limited hospitality.

Thea, meanwhile, sat in perfect tranquillity. Though her own voice was true, if small, Nan had long ago given up all hope of overcoming her uncontrollable shyness. As a child, she had been persuaded by Belle to play five bars of 'The

Merry Peasant' at a party, before dissolving into such hysterical tears, that she had since been left unmolested. She was the more proud of Paul's powers of entertaining, his simple good humour in accompanying, his lack of embarrassment when asked to sing. She did not ask herself why she was proud of him, why she smiled as she compared him with Ronnie, why she was content to sit near him and listen to Mr and Mrs Winter in their pitched battle of wind and weight. He was a friend of the family, she told herself. He was a foreigner, and lent distinction to the circle. So she sat and smiled, unconsciously, and Paul watched her.

When Mr Winter had unscrewed his flute, and blown down each part with mournful distaste, Ronnie avowed his undying attachment to the lady of whom he had caught only a brief glimpse. He constantly raised and lowered his eyebrows as he sang, looking meltingly at Elsie the while. If he sang the words with somewhat startling emphasis, it might be attributable to the exertions of Mrs Winter, who accompanied him. She habitually played with considerable force, and was apt to play even more loudly when uncertain of the notes, as though to cover any errors. Ronnie's windy tenor, in these circumstances, was hard put to it to compete in volume, and, at the same time, to sound tender.

"Now, Herr Bruner," said Nan, trying hard not to sound triumphant, "I wonder if you would sing for us. Perhaps that one you sang the other evening?"

Paul looked at Thea. "But, won't you sing? Can't I persuade you?"

"No, no!" cried Thea, looking startled. "No, I'm afraid I can't."

"Why, then," said Paul. "I will make a bargain with you." Then, seeing her anxiety, he finished, smiling, "If I must sing, then will you turn the page for me?"

Thea laughed at that, and went with him to the piano. Then she must lean over him to reach the page of the music, and he must show her how well-occupied both his hands were in

playing when the page had to be turned, and they whispered,
like conspirators, while Mrs Winter installed herself comfortably, assuring Nan that there was no draught, and that she
did not want another cushion.

Paul's voice was pleasing, and he sang with charm and ease.
The simple German love song was suitable to the occasion. He
found time to smile up at Thea, and, when Mrs Winter was
heard to remark in her powerful whisper, "Germans. Always
so musical," their eyes met with a delightful sense of a shared
secret jest.

"What do the words mean?" Thea asked, under cover of the
bustle which followed the end of the song.

Paul glanced over the sheet, as though about to translate it,
and then looked up at her. "All it says is, 'I love you'," he said,
and they stayed motionless for a moment, as though, like the
lovers in Keats' 'Ode to a Grecian Urn', they might stay thus
for ever, their love undeclared, sweet and silent between them.
Forever wilt thou love and she be fair. Then Thea turned away,
and for the rest of the evening, she avoided his eyes and was
careful not to address him with any hint of intimacy. She did
not know what she feared, but the moment's silence lingered
in her mind with a strange mixture of panic and joy. She was
like a child playing hide-and-seek, running away, half afraid,
yet half eager to be caught.

Nan's anxiety about the refreshments proved to have been
unnecessary. Emily served them, with the air, it is true, of a
Welsh Calvinist minister supervising a banquet of cardinals,
but her disapproval was only demonstrated by her facial
expression. She even closed the door ceremoniously behind
her, instead of hooking it shut with one foot, while hopping
upon the other. And Mrs Winter, whose habit it was to
remember the names of her acquaintances' maids, and greet
them condescendingly, as the lady of the manor would once
have hailed her tenants, was too intimidated by Emily's robes
of state to show her any such familiarity.

When Mrs Winter had said, "No. No more. No, really,

thank you," for the last time, Ronnie was persuaded to give a recitation. His bashful refusals were prolonged only until he had been able to decide whether to render 'The Burial of Sir John Moore', or 'the Charge of the Light Brigade'. He had a larger repertoire of humorous recitations, but felt that his future mother-in-law expected something worthier of him upon the present occasion. So the cannon volleyed and thundered, and the mouth of hell gaped wide, and Thea and Paul were once more united in delighted hidden mirth. For who could tell that Ronnie, with his receding chin and lamentable taste in ties, would in so few years be staggering across a muddy field in France, at the head of his platoon, or that he, who spoke now of Death with such quavers of emotion, and fine gestures, would learn to live so close to death that he noticed it no more than he would a sparrow in the hedgerow?

It was late when the guests departed. Ronnie volunteered to walk with Paul, since their way lay in the same direction, and Thea hoped that Ronnie wouldn't feel called upon to murder Elsie's admirer in a fit of jealous rage outside Abbot's Green station, and then was nearly overcome by an uncontrollable gurgle of amusement, at the thought of Ronnie killing someone. She felt no anxiety this time lest Paul should not come again. His visits were as regular as his business engagements and his sense of fitness would allow. So she said good-night to him rather perfunctorily, turning quickly to take Ronnie's proffered hand, and when he was gone, had a strong impulse to run after him and look into his eyes and part with him more satisfactorily, but instead she went up to bed and fell asleep smiling, and had no dreams.

Thea's love for her mother had been violent and passionate, tormented by jealousy and fear of losing her. Her feelings for James were tangled and troubled, inextricably linked with the disillusion and pain caused by her father. It was as though in recompense, that her love for Paul Bruner was so tranquil, growing almost unperceived out of friendship and liking.

Even the time between her discovery of her own love, and Paul's avowal of his, held no suspense and the days drifted by in such happy calm as she had not known since her early childhood. Time did not slip under her feet perilously, like a ball, but wandered caressingly past, like a butterfly in a summer meadow. For the first time for many years, the future cast no shadow. She did not long for the days to pass, or dread lest they should pass too quickly. She was still content to see Paul Bruner in Nan's company, content often to sit back and listen to them talking, while she herself kept silent. She knew that it could not always be like this, that some sort of change must come. They were drifting downstream in the sunshine, the current taking them gently towards their destination. But evening brings cold winds, and even river-picnics cannot last for ever. She knew all this, but smiled and forgot it. It was enough that Nan grew younger and less worn, and that Paul came often, and did not frighten her.

One fine day in July, Paul came early in the afternoon, dressed not in his city clothes, but in a grey flannel suit and straw hat.

"The first day of my holiday!" he proclaimed. "I want to go for a country walk, but I need a guide." He glanced towards the kitchen. "I wondered if Emily would take me."

"Emily would take you round London," Nan answered. "She was born within sound of Bow Bells. She's told me so often. But she has a rooted aversion to the country. For one thing, it's so untidy. For another, there are too many animals about. The only young man that Emily ever had spoilt his chances by taking her for a country walk. Her hat blew off, and a cow trod on it, and Emily abjured men and the country from that very hour. You will have to find someone else."

"Thea, you will have to take pity on me," said Paul. "For a country walk is essential to the first day of one's holidays."

"It's rather a long walk to the country from here," Thea protested.

"Yes, I thought we would take a train from here to the

nearest bit of country, walk, have tea and then return by train."

"Now, that's the sort of walk that seems to me sensible," said Nan approvingly. "Thea, I should get your hat, before he decides on something more energetic."

"And put in an extra hat-pin," Paul called after her, "just in case."

Thea felt something like resentment, as she set off with Paul, as though she as being hurried faster than she wanted to go, as though someone was trying to take away one course of a meal before she had finished it, and was placing the other in front of her before she was ready for it. So she walked along, demurely, and aloof, by the sun-warm fences and the rich-smelling stocks in the little front gardens, and pretended not to see Paul invitingly bending his arm to receive her hand.

"Where shall we go?" Paul asked, more soberly, and Thea felt a pang of guilt at having even so little spoilt his day.

"There is some nice country round Enfield," she suggested, and he said quickly, "Where your cousins live?"

"Beyond their house," Thea answered. She had an impulse to link this day with her first visit to Enfield, when she was such a child, and so happy.

"Were you thinking of calling on them?" Paul asked, and his face and voice were expressionless.

"Oh no." She glanced up at him, and smiled to herself at the relief in his face. "Unless you'd like to?" she added, and laughed outright at his hasty, "No, no." He smiled too, but said meaningly, "I would like this day to be ours alone," and Thea walked faster.

How familiar Enfield station was, as Thea looked about her, and how clearly she remembered Windmill Hill, where she had walked first with Lydia, and where, not long after, Andrew had run out into the road.

She was forced to accept Paul's arm up the steep incline, and he tucked it possessively away, as though taking it permanently into his keeping, and Thea found the support pleasant, and yet rebelled against it. They left the town behind, and turned into the country road, with its tiny, rough footpath, and the trees on each side. Thea's mind was busy with memories, as though she were stocktaking, before a new year. Paul kept her hand in his arm, and watched her.

When they reached the stile, Thea turned towards it, and they both, with one accord, stopped and leant on it, looking at the view.

"We came to fly our kites in this field," said Thea, dreamily.

"You and . . . ?"

"And James, and the others."

Paul was silent. Thea was trying to thrust back the years. It seemed to her that childhood, after all, was best. Andrew had the best part, running, laughing, into the sunlight. Where was James now, she wondered, and what was he thinking of? And what would become of Charlotte, plain, awkward Charlotte? Her mind rested on Janey, with the usual relief. Dear Janey, who would marry and have nice children, without any agony of self-questioning or any regrets for her lost childhood! Thea closed her eyes, and tried to imagine that she was in her second-best white frock, with the lace petticoat, that she wore black stockings, that her hair was in ringlets down her back, and that she must climb the step to reach the top of the stile, instead of being able to rest her elbows comfortably upon the bar. She rubbed the grained wood with her hand, and it was smooth and shining. Here, she thought, my hand rested. Here James put his hand and vaulted over, not as though he was showing off, but as though it was the natural way to get over a stile. Perhaps when I am dead, children will come to climb this stile, to fly their kites in this field. Perhaps James's children will come here. She tried to imagine James married, respectable and prosperous, like his father, but the image was blurred and unreal. She could see him only insouciant, and laughing and incalculable. His irresponsibility seemed an indispensable part of his character. Oh, why do we grow up, she cried to herself, why must there be change? She closed her eyes again and for a moment the meadow was peopled. James ran, knee-high in grass, Janey stood with feet apart, her round face shaded by the wide frill of her hat, Andrew jumped up and down in his blue sailor-suit, while his kite bobbed a few feet off the ground. Charlotte lay on her back, holding the string tenderly between her thin fingers and Nurse sat on the little wooden seat by the hedge, and knitted and presided over the revels like a diminutive Goddess. Thea opened her eyes, and the summer haze lay on the still, green fields, the trees rustled and whispered gently. Beside her, Paul stirred, and took a breath, as though about to speak.

Thea caught up her skirts and ran lightly up on to the step and over the stile. She turned, and laughed at him.

"Down at the bottom of the valley, there's a farmhouse," she said, "and there we can get tea." She took off her hat and shook her head, as though shaking long hair out of her face. Paul did not vault the stile, but climbed slowly over it, treading heavily. Thea's eyes were alight with mischief. "I'll race you to the end of the field," she cried, and set off through the long, dry grass, catching grass-seeds as she ran, and swinging her hat in her hand.

The farmhouse had not changed since Thea had last seen it. The same white gate opened on to a neat brick path, the same green-painted door stood invitingly open.

"Is this where you came, after flying your kites?" asked Paul, when they were seated in the sunny parlour, and the farmer's wife had welcomed them. His tone was very grave for such a casual question.

"Yes," Thea replied. She leant back against the wall, her senses dulled by memories, as with an opiate. "And Nurse was so angry because Andrew went out into the kitchen and started eating his tea there. Mrs Bates said she didn't mind, and Nurse didn't like to go into the kitchen herself and get him back. So Andrew stayed there, and Mrs Bates said, 'Bless the little gentleman, he could stay all day if he felt like it!' and that made Nurse crosser than ever. She said Andrew would make himself sick, but of course, he didn't."

"Her name is Mrs Bates?" asked Paul.

Thea started. "Yes. Yes, it is, but I didn't think I'd remembered that. Isn't it strange the details you remember, when things like the dates of the Kings of England, or capitals of the Countries of the World, which you try to remember, just don't stick?"

"Do you remember when we first met?" Paul asked, tenderly.

"Oh yes," Thea replied. "You offered me a sandwich, and I didn't dare take one, though I was dreadfully hungry."

Further reminiscences were cut short by the reappearance of Mrs Bates, bringing home-baked bread, home-made apple jelly, and a large, round, home-made fruit cake.

"If you are hungry now," said Paul, "you have chosen the right time for it."

"Excuse me, sir," said Mrs Bates, pausing with the tray resting on her hip, "but are you from Scotland?"

Paul looked startled and at a loss.

"It was only that I thought you spoke like a Scotsman," she explained. "You see, my father came from the North," she spoke the word reverently, "and he does so like to talk to anyone who comes from there."

"I'm very sorry," Paul smiled, "but I am from Germany."

"Well, fancy that," said Mrs Bates. She looked at him wonderingly, evidently surprised that he looked so like any normal human being. "Fancy you coming from there! Such a long way away. I must tell the old man. He *will* be interested to know that." She went off, quite reconciled to the fact that Paul did not come from 'the North.' Thea chuckled.

"You can never say that your accent isn't good enough now," she said.

"Fritz would say that it was disgraceful to be taken for anything but German," Paul replied, frowning a little.

"Fritz – your brother?"

He nodded. "Fritz is so proud of being German, that he won't even try to speak any other languages properly. He thinks that the only composer in the world is Wagner, and the only poet Goethe. He is always saying that he wishes he had been born in time to fight in the war against France."

"I suppose all boys want to be soldiers," Thea said easily. "Or sailors," she added.

She lost interest in the discussion, while she began to pour out the tea. "You take two lumps of sugar, I believe," she said, pleased to have remembered his tastes, and expecting him to be flattered. But Paul took the cup abstractedly, and returned his frowning gaze to the window.

"I wonder if I am too English," he murmured. "Fritz would say that I was."

They enjoyed Mrs Bates's apple jelly, and her home-made cake, but some of their friendly companionship had been lost. Paul still seemed absent-minded, and Thea fancied that he was thinking of Berlin, of a house she had never seen and of a sixteen-year-old boy who liked nothing that was not German. The sense of intimacy against which she had rebelled had vanished, and, having herself tried to banish it, she felt betrayed now that it was gone. Paul was courteous and friendly but withdrawn.

Paul paid Mrs Bates for their tea, and they sent messages to the aged Scot, who, after forty years in the degenerate South, still pined for the broad richness of his own tongue. Mrs Bates proudly pointed out her son, a tall, handsome lad in the yard, amid the jostling bodies of a herd of cows.

"Is *that* your son?" cried Thea, in amazement. She was remembering the sturdy little boy, in heavy, muddy boots, who had leant against the gate and stared at them. James had gone and talked to him, and ended by giving the farmer's son his best pocket-knife, for no better reason than that he didn't possess one.

They retraced their steps through the deep meadows, while the sun paled to yellow from gold. The western sky had turned to cream, and the indefinable country scent of grass and earth and meadowsweet sweet hung in the evening air. Beyond the stile, they turned once more to look back over the valley.

"How soft the English countryside is!" said Paul. Thea was unpleasantly struck by a shade of contempt in his tone. What should she say, she wondered, in defence of her land? She could say that the softness was not that of bogs or marshland, but as firm, beneath its gentleness, as good turf. She could say that, while some men held in their hearts the bare bones of the Welsh mountains, or the rocky beauties of the Lake District, the misty heights of Scotland or the wild moors of Devon, yet for most Englishmen, there could be nothing finer, and better worth fighting for, than just such green fields as they were looking out on, just such huge oak trees and horse chestnuts, just such broad, rough stiles, worn smooth by the hands of children and the elbows of lovers. The incense-tang of the meadowsweet came to her nostrils like a holy scent, and the white and gold of the buttercups and daisies cried to her with the appeal of littleness and unpretending humbleness. She put her hands on the wide wooden bar, as one who touches an ancient relic, but kept silence.

"You must come to Germany," said Paul, "and see the mountains, and the Black Forest." He turned to look at her, and Thea was suddenly angry, thinking that he was offering her his land, as a German, instead of his love, as a man.

"I could never love any country but England," she said, her colour higher than was warranted by the lessening heat of the sun. She added in low tones, "Not even France, or Monaco," and there were tears in her eyes. She stepped on to the dusty path and walked along beside the hedge, in the shadow of the tall trees. Paul followed her slowly and when he caught up with her, he did not take her arm but walked beside her in silence.

Thea went to bed early that night, complaining of a headache, which was due, she said, to walking in the sun. The familiar little room seemed too small to contain her troubled spirit, and she leaned out of the window to cool her forehead in the night breezes. The Milky Way glimmered faintly above in the madonna blue of the summer sky. She was tormented by the struggle within her. At one moment she cried out at herself for having stopped Paul from speaking when they first stood by the stile. Then it was as though Jimmy Stainforth's face came between her and Paul, and she heard his thick voice saying, "Thea!" and felt his lips on hers, and she shuddered in the old repugnance. She remembered Uncle Robert and her childish dreams of her father, and how sweet it had been to know the loving protection of a strong arm and a steady affection. But at once she remembered Ambrose and his possessive hand upon her mother's chair, and she put her hands on her breasts in a sudden gesture of defiance and rebellion. Her body was hers alone. Her virginity was very dear to her. At what price must she purchase the safety and protection for which she longed? It seemed to her that, no matter when Paul turned to speak to her of love, though her mind leaped to meet him, though his face and his smile and his voice had become very dear to her, yet always her body would shrink from him and her hands would push him away, because she was afraid.

Seventeen

T he day after his walk with Thea in the country, Paul did
not come to visit the house at Abbot's Green. Nan, as
discreet as always, accepted Thea's explanation of her low
spirits that her headache was still troubling her. Emily, ex-
hausting her culinary skill in fabricating a jelly to tempt
Thea's appetite – a jelly whose glutinous substance clung
fiercely to the spoon, and which gave off a strong odour of
pear-drops – was heard to mutter that People ought to have
more sense than to take other People out to walk for miles in
the sun, what were trains for anyway.

"It was my fault," said Thea, thus provoked, "I took my
hat off." To which Emily merely replied, "Huh! Country!"

The day passed slowly, and Thea once more went early to
bed, and cried herself to sleep, with some faint notion that she
was crying because she was an orphan. The next morning saw
her restored to her usual tranquillity, and in the afternoon,
Paul arrived, humbly announcing that he had come to tea.

"I'll get another cup and plate," cried Thea, as he joined
them in the garden. She felt like the Ancient Mariner, when
the Albatross dropped from around his neck. Her feet were
light on the flagged path.

"I wonder he don't come and live here," said Emily,
sarcastically.

"Don't you like him, Emily?" asked Thea, pausing in the
kitchen doorway.

"I've known worse," replied that unyielding worthy. She
emerged from the larder, bearing a pallid sponge cake.

169

"Here," she said, "you'd better take this. I was keeping it for tomorrow, but them buns won't be enough with Mister Brooner here." Emily scorned to use foreign titles.

"Oh, Emily," said Thea, half laughing, half moved, "thank you." She bore her spoils triumphantly to the garden, and told Paul at what rate his appetite was assessed by Emily.

"One of these days," Paul promised, "I will gather my courage together and bring Emily a bouquet of flowers. What do you think she would say if I did?"

"She would say, 'waste of money!' " Nan predicted. "And then she would look for the vase with the smallest neck she could find, and she would cram the stalks well down into it, and stand it on the dresser, and leave it there until the flowers decomposed."

"I will venture it," said Paul, "just to see if your prophecies come true."

"But she would be very pleased," Thea protested, "and if there was a card with the flowers, she would put it in her treasure-box. She keeps all her Christmas and birthday presents there, and never uses them."

"There shall be a card with the flowers," Paul replied, "but I'm not sure that Emily approves of me. The first time I came here, she frightened me so much that I nearly went away again."

"That was because she couldn't 'catch your name'," Nan explained. "Still, I'm glad she didn't quite frighten you away."

Paul smiled, and glanced enquiringly at Thea, as though half expecting her to second Nan's remark, but she seemed to be engrossed in cutting Emily's sponge cake.

Just as they had finished tea, they heard the sound of the front doorbell.

"Oh bother!" Thea exclaimed. "Who can it be, Nan? Were you expecting someone?"

Nan was already on her feet. "I wasn't," she said ruefully, "but I expect it's a customer. It's probably Mrs Harmon, to say that she 'just couldn't manage tomorrow, so came this evening instead'.'" Nan mimicked the good lady's rounded vowels and drawling tones with wicked pleasure, before she went quickly into the house, to forestall Emily, who was apt to treat Nan's clients like unwelcome parish visitors.

It was very quiet in the garden, more quiet than it can ever be in the country, where living creatures stir softly in the hedges and the long reeds. The fact that the small patch of grass and stones was in the middle of hundreds of houses, gave a sense of suspended animation, like the silence of the Sleeping Beauty's palace. The snapdragons stood motionless, the aubrietia and Little Dorrit clung to the rocks like embroidery, the very roses seemed to hold their breath. The houses on each side, and at the end of the garden, might have been under an enchantment which held them silent, and the curtains at the windows did not stir. Then, into the stillness, the thrush, perched on the laburnum tree, suddenly flung his song, as thrilling and uplifting as the bugle which plays the Last Post, and every note lingered in the summer air, rounded and golden, the eternal song of love.

As though the birdsong broke some spell, both of them moved at once. Thea, noticing that the butter was melting in the sun, leant forward to cover it, and, at the same moment, Paul reached out and took hold of her hand, saying softly, "Thea. Thea, my dear." Thea left her hand in his cool, firm fingers, but said confusedly,

"I must . . . I must cover the bread-and-butter."

At that, Paul threw back his head and laughed aloud, and Thea, turning to look at him, saw the sun glinting gold on his hair, saw his blue eyes shining with amusement and tenderness, and slipped into his ready arms as easily as a child climbs on to its father's knee. She hid her face in his coat, and for a few minutes she was conscious of nothing but a great calm. Paul's arm was close and strong about her, but gentle, as though anxious not to frighten her. She clung to him in silence, while above their heads the thrush still sang his challenge to happiness. After a while, Paul loosened his grasp,

171

and put a hand on her shoulder. She raised her head, and he bent and kissed her, not fiercely or passionately, but with deep tenderness, and the ghost of Jimmie Stainforth was laid for ever.

"Thea," said Nan, some fifteen minutes later, coming out into the garden, "what do you think? Mrs Fairs—" She stopped. Her visitor sat where she had left him, but on his knee was Thea, with her arm round his neck. "Good heavens, the neighbours!" cried Nan, and glanced hastily up, half expecting to see Miss Luke at the window on one side, and Mrs Winter at the other. No one can live in the suburbs of a city without acquiring a respect for the female Intelligence Service which it boasts. She was relieved to find no heads bobbing hastily behind the curtains. Thea and Paul started up guiltily, and stood hand-in-hand.

"Please," stammered Paul, "please, may we be married?"

For a moment, Nan stood still and looked at them. From the other side of the high fence came the sound of a lawnmower, as Mr Winter began to cut his lawn. The dear summer scent of new-cut grass came freshly to them. The thrush was no longer singing, but sparrows were twittering in the apple tree, and, a few gardens away, they could hear children laughing and shouting as they played out the last bright hours before bedtime. The narrow garden was no longer set apart in a silent world of its own, but hedged about with the familiar and friendly things which Thea remembered from her childhood. The rickety wooden table was the one that had been used for tea in the garden ever since Thea had been at Abbot's Green, the apple tree cast the same dappled shadow in the evening sun, the garden chairs had the same frailties and were coloured the same dull green, with brown patches where the paint had flaked off. Thea felt the ties of the old life dragging at her heart. In those few seconds when Nan stood silent, she felt a painful sense of loss and parting.

Then Nan came forward, put her hand on Paul's shoulder and kissed him.

"My dear boy," she said. She drew back and looked at him, with a radiant happiness on her face. "I am so glad for you both."

Thea flung her arms round Nan's neck. "Oh Nan," she whispered. "Oh Nan." There was so much she wanted to say – that this was not an end, but a continuation, that she had not planned this thing, but it had come upon her with the force of the predestined, that her feet still lingered in the old paths and though she was drawn out of them into an untrodden land, still she would look fondly back over her shoulder. "Dear Nan."

She returned to Paul's side, slipping her hand into his and turning her face up to be kissed, just as Emily came out into the garden.

"I've come for the tea-things," said Emily stiffly.

"Oh, Emily, we're going to be married," cried Thea, her momentary sadness bubbling into gaiety.

"Yes, Miss Thea, so I should think," Emily replied. She stacked the crockery noisily on to the tray. "You ought to've covered this bread-and-butter," she said. "It's all melted."

Paul clutched convulsively at Thea's hand, and she leant against him in an agony of silent mirth until Emily had folded up the green checked cloth, put it over her arm, and trodden heavily away into the house carrying the tray. Then they looked at each other and laughed.

Nan did not ask why they were laughing, nor did they tell her. Perhaps in that moment, they all three felt that Paul and Thea had already begun to live their life apart.

"Nan," said Paul, some time later, "how soon may we be married?"

"Well . . ." Nan paused to consider. "Well, I think that you should wait a year at least."

"A year!" Paul exclaimed. "I had rather hoped . . . That seems a long time."

"Thea is so young," Nan pleaded. "And you haven't known each other for very long. I think that you should certainly wait a year."

173

Paul was silent, his eyes on the grass at his feet. He was frowning a little, almost as though he was working out an abstruse mental problem in arithmetic. His boyish eagerness had vanished. He looked stern, even, Thea thought, angry. Nan watched him with a shadow on her face, and Thea knew that she was remembering Tom Lawrence, and how soon he had married Belle and taken her away into his life of uncertainties and cheap shifts. Then Paul raised his head. He smiled his devastating smile at Nan.

"You're quite right," he said. "I hate to wait, but I'm sure we should. You will want to sew Thea's dress and make other arrangements. The time will pass quickly." He straightened his shoulders, like one who feels relief after making a difficult decision. "A year, why, we shall need a year to find a house we like, and furniture." Nan, too, was looking relieved.

Thea had a strange feeling that none of this concerned her very closely, that from the moment she had slid into Paul's arms, she need never more worry about the future, need never more make decisions. She leant against Paul's shoulder and listened to them talking, as though she were at a play, watching with pleasure, but from a distance. The thrush was singing again and the air was full of the fresh scent of the grass, the children's voices sounded more sleepily and a train puffed breathlessly out of Abbot's Green station. These things were more real to her and more immediate than the question of when she and Paul would be married. Her contentment was almost like that pleasant detachment of illness, when time ceases to have any meaning, and the firelight on the ceiling or the pattern of leaves on the sunlit wall mark the boundaries of reality. It was only as Nan shivered in the freshening breeze and they rose to go indoors that she asked Nan a question.

"What were you going to say about Mrs Fairs?"

Nan laughed. "Why, she called to ask me to make her a new dress."

"I don't believe it! What colour does she want it?"

"Black," Nan replied. "Black satin, and *exactly* like the

other. She started by saying that she thought it was time she had a change, so I suggested a nice maroon or dark blue, but she said, no, she wouldn't like anything but black."

"Oh no, Nan," said Thea, "we couldn't possibly exist without Mrs Fairs's black."

"No, and we're not going to get the chance," Nan laughed. "Well, I must go and see Emily and try to coax her to give us something special for supper." She went indoors and Thea and Paul lingered behind. Thea was suddenly grave. She was thinking of Mrs Fairs's black. How Belle had disliked it! It had been that hated black satin dress which she had flung on the floor, that afternoon when she cried out against the prison bonds. Thea sighed quickly, and found Paul looking at her. His face was troubled.

"Thea," he began, and stopped. He turned to face her, his hands at his sides. "If you ever feel that you regret it," he said, "you have only to say so. I shall understand. I am ten years older than you, and I am a foreigner. Perhaps I have hurried you too much, but you see . . ." He stopped short again, as though he had nearly said something indiscreet. "You are free," he finished. "I want you to feel free."

"Ah, no, Paul," cried Thea, "I don't want to feel free. I don't want to be free." She reached up to put her arms about him and held him fiercely, whispering, "Hold me close, Paul. Hold me close. Don't ever let me go. I feel so safe when you hold me."

Eighteen

"I wonder," said Thea, "whether we are getting married too soon."

"Too soon!" Paul protested, "but . . ."

"I was thinking of Nan," Thea explained. "She'll be so lonely here alone."

They had spent a pleasant evening looking at houses through the rose-coloured descriptions of house agents. They were astonished to find how many desirable residences or charming semi-detached villas appeared to be exactly what they wanted. The time was yet to come when they would tramp wearily from house to house, discovering that Laburnum Cottage was a gaunt, four-storied mansion, craning its top attic over the railway-lines, and that Ivy Lodge was the smallest of a row of workman's houses. They had yet to pursue the elusive bathroom, to count the stairs, and to observe that 'within easy walking distance of the station' might mean a quiet amble of five miles. They were still implicitly believing the glowing advertisements which lay before them, like amateur gardeners fondly awaiting the riot of luxuriant blooms promised them on the seed packets. Paul thoughtfully glanced over an account of one of the larger houses at Muswell Hill.

"I don't want you to worry about her," he said slowly. "I was wondering whether you would like Nan to come and live with us, and –" he faltered, but added with determination – "and Emily, too, of course."

Thea was silent, trying not to let the dismay she felt show in her face. As the weeks of their engagement had passed, she had been finding increasing pleasure in planning their home, the neat little house which should belong to them alone, the meals which she would arrange, the welcome which would await Paul when he got home from the office, the long evenings alone together, beside the fire, or in their own small garden. She loved Nan and was angry with herself for the bitter disappointment she felt at the thought of having her always with them, or having Emily still ruling the kitchen with complete autocracy. Surely *she* should be anxious to have them, and Paul, not even related to Nan, should deserve her gratitude. But then, he will be out all day, she thought resentfully. I have the right to have my own house. She very much regretted her ill-fated words about leaving Nan lonely, which had prompted him to offer such a solution, and found herself thinking that she must watch her tongue, and that it was just like a man to make such a suggestion without counting the cost to her.

The moment's silence lengthened into minutes. Thea was afraid to speak in case she could not control her voice. Her temper, so slow to arouse, was fighting to possess her. She felt caught in the clinging spider's web of family ties, cloying, inescapable, because one could not even try to escape from it. I don't want to be tied like that, she told herself, and with the words, the tide of angry emotions turned. What had Belle said? Most selfish people put it that way. She turned to meet Paul's eyes, and smiled, reassured by the understanding and regret she saw there.

"How good you are!" she said softly. "Dear Paul, I know we ought to do that. We'll ask her tonight. How could I think of leaving Nan alone!" Paul took her hand and she pressed it convulsively, but went on, "She could have her own room for dressmaking if she really won't give it up, though perhaps she will when she moves to a different place. And then, how nice it will be to have Emily in the kitchen still, and later on we might have a girl in to help her, if we can afford it, and that might sweeten her temper."

People make sacrifices worse than this every day, she told herself. She remembered the woman in the next street, who had refused to go out to India to marry a man, because her mother was dying of a slow and painful disease and she would not leave her. She remembered the young married couple two doors away, who could never go out together, because his crippled father lived with them, and hated to be left. She thought that even Mrs Winter had for many years cared for her husband's sister, who had been jilted in her youth and was subject to hysterical fits, until she at last died of an overdose of sleeping tablets. This offer which she and Paul would make to Nan was part of the duties recognised by middle-class English people. They did not ride out to rescue strange princesses or search for mystic signs. Yet this opening of their dearest possession, their home, to receive relatives in want or trouble, was a part of their code of Christian chivalry, as fine as that of King Arthur's knights. With many other middle-class conventions, it formed the barrier which divided them both from the very poor and from the aristocracy.

So Thea folded up an account of a dear little house with two living rooms and three bedrooms and 'a mass of roses round the front door' and turned her attention to the smallest 'desirable' residence which would leave room for Nan to live with them comfortably. They resolved to speak to her that evening, and indeed Thea thought it best to leave no time in which her resolution might waver.

"Nan," Paul began, a little nervously, "we've been looking at these houses for sale and to let. There seem to be one or two that might suit us, but we're waiting to know which district you would prefer."

"That's up to you, my dears," Nan answered, "only," she added, smiling rather wistfully, "only, perhaps somewhere not *too* far away."

"But, Nan, you'll be coming with us," Thea put in, "so, of course, you must say—"

"Coming with you?" Nan interrupted. "Good gracious, no! I might come and stay with you perhaps."

"But we had so hoped that you might come and live with us," said Paul. "Thea will be alone a lot while I'm in the City, and with Emily in the kitchen, it will seem more like home."

"No, I wouldn't dream of it," Nan said firmly. "I don't ever think it's good for a young couple to have relations living with them."

"But, Nan, you're not 'relations'," said Thea.

Nan shook her head. "No matter who it is," she replied, "It seems all right at first, but after a week or two, you find that you want to have your house to yourself."

There was a short silence. Paul and Thea were so convinced of the truth of this, that they could think of nothing to say. Thea was wishing with all her heart that she had not so grudged the necessity of asking Nan to live with them. Nan's unthinking selflessness threw into sharp relief her own reluctant sense of duty, which had been strengthened, moreover, by the knowledge that if she did not obey it, she herself would not feel comfortable.

"Besides," Nan continued, almost as though she knew what Thea was thinking, "I am getting too old to move now. I used to hate this house when I first came here, but now that I am accustomed to it, and have been here so long, I shouldn't like to leave it." She might have added that from this house her two daughters had been married. She might have said that in leaving it she would lose even that faint sense of association, that painful comfort of living in the house where they had lived, of seeing about her the things which they had touched, and that it would make them seem still farther away from her. But, being Nan, she only added, "I like the people round here too, now I've got to know them. I couldn't face making new friends at my age."

"I'm afraid you'll be so lonely, Nan," said Thea.

"Nonsense," said Nan, staunchly. "People are always coming in, and the dressmaking keeps me busy. I have all my possessions about me, and Emily and I are used to each other's ways, and I have the whist drives and the church fêtes to go to, quite apart from concerts."

"Paul . . . I . . . we wondered whether you wouldn't give the dressmaking up," said Thea.

Nan stiffened. She sat up even straighter than usual (and she had been trained to keep her back straight as a girl, on a backboard) and raised her fine head. "I wouldn't dream of it," she said. "It gives me something to do, and besides, I like to be independent."

Thea was suddenly proud of her lineage, proud because she did not come of a noble family, strewn with illegitimate children and poor relations, with mortgaged estates and aristocratic debts, but of an obscure line of non-conformists, who were 'in trade', who held immorality to be shameful and not clever, who were just, even when they were not kind, respected, even though they were not famous, and who held self-reliance, hard work and independence to be the cardinal virtues. They stood upon their independence as a captain upon his bridge. If the ship went down, they went with it, but kept their self-respect.

"Then, if you have really made up your mind," said Paul, "we must just try to find somewhere very close, so that we can see you every day."

"Oh, Nan, are you *quite* sure?" Thea asked, and she was pleading, not only that Nan should not make a decision she would regret, but also for Nan's forgiveness for the fact that years of companionship could be so lightly set aside.

"Quite sure," Nan replied. "And I will come to call on you so often that you will wish that I *was* living with you."

They all laughed and the matter was finally set aside. Whether Nan was making a sacrifice, or whether she really preferred her own dark little house, alone with Emily, Thea never knew. Behind all her sweetness and pleasant good-temper, Nan never lost the unobtrusive barrier of reserve which had sufficed to defend her from the hostile curiosity of the ladies of Abbot's Green, and now sufficed to defend her from the loving pity of her granddaughter. So they found their house, in what had once been the next village, but now was the next tram-stop. There was no may tree at the corner of their road, but chrysanthemums in their small front garden and a rose-arbour outside the french windows at the back. It was a small house, in a row of others, very much like it, but their house, as Thea pointed out, had an extra and totally unexpected gable, which the architect had obviously included as an afterthought, and which distinguished it from its semi-detached neighbour, which only had a bay window. The little front gate bore upon it the word, 'Barramour', which, as Paul said, sounded like a swear-word.

"Yes," Thea agreed, "we can't possibly live in a house called Barramour. We must change it."

They discussed alternatives, from The Nest to Brunerhouse, but could never decide upon a name, and so the board with Barramour on it remained on the gate, almost unnoticed, and their letters were, in any event, addressed to Number forty-two.

"When I marry," Thea had determined, as a child, "I will have to my wedding only those very dear to me." And now she found that she did not mind who came. In fact, she felt that she would like everyone she had ever known to come to her wedding – the small boy who had hit her on the head with his satchel the first day she went to school and had made her cry; the old flower-woman who came round from door to door with her huge basket and always gave Thea a bunch of violets, not knowing that she disliked violets; the old gentleman who had lent her his handkerchief in the train to Enfield. Was he still alive? She would like to show him that the child who had cried so bitterly that day was now happy and protected, never to be lonely or frightened again. She thought of Mrs Van Dutyens, and spent most of a night planning the letter she would write to her, the gracefully worded thanks, the pretty invitation to come and see her little Thea again.

In composing the letter, Thea found all the faces and scenes of Monte Carlo vivid in her mind, as though she returned there on a visit. She could not sleep for Belle's smiling face under the light straw hat, for the thick coils of hair shining in the light of the dressing-table lamp. She planned her words of welcome to Mrs Van Dutyens, gracious and affectionate, as Belle's would have been. No longer would she be the sulky, tongue-tied girl. "Sadie," she would cry, warmly, "how lovely to see you." Then she would introduce Paul with pride, the man who was a little older than her, as Sadie had recommended, the man who was to take care of her. But in the morning, she knew that she would not write to Mrs Van Dutyens. She imagined her coming to the little suburban house in her perfume and jewels, and her over-elaborate dress and hat. She imagined her loud voice and laugh, and thought how she and Nan would have nothing to say to each other, and how the ladies of Abbot's Green would be scandalised by her. She wanted to remember Sadie as she had seen her last, dressed in the plain black frock and hat, with that air of detached responsibility which Nurse had. For the last time she saw the wise, faded blue eyes. For the last time she heard the husky voice with the American lilt in it, saying, "I want you *should* forget it. I want you should forget *all* of it, 'cep' the time that went before." It was as though Sadie had known and spoken for this moment. For the last time, her bulky figure passed behind the barriers of Thea's mind, and out of sight, into the untrodden past.

The hired car was full of the scent of white lilac, and its fragrance blurred Thea's senses like intoxication or the near approach of sleep. There was an unreality in the familiar streets, in the driver's back, in Uncle Robert's nearness, in her own white satin dress and the veil over her face.

"I am going to be married," she thought, and the words had the fantastic half-truth of a dream, where events are comprehended, but never really happen. It seemed strange that Nan

183

should not be with her on this last journey of her single life, and yet the fact that Uncle Robert was with her in the car had, again, the unreal logic of a dream, since he had been for so many years her ideal of a husband and a father. His hair was grey now, but still plentiful and waving. His imperial was clipped rather closer, so that he bore some resemblance to the new King, George the Fifth. Thea looked down at his legs in the formal striped trousers, cramped even in this roomy car, and the fine hand resting on his knee, the long fingers, like James's, and the single gold signet ring. As she looked at it, the hand came up and took hers, cool and firm round her trembling, clammy one. She pressed it gratefully, thinking that this was the last time she need long to have him as her father. From now on, she had her own protector, kind and strong and loving. The dream dissolved into one clear reality, Paul. It was as though he had kissed her and she had awoken from a long sleep, to see his face above her.

When Thea left Uncle Robert's arm to stand by Paul, she felt about her what Malory calls 'a great clearness'. The unreality of the past months fell aside like a curtain and she saw her path plain before her. As she took her place at Paul's side, he turned to look at her with such an obvious appeal for help that she knew then beyond all doubt that never on the earth would she find that freedom from all responsibility, that complete protection from all worry and anxiety, which she had hitherto demanded for her happiness. She took Paul's hand in hers, thinking that now her married responsibilities had already begun, and turned to glance at him so that she should carry away from her wedding the picture of her husband praying at her side. But Paul, though kneeling in front of the altar, was looking at her, his eyes upon her face. I must pray for both of us, Thea thought, but with a faint chill, because their unity was already broken to that extent.

In the vestry the dream came back again, and Thea watched herself signing the register with surprise. May 5th, 1914 was on the page (Nan had relented before the end of the stipulated year) and there, in her childish, thin writing, leaning back a little, as was taught at the Abbot's Green School for Girls, were the words 'Thea Lawrence'. That's the last time I shall write that, Thea thought, the last time I shall use the name my mother used. She thought, too, that it was the end of her tenuous, uncertain link with her father. He had left her only one legacy, his name. At last she felt that her father, too, was dead. She had buried her mother in a rock cemetery by the Mediterranean. Now she buried her father, all he had once meant to her, all he might have been to her, all that he had been to her mother, in this parish register in Abbot's Green. She looked up at Paul, and he nodded soberly. Someone made a joke, and the little party in the vestry laughed, but she and Paul plighted their troth gravely and earnestly, and she was glad that he did not kiss her.

Aunt Mary had offered to lend her house at Enfield for the wedding, but Thea had refused, thinking Nan would prefer to have it at Sunnyside. Mercifully it was a fine, warm day, and she and Paul stood in the garden while Nan welcomed the guests by the rockery and passed them on to what the local photographer called 'the Bridal Group'. Charlotte and Janey were bridesmaids in identical dresses; Janey looking very pretty, and Charlotte very plain. Lydia's small boy, Drew, was alleged to be train-bearer, that is, he fidgeted during the service and ran about shrieking afterwards. Lydia had ceased to be The Misunderstood Genius, and had become The Mother. Drew was a small, pale, dark child, bearing no resemblance whatever to Andrew, for whom he was named. But to Lydia he *was* Andrew. She was determined that he should be like her brother, and the naughtiness which in Andrew had been constantly reproved in Drew was encouraged. She refused to see his obvious likeness to his father, as though Tony were merely the means whereby Andrew was reincarnated. Drew was clumsy with his hands, yet he was always given mechanical toys. He was a backward child, yet he was always being cited by his mother as an instance of startling precocity. Her real affection for her brother, the normal and reasonable affection of an elder sister, had become magnified and metamorphosed by Andrew's death, and by her own romantic imagination, into an undying passion that was now violently poured out upon Drew. Only Aunt Mary sympathised with her in this. There was no doubt that she was genuinely devoted to her son, but her habit of self-dramatisation made her family shrug their shoulders, saying, "Oh, Lydia, playing up as usual." They resented too the suggestion that a child of Lydia's could take the place of the incomparable Andrew, resented that she should flaunt the tragedy which all of them had felt, as her own particular grief, and hated to see her drawing Tony's son to her knee, stroking his hair, and saying fondly, in front of strangers, "This is my little Andrew," a pause, to master her emotion, and then, "named after his uncle." Thea felt sorry for Lydia in her desperate attempt to undo time's work, to cling to what was gone, but then, as she told herself, Andrew had not been her brother.

Early among the guests was Mrs Winter, in a hat so obviously bought for the occasion that it rather seemed to accompany her, than to be part of her clothing. Her big round face was shining with the heat and she was out of breath and flustered. She kissed Nan as she shook hands with her, and took Thea's hand in both hers and then kissed her too, warmly on the cheek. "She's fond of me," thought Thea, astonished by the discovery.

"My dear," said Mrs Winter, and suddenly, terrifyingly, dropped two aitches. "I 'ope you'll both be very 'appy," she said. A gust of affection for Mrs Winter swept Thea in return. She saw Mrs Winter, not sure of herself, awe-inspiring and overbearing, but gallantly clinging to her pretensions to gentility, valiantly striving after culture. Her singing, like her new hat, was part of this endeavour, and she knew that she sang off the note, as she was now uneasily aware that the hat was too big. She did not hope to deceive others, or herself,

186

but asked only that others would pretend to be deceived, as she did.

"Dear Mrs Winter," said Thea, "how lovely to see you!" and she was delighted when Paul insisted on kissing Mrs Winter, claiming that it was an old German custom for the bridegroom to kiss the guests. She noticed, however, that he carefully shook hands with Elsie, following close behind and escorted by a perspiring and tongue-tied Ronnie.

James had not come, being unable to leave his office in the North of England. But he had sent a telegram, wishing them both all happiness. When it was read out, Paul put his arm round Thea and held her to him, and she was pleased at his possessiveness. James should marry some nice girl, she thought maternally. Someone who would look after him. She leant back against Paul, her hand in his, smiling.

"Isn't it *too* romantic?" cried Miss Luke, in a loud aside to Nan. She had arrived late, having called in on her way back from the church to make sure that Mrs Luke was all right. She had laid aside her acidity, but the eager look was there, the sharp, hopeful look that always made Thea want to be God, with power to satisfy that hunger. There are people who spoil children, because the things they want are so easy to provide, the sugar cake, the pretty toy, the half-hour more before bedtime. Thea thought that if she were God, she would give to all her children the pathetic joys they begged for: success to the little-minded, safety to the fearful and love to the lonely. But Miss Luke, in her flowered print dress and her straw hat, was shrill and in high spirits.

"Quite a love-match!" she exclaimed, and ran at Thea and Paul, her eyes bright behind her glasses. "Such a lovely wedding! I just ran in to Mother, and she was ever so excited." Thea almost started, so incongruous was the thought of excitement and Mrs Luke. "I told her what the bride was wearing, and the bridesmaids." Her little eyes flickered over Charlotte and Janey, and returned to rest a moment upon Charlotte. "So I said, 'Well, Mother, I'll just pop round for a minute or two, but I'll soon be back to tell you all about it'. She gets rather low, you know, if she's alone for long."

"Perhaps if we were to call in to see her," Thea suggested, "before we go, she might like it?"

"Oh, she'd love it," cried Miss Luke. "Oh, she *would* like that. She'd like to see you in your white." Thea longed to give away some of her abundance to placate the jealous gods. When Miss Luke turned to glance at a noisy group of guests nearby, who were laughing at one of Ronnie's jokes – Ronnie always, as Mrs Winter said, "the life and soul of the party" – Thea clutched Paul's arm and whispered quickly, "Talk to her, Paul, be nice to her." She was like a queen, she thought, who gives a penny to a beggar-woman, before entering the palace and leaving her outside in the darkness and the cold rain. So Paul talked to Miss Luke of music and art, while she laughed up at him, the ugly hat perched on untidy, greying hair, the dress loose over her flat boniness. Thea felt for her an agony of pity, but she knew that in that moment Miss Luke felt young and attractive. Thea wondered if Miss Luke was thinking that what Paul wanted was not an ignorant young girl, but a slightly older woman who could appreciate good music. A woman who was cultured and spoke a little German. Thea hoped that she was thinking that.

Before she changed her dress, Thea went with Paul to visit Mrs Luke. Despite the warm day, there was a fire in the hearth, and the old lady was wrapped round with woollen shawls and blankets. She smiled calmly up at Thea.

"Well, my dear, so Mr Right did come along." She included Paul in her smile, and Thea thought how angry and embarrassed she would once have been. She stood at the end of the bed, listening to the clock ticking and the faint voice speaking like a scratchy pen. "You do look pretty in your white. And what a lovely bouquet. I had lilies for my wedding. Mr Luke was ever so fond of lilies."

Don't put lilies on the grave, Belle had said. *They always make me think of funerals.*

"Well, my dear, and so I suppose you're very happy?"

188

"Yes," said Thea, "oh, yes." She supposed that she was happy. Surely she was. If only things would stop whirling about her, with unimportant thoughts catching like brambles at her mind, and important and vital ones dissolving into mist. If only she could lose that sense of breathless apprehension, and trust in Paul as she wanted to. If only the bright sun of their future life were not suddenly eclipsed by a dark shadow which had crept between.

"Where are you going for your honeymoon? Mr Luke and I went to Bournemouth, and it was ever so nice."

Paul answered for her, and Thea was thankful. Had she and Mr Luke set out on their honeymoon like two adventurers, only to return to this still room, with the antimacassar and the stag at bay and the glass with the beaded-net cover? And from that voyage did nothing remain but the photograph of Mr Luke on the table and the un-beautiful Andromeda, Miss Luke, chained to the rock of duty, waiting for the monster, old age, from which nothing but death could set her free? Oh, God, let ours be a joyous adventure, thought Thea. Let us be together. Do not leave one of us to grow old alone.

"Well, Mother, I expect Thea should go and change now," said Miss Luke, and she smiled at Thea as though there was a secret understanding between them. "They've got a train to catch, you know." Thea bent over Mrs Luke to kiss her. The old cheek was plump and soft.

"Goodbye, my dear. Thank you for coming to see me. I hope you'll be very happy. Such a fine day. I like to see a fine day for a wedding." Thea felt a ridiculous stab of superstition, as though Mrs Luke's benediction could be unlucky. Then they went from the quiet room and the ticking clock, down the stairs with their shiny banisters, across the cold and silent hall and out into the May sunshine, where birds sang and flowers scented the air. Thea took Miss Luke's arm.

"You will come and see us often, won't you? You know we always like to see you, and we don't want to lose all our friends when we move."

"No, indeed," Paul agreed, courteously, but already he was impatient to be gone, and Thea knew it, if Miss Luke didn't.

"That would be lovely," Miss Luke said brightly, and so they parted, Thea and Paul to change for the journey, and Miss Luke to join the other guests before returning to her bondage.

That night, Thea and Paul stood on a cliff-top, looking out over the sea. They had talked and laughed over dinner, and then they had decided to stroll out to see the moonlit Channel, and a silence had fallen upon them. The moon's shaft lay upon black waters. Thea strained her eyes into the distance.

"Over there is France," she said softly.

"And beyond that, Germany," Paul replied. "I am longing for you to meet my mother. How you will like each other! And my father – he always wanted a daughter."

Thea said nothing. It was true, what Charlotte had said. Everyone stands alone. No one can share our thoughts. No one can weep our tears, or bear our pain. It was possible to stand, as she stood, with a man's arm about her, feeling the warmth of his body and hearing his breathing, and yet be so far away from him that he could not hear her cry for help, nor feel the torment which twisted her heart.

Thea shrank under the silence of the country, the blind stare of sea and Downs – blind because it still looked upon the past. Beneath the cliff, high ships tossed, the Anglo-Saxon steersmen bitter with longing for their lords, for the smoke-filled hall and the cup of friendliness. Round behind them lay Battle, the land heavy with the blood of the last Englishmen. The beacon fires gleamed their welcome to the great Spanish ships, and, older than all, the Long Man stood white and silent against the hill, the guardian of the past, the shepherd of the unchanging land. And Thea knew only that she was a stranger here, that the land was not hostile, but unseeing, as a giant does not notice the fly beneath his boot. The sea mist which crept up over the edge of the cliff was white and chill, colder and more unfriendly than the familiar London fog. Thea's soul cried out for the companionated town, for the lighted windows, the garden fences, the smoking chimneys, where the silence of evening was broken by the trams, the silence of night by the policeman's tread on the pavements and of early morning by the rattle of the milkman's cart. The flickering stars were too far and dim for her, used to the ready glow of the street-lamps. The white mist licked hungrily about their feet, and Paul had never known her mother, and did not care that she was dead.

Then Paul spoke, and Thea knew from his tone that he was afraid of hurting her, and desperately anxious to help her. "She knows about us," he said. "She would want you to be happy." And because he took it for granted that they were both thinking of Belle and because he used the very words Belle had used, "I want you to be happy, darling," the loneliness fell away from Thea. She smiled up at him through tears, and said, "Yes," and that was enough.

They were silent again, and Thea thought how beautiful the dancing waters were, how sweet the fresh sea air, how kindly the waves murmured at the foot of the cliffs. She nestled close, whispering, "Dear Paul. Oh, dear Paul." He turned suddenly and strained her to him, saying breathlessly, "I suppose we should get back to the hotel."

At once he felt her trembling within his arms, as a captured butterfly flutters in a closed hand. He relaxed his grasp, and said very gently, "Thea, don't be afraid."

For a moment she remained tense, and then she sighed. He was conscious of her slight weight leaning against him without reserve. Only once before had she made such a surrender of herself, lying before the altar in the church in Monte Carlo. Now Paul knew that she gave into his keeping, not only her body, but her soul, her mind, her heart. Without reservation, she clung to him, her head on his shoulder.

"No, Paul," she said. "No, I'm not afraid."

Nineteen

H appiness is like a bubble blown from a clay pipe. It has about it always an unexpectedness, a wonder. There were times, during the weeks which followed their return from the honeymoon, when Thea would stand still and hold her breath in amazement, not only to find herself so happy, but because the ingredients of her happiness were so simple. She would pause, duster in hand, by the dining-room windows, or stand under the rose-arbour in the back garden, with her face lifted, her head a little tilted, as though she were listening for something. For what? She did not know. For the imperceptible passing of time, perhaps, or for the past and the future jostling against this present which lingered, rounded and beautiful, and never failed to astonish her.

Thea never quite got used to issuing orders, and to being expected to give advice.

When a huge blackbird found its way into the bedroom and went immediately mad, beating its wings against the windows and hurling itself desperately upon the unyielding glass, there was no Nan or Emily to deal with the situation. The young maid, Agnes, crumpled her apron in her two hands and bleated in terror, and Thea must herself venture into the arena, through the flapping anguish and sharp beak, to set the windows wide open for its escape.

When Agnes, cutting bread, gashed her hand, it was Thea who had to answer her shriek, hold the bloody wound under the cold tap and tie it up with a perfectly good table napkin. She was surprised to find how many crises could occur in an ordinary household, crises which had seemed no more than minor events when someone else was dealing with them, but which called for all her small stock of courage when she alone was responsible.

A more experienced servant might have saved her from much of this, but Agnes was seventeen, and nervous. She had been for three years a vegetable maid in a big house. The mistress had been kind, and the household generously run, but her fellow-servants, particularly the cook, had bullied her into something like a nervous breakdown. She had returned home in a state of tearful despair, and this was her second excursion into domestic service. Emily's married sister lived next to Agnes's mother. Thea had interviewed her at Sunny side before the wedding, Emily introducing her into the sitting room, like a Roman thrusting a Christian into the lion's mouth and Thea sitting on the sofa like a Christian waiting for the lion to appear. Emily had withdrawn, leaving mistress and maid regarding each other with equal apprehension.

"Good . . . good afternoon, Agnes," said Thea, wondering if she should have used instead the surname on so slight an acquaintance. Agnes blenched.

"Good . . . afternoon, Madam," she faltered.

There was a silence. Thea wondered if she might run and fetch Nan, who had firmly retired, leaving her alone with this terrifying being. She supposed that she should ask for a reference, but how could one enquire of a fellow human being if she was sober, honest and industrious? An inspiration seized her.

"Do sit down."

Agnes poised herself on the edge of a chair, her feet close together, her handbag and her umbrella (marks of respectability) tightly clutched. Thea noticed that, although her hair was dragged severely back from her face, her eyes were round and frightened, her mouth childishly soft. Thea suddenly smiled.

"Emily said she thought you might come to me, to do some cooking and help in the house."

"Yes, Madam." Then, in a burst of confidence, "But, I don't cook very good, Madam."

"Well, nor do I," said Thea cheerfully. "We'll learn together." She sighed in relief. The matter seemed to be settled more easily than she had hoped. She told Agnes the address of their house, and the date of their return there. "I'll see you then," she finished. "I think Emily is making a pot of tea for you." She smiled again in light-hearted dismissal, and escorted Agnes out to the kitchen, to the watchful Emily. Engaging a servant was, after all, quite a simple affair.

Emily came in after Agnes's departure. "You said you'd have her then?" she enquired, sourly.

Thea, still self-satisfied, replied that she had.

"And you fixed her wages, I suppose," said Emily. Nan, just returned, looked at Thea and smiled. "Huh," said Emily. "I thought so. Well, I did. And she'll go to the house with me for the week before you come back, to get it ready. *And* she's got some proper uniforms from her last job, so you won't need to get her any."

"Thank you, Emily," said Thea meekly.

Emily stood in the doorway, one hand in the pocket of her apron. "She's a poor thing," she said, with immense contempt, "but she'll do what she's told." The oracle had spoken. Agnes had been examined and assessed by an infallible valuer. There was no more to be said.

So Thea and Paul were greeted on their arrival at their new home by flowers in every room, arranged by Nan, by a meal, planned and prepared by Emily, and by Agnes, somewhat battered by a week spent in Emily's company, but smiling and neatly dressed in her uniform.

Looking at Agnes, shining with cleanliness from her white cap to her well-polished shoes, and at the small rooms, all spotless and unused, Thea felt as though she was stepping into a dolls' house. She remembered that one of her games as a child used to be to pretend that she had become very small, like Alice, and could live in the same house as the Bloggs family, run up their tiny stairs, sit in their little chairs and use their minute knives and forks. It had always seemed to her that their house, by its very smallness, had a safety of its own, as though the winds of mischance which swept through other houses would merely skim harmlessly over their little red-tiled roof. Number forty-two, Rose Avenue was her dolls' house, hers and Paul's. They stepped into it, slammed the front door, and no one could touch them.

They had taken the house furnished, because Paul said that his future plans were somewhat unsettled. It would be better to wait until they finally settled down before buying furniture. So the first week saw some anxious searchings for cooking utensils and articles of tableware which were known to be somewhere in the house, but had mysteriously concealed themselves. But in a fortnight it was as though they had been living there for years. The pleasant routine of suburban life enclosed them. On Saturday morning, Thea went shopping, with an air of importance, a large basket, and a list, jointly achieved by herself and Agnes. On Sunday morning, they went to church, returning to roast meat and a fruit pie. On Sunday afternoon, they lay in the garden, and made tea themselves, Agnes being out. On Monday, Thea helped Agnes with the washing, and prepared the laundry, with its cryptic list of shts. and twls. lrge. They visited Nan regularly, and she as often came to them. And every alternate Wednesday, Agnes again had the afternoon off. It was an unchanging and unfailing routine which would have driven many people, including Belle, to a state near to insanity, but to Thea it was perfect, the answer to all her longings, the end of all disquiet. Every weekday she kissed Paul goodbye before he left to catch his train, and stood at the gate to watch him go. He always turned and waved before passing out of sight round the corner into the main road. Every evening, she was ready to open the front door to him, listening for the latch of the gate, or for his footstep on the pavement.

Had she never loved him before, she would have loved him

now, for his sweetness of temper, his thoughtfulness, his love of home, his appreciation of everything she did to make the house comfortable. They played at housekeeping like two children, yet there was in their relationship something of that of a long-married couple, a certainty and tranquillity. They were oddly sure of each other. They found great pleasure in the little intimacies of their daily life, breakfasting together, reading each other's correspondence, working in the garden.

Thea had never before enjoyed gardening, but here they had all the excitements of treasure-trove and of reaping where they had not sowed. Each lupin, each peony was an unearned triumph. She loved the golden summer evenings, when Paul took off his coat and rolled up his sleeves to mow the lawn, while she snipped dead blooms or tied up the rambler roses. For weeding, she wore a gardening apron, like Aunt Ruth's, and she sometimes thought how strange it was that she had only the things which Aunt Ruth had, the little house, the husband, the one servant, and yet she was so happy, while Aunt Ruth's life had been a burden to her. After dinner, she and Paul would frequently return to the garden, to admire their work and to water the plants after sundown. The moist earth had a strong perfume and the flowers brightened gratefully. The bird-songs were reduced to twitterings and, walking in their small patch of land, they might have been on a desert island – or perhaps in that first garden of all, where the one man and the one woman walked, and were content.

One evening, towards the end of June, Paul was late home. For two hours, Thea wandered distractedly between the garden and the dining room, which was in the front of the house, and from which she could hear his footsteps. At first she thought that he had missed his train, and thought how hot and tired he would be. Then she thought that he had been delayed, and felt annoyed because he hadn't somehow let her know. Then she was quite certain that he had been knocked down and killed. Agnes enquired what she should do with the dinner, which was ready, and would spoil.

"Oh, Agnes, I don't know," Thea sighed. "The master has never been as late as this before. I'm afraid something must have happened to him."

"You don't want to worry, Ma'am," said Agnes, hopefully. "P'rhaps he's had an accident or something."

"Agnes, what a thing to say!" cried Thea furiously. "Just put the dinner in the oven and keep it hot. I expect he won't be long." Agnes, much astonished at such bad temper from her amiable mistress, retired hurt to her kitchen, and Thea was left to the suggestions of her own sufficiently agile imagination. By half-past seven she was standing at the gate, staring up the road, and at twenty to eight she retreated to give way to hysterical tears. But by the time Paul arrived, soon after eight, she was no longer crying. She came in from the garden, where she had been cooling her hot cheeks, to see Paul hanging his hat up in the hall.

"Hallo, dear," he said. "I hope you didn't wait for me."

Thea did not raise her face to his when he bent to kiss her.

"Where have you been?" she asked, and what was meant as a plaintive enquiry sounded, because of her tight throat, like a demand. Paul stiffened.

"I met an old business acquaintance from Germany, and he asked me to have a drink with him." He looked at her compressed lips. "I am sorry that I am late."

"But you might have let me know," Thea burst out. "You must have known that . . ." She might have broken down here, but at that moment Agnes forcefully sounded the gong.

"I couldn't possibly let you know," Paul answered. "I didn't meet him until this evening."

Agnes emerged from the kitchen, with the soup. "Shall we go in to dinner?" Thea suggested, with elaborate courtesy.

"By all means," Paul replied.

When Agnes had left them alone, Paul said, "Next time I am late, I suggest you have dinner, and keep mine hot for me."

"Perhaps that would be best, if you are going to do this very often," Thea answered.

Paul let his spoon fall with a clatter against his plate, and a splash of soup fell on one of Thea's best table-mats.

"If by 'doing this' you mean going out for a few minutes to talk to an old friend," he said, "I think it possible that it may occur again. I am sorry that you do not approve."

Thea allowed her eyes to rest upon the soup spot in an irritating way. "I don't disapprove. I merely suggest that you let me know ahead, so that the dinner isn't spoilt."

Paul took a breath to reply, glared, and then turned his attention to his soup. Agnes entered upon a chill silence.

"I saw Mrs Winter today," said Thea, pleasantly conversational. "Elsie has a daughter."

"Really?" Silence threatened once more. "How nice," Paul finished, frigidly.

"Thank you, Agnes," Thea smiled, and waited until the door was shut. "If you are in a bad temper," she said, "at least you needn't let the servant know." She never spoke of Agnes as 'the servant', but always by her name, and Paul, knowing this, was further annoyed. He said nothing, however, until Thea had served the chops. She was thankful that she had decided that Agnes should not wait at table. The chops, she was pleased to observe, were distinctly over-cooked.

"Perhaps," said Paul, wrestling with hard brown meat, "you would prefer me never to go out in the evenings."

"Oh, for goodness sake, stop nagging," cried Thea.

"Nagging!" Paul shouted, and was struck speechless with rage.

This is the end, thought Thea, gloomily tearing at her chop. Paul doesn't really love me. He couldn't or he wouldn't be so cross. He must have known I'd worry, but he doesn't even care.

She saw a pallid and loveless future, with the two of them sitting silently opposite one another at meals and quarrelling in between them. Her marriage was a failure, just as her mother's had been. Paul would probably leave her, and she would return to Nan's house, old and broken before her time, while he went back to his beloved Germany. She had difficulty in swallowing, because of the tears which threatened to overcome her, but she concealed what she had not eaten under the bone, and glanced at Paul. He had had a busy day, and was eating with good appetite. Thea offered him a second helping, which he accepted, and the strain of the silent eating became almost unbearable. At last he had finished, but even Thea was not able to make conversation while Agnes cleared the plates and brought the sweet, and she went away wide-eyed and anxious, and closed the door softly, as though she was afraid of waking someone. Thea put her spoon in the sweet, raised it to her mouth, put it down again, and burst out crying.

"My darling," cried Paul, getting up and coming round the table. But she pushed her chair back and flung herself upon him, taking hold of his coat and shaking him, while she sobbed, "I thought you were dead. Oh, Paul, I thought you were dead!"

So ended their first and only quarrel. They ate their sweet sitting on the same chair, and Paul's handkerchief was used to wipe her eyes.

"Do you know," said Paul, after a while, "I thought you were jealous."

Thea looked up in amazement. "Jealous? I never thought of it." She began to smile a little. "Should I have been?"

Paul laughed, and then became very serious. "Do you remember the day we first met?" he said. "I came into a room, and it was full of people talking and eating. And then I saw your face. You were standing by Janey, talking to her. And I stayed where I was and looked at you, and I said to myself, 'If I ever marry anyone, it will be that girl.' After that, there wasn't anyone else in the room."

Thea nestled against him, as though he were telling her a fairy story. "And then you came over and spoke to me. Without an introduction, too," she added, and smiled as she said it.

"And you told me that you were going to France. I had to return to Germany, and I thought, 'It is over already. I shall never see her again.' Then, when I was offered this temporary job in England, I accepted, although . . ." He stopped dead, and then continued, "Although I hardly hoped to see you." He laughed and kissed her. Thea thought for a moment that if her mother had not died, she and Paul would not have met again, but she was not yet ready for the thought. She thrust it to the back of her mind, and said lightly, "So I needn't be jealous?"

"Now and for ever, you are the only one for me," said Paul. He bent his head and kissed her hand, and said again, as a man reaffirms a sacred vow, "You are the only one for me."

The lupins drooped, the peonies opened their heavy heads and cast their petals, the first crop of roses reached their full, rich blossom. The warm days of July fled past, and Thea lived contentedly in her dolls' house, pausing often to wonder at her happiness.

Thea had always been afraid of thunderstorms. There are those who are excited and exhilarated by a storm, greeting it like the witches of old, sending their spirit out to ride upon its furies, flame answering flame in a glory of defiance. But Thea cowered beneath the thunder and lightning as she did in the face of anger or cruelty. That answering spark which turns fear into rebellion, awe into joy, had no place in her. She was glad that Paul was home when the first thunder rolled out of a cavernous purple sky and the wild sheets of light swept through the house, fierce visitors who claimed admittance – entering then gone, before it could be denied them. They sat near the window and watched the storm, because it was impossible to ignore it or to pretend to any other occupation. The lawful pursuits of civilised man dwindled away, and for an hour there was nothing real but the thunder and the numbered pauses, the beautiful cracks of forked lightning and the dazzing flashes in between.

"It is lucky we don't live in a castle," said Thea, still clutching Paul's sleeve after the last grinding explosion. "I like our little house. Nothing can touch us here."

She glanced up in time to see Paul's quick frown, as though she had said something to hurt him. And quite suddenly she forgot the storm. Many small things which she had noticed but laid aside in the past weeks linked up with that involuntary frown and unresponsiveness, to become an unmistakeable threat and warning, just as tumbled white clouds form at last into a dark, heavy bank. Paul was worried, and she had pretended, even to herself, not to notice it.

"Something's wrong," she said, and, as he began to deny it, she cried quickly, "Please, Paul. Please tell me."

He sighed and bent to lay his cheek for a moment against her hair, saying under his breath, "*Liebchen, liebchen.*" Another peal of thunder echoed round the sky unnoticed. Perhaps something has gone wrong with his business, thought Thea, and her heart lightened. Poverty held no fears for her. She could manage without Agnes, and economise in many small ways. Nan's granddaughter would not be daunted by such a thing as poverty.

"Tell me what it is," she said soothingly.

Paul straightened his back and put his arm round her. "You remember," he began, "the evening that I was late home?"

Thea laughed and nodded. "I remember."

"I told you that I had met a business acquaintance from Germany. We talked, and he told me –" Paul hesitated, then continued more slowly – "he told me that there would almost certainly be a war between Germany and England."

"No, no! Paul, you don't believe that?"

"At first, I wasn't sure. But now I think that he is right. In fact, I'm certain of it. Unless there's a miracle, there will be war."

"But no one seems to expect it here."

"Anyone who is in touch with Berlin expects it. There will certainly be a war, and England will be on the other side, I think there is no doubt."

202

"But when?"

"Very soon now."

Thea looked up at him wild-eyed. "What shall we do? Should we go to Germany?"

"No," Paul replied slowly. "No, I couldn't take you there if the two countries were to be at war. Besides, if I went back to Germany, I should have to fight, and I could not fight against England now. It has given me my love and my home, and very happy years. I could not fight against your country."

"But, will you be safe here?"

"Yes," Paul answered, and smiled ruefully. "Yes, I shall be quite safe. They cannot make me fight against my own people." They were silent, and Thea knew that their thoughts were far apart, Paul's with his mother and father and his brother Fritz, who had always wanted to be a soldier, Thea thinking only of the little house which held their peace, so small a house that one would have thought that the world's forces could have fought their battles without stamping into its inoffensive territory.

"Why should there be a war?" cried Thea in desperate resentment. The thunder rumbled mournfully, like the roar of an old lion whose strength is nearly spent. It seemed to Thea that a fiercer storm now beat on the red-tiled roof. How could she know that she felt the first keen blast of a hurricane which in thirty years would not be blown out, which would sweep through every house in the land, and in many other lands, and which would rip up the old way of life by the roots, leaving in its place only confusion and a great and disordered striving? She looked round the beloved drawing room, where she and Paul would sit by the fire in the long winter evenings. It seemed very distant and small and yet clear, like the stage set for a marionette show, or like the picture seen in a lighted window.

They sat by the window for a long time, until they shivered in the fresh breeze which had followed the oppressive heat of the storm. At last they stirred and went up to bed, still silent, and all night they lay and held each other in the darkness. They had never loved each other more, but the frail and shining bubble of happiness was broken. Or perhaps such a bubble is never broken, but sails through the open window of life, out of reach, indeed, and beyond recall, but never quite lost, never quite wasted.

Twenty

T hea sat in the afternoon sun, writing to Paul. The notepaper on her knee was only half-filled with widely spaced words, and yet already the pen lay lifeless between her fingers and her eyes gazed wearily up the street. She sighed and bent her head.

"Elsie Winter – I mean Steadman – has just passed by, with her baby. She is a lovely little girl, with long fair curls." Her thoughts wandered again. If she had a child of her own, she thought, it would be easier to write to Paul, and he would seem nearer to her. She could describe the first tooth, the first conscious smile, the first recognisable word. And she could feel that, in holding the child, she held close to her the reality of her marriage and her love for her husband.

Once more she remembered the day when Paul had walked away from their house in Rose Avenue, to his internment. Carrying his suitcase, he had looked to her like a small boy going off to school for the first time, lost, friendless, hurt. She had stayed at the gate to watch him go, and he turned at the corner, and waved to her, as though he were only going up to his office for the day, and would return in the evening. Thea had gone slowly into the house and it was as if she stepped into a long-vacant mansion, where each movement echoed and the silence whispered like a ghost. She went up to the bedroom to tidy Paul's clothes, and found that he had left his razor behind. She stood with it in her hand, with a sense of overwhelming disaster, greater than she had felt when she saw him turn the corner out of sight. Part of the bitter jest of life is that we always feel our great griefs through trivialities. It is not the sledgehammer blow of tragedy which breaks our resistance, but the sharp needlepoint, striking unawares to the heart. So Thea, in the face of a world war and her husband's internment, was anguished by the thought of Paul, so careful of his personal possessions, being forced to borrow a razor from a stranger, one of his fellow-prisoners, perhaps, or one of the officials.

He had not warned her of his almost certain internment, preferring to make unobtrusive arrangements to let the house and to see that she was cared for, while saving her the pain of anticipated parting. When the summons came, he found time to tell her what he had done, that she was to go back to live with Nan until he was released, that his firm would pay her his salary as though he were still working for them, and would keep his place open for him, that all debts were paid up to date. He found time, too, to tell her that he would not be gone long, would write as often as he was allowed to, and would let her know when she could visit him. He found time to tell her that he loved her, and that she must keep her spirits up and take care of herself. The only thing he had not found time for was his own comfort, and they had thrust his belongings into his suitcase, under the eye of the unyielding police officer, in the last few minutes before he left. And so his razor was left behind, and Thea fell on her knees beside the bed, put her face down on his old gardening jacket, and closed her eyes. It seemed that her heart must stop beating until he returned.

The familiar old house welcomed her back, almost, it seemed to her, as though it would take her in its arms and wipe out all memory of those short months away. When she had returned from Monte Carlo, she had been glad to surrender to her well-known surroundings and pretend that she had never left them, that her mother was only in France, instead of in a more strange country. But now she tried to struggle against the charm that would rob her of her memories. Each day Paul seemed farther away from her, receding into the past with Sadie and Fanny and Ambrose. The Christmas which was to have seen the end of the war came and went, and her brief visits to his place of internment did not draw them together, but rather thrust them apart, for she felt more than ever before that he was a foreigner and an alien, and he was stiff and awkward in those unfriendly surroundings, while there was so much to say that they could think of nothing, and spoke of the weather like two strangers. And when she was home again, she would think of him in that place, living with other men who had brown faces and blue eyes, light hair and white teeth, and talking the language of his own country, the language which she could not speak.

Agnes had returned with her to Sunnyside and it was a pleasure to Thea to have her there, enquiring after 'the Master' and addressing her as Madam, or Mrs Bruner. But Emily struck such terror into Agnes's simple soul that she came to Thea after a time, with tears in her eyes, declaring that she would "Rather go into the tiger's cage at the Zoo, Ma'am," than stay in Emily's kitchen. Emily snorted her satisfaction and contempt, and Agnes departed, weeping, from her beloved mistress and terrifying fellow-worker, and now there was no one who called Thea by her husband's name, for Emily called her Miss Thea, as before, and Nan tried in vain to hide her pleasure at having Thea once more to herself. For a while, Thea rebelled, but as the weary months went by, she began to think of her married life with a faint wonder, as one recalls a dream, and to remember Paul tenderly and remotely, as one remembers the dear dead.

At first she wrote to Paul frequently and at length. She told him of all the minute happenings of her life, so that the seasons were marked for him by the cycle of flowers in the garden, and the daily visitors to Nan's dressmaking appointments trod diligently through her letters, with Emily's sharp remarks and Nan's small jokes. For thus, Thea thought, they could be together and share the memories of even this time of absence. But in the life of seclusion which Nan and Thea led, there was soon nothing new to write about. They never went out now, and had no guests but Nan's clients. Thea had proposed to offer her services to a canteen, run by Mrs Winter for 'the boys'. But Nan, surprisingly enough, had dissuaded her, and Thea was the more ready to relinquish the idea because her shyness quailed at the thought of it. Even the 'musical evenings' had been allowed to lapse. Thea, her eyes absently following Elsie's figure down the road, was suddenly struck by an idea. Why should they not have a musical evening once more? Nan enjoyed entertaining, and it was time that they had some company apart from their own. Besides, she thought, painfully, it will be something to write to Paul about.

A few minutes later, Thea saw Nan coming down the road. She was walking slowly, enjoying the sunshine and the blue sky, and Thea thought that she had never seen her looking so contented and happy. She was even putting on a little weight, and her cheeks had filled out, the haggard, harrassed look almost vanished. Life had struck at her its harshest blows, and she had bent under them, patiently suffering where another, more self-engrossed, would have broken. Now the meadows were calm and the skies clear, and the war meant nothing to her while she had her last and dearest child living with her once more.

Nan and Thea found restfulness in each other's company, and Thea sometimes wondered whether she was not happier as she was now than she would be in returning to the more demanding life of marriage. She was wondering that as Nan came into the house, and bent hastily to her letter.

"I will send the parcel to you tomorrow. I only wish that I was allowed to send you more. If there is anything you want that I can get for you, you will let me know, of course." She could think of nothing more to say. Her wordlessness was a reproach to her. She wrote in desperation, "I must hurry now to catch the post. With all my love, Thea." As she folded it and addressed the envelope, she was thinking that she had never lied to him before, and that it was more treacherous to lie to him by letter than by speech. There was yet more than half an hour before the next post went. She unfolded the sheet of paper, and scribbled at the bottom, "Paul, I love you. I love you," and prayed that he would not know that she wrote the words less as a message to him than to convince herself that they were true.

"Nan," said Thea, "we must have a musical evening. We haven't had one for ages."

Emily was laying tea, and Thea saw her exchange an alarmed look with Nan, the sort of glance they used to exchange when she asked an awkward question as a child. But Nan answered composedly, "No one does much entertaining in wartime."

"Just a quiet party," Thea insisted, "the Winters, perhaps, and Miss Luke and the Bensons, and a few others."

Emily never hesitated to join in the conversation if she thought it was of any interest to her. She straightened her back and stood with the tray in her hand.

"What do you want that lot for?" she demanded. "Just a lot of trouble for nothing."

"You're both getting lazy," Thea told them. Once more she was aware that they glanced at each other surreptitiously, with apprehension. "We haven't had any company for so long that we're becoming hermits. Even in wartime, a small party is quite all right. In fact, it's good for everyone's spirits."

"But, when people have been bereaved," said Nan, rather hopelessly, "they don't always feel like going out."

Thea's rare obstinacy was aroused. A suspicion that she was in the wrong served to strengthen it. "I should *like* to have a party," she said. She stood up with Paul's letter in her hand and shook her shoulders, as Belle might have done. "It's so dull never meeting anyone," she finished. Nan gave the faintest of sighs.

"Very well," she said. "But I think we'll have a tea party. It's easier." Emily opened her mouth to protest, and then stamped out to make the tea. Thea ran across to post her letter. The street was very quiet. From one of the houses came the friendly sound of someone practising the clarinet. Thea paused by the pillar box, feeling for a moment that the house was a prison, and that she would like to stay under the pale blue sky, listening to the ripple of the notes, and pretending that there was no war, and no sharp harvest of young men, but a universal peace and gentleness and safety. She posted the letter to her enemy alien, with his prison number, and went back across the road to tea.

In the end, the tea party was represented only by their old friends, the Winters, Miss Luke and Mrs Benson, the Vicar's wife.

Emily wore her best cap with the streamers flying out behind, in which she always reminded Thea irresistably of the Flying Dutchman. Thea put on her best afternoon frock, part of her trousseau, and awaited the guests with a feeling of excitement and pleasure. She might have been a child in a pink party dress, waiting for the knock at the door.

Mrs Winter, in peacetime, had never been the type of woman who was overlooked. Placed in the middle of a Bank Holiday crowd, or in a seat in the Albert Hall, she would nevertheless have remained a landmark, a monument of indestructible energy, the concentrated essence of British housewifery. The Great War came to her like a personal mission. In her canteen at one of the big railway stations she served the soldiers with thick mugs of very strong tea, harried them, and loved them like the sons she had never had. They called her Ma, laughed at her and liked her. She drove the organisers of the canteen nearly to distraction, because she quarrelled with all her fellow-workers, but she was so reliable and energetic that they could not bear to lose her services. She never tired of talking about 'the Tommies,' or 'the dear boys'. She told long stories of their humorous remarks, or of the letters they gave her to post, the photographs they showed her. She had a facile sympathy which was none the less genuine because it did not move her very deeply. She would have worked herself to death to relieve suffering, but would never have been tempted to kill herself because of it. When she told of the little red-headed man, who showed her a photograph of his 'wife and bairn' in a remote part of Scotland, remarking, "Well, mem, yon Hun wilna trouble them while Sandy MacTavish is alive," her heart expanded with sympathy, but did not contract with pain. This sense of drama and romance was typical of The Great War, the last echo of the spirit of Balaclava, never to be repeated. The marching feet, the London buses behind the lines, the song 'Tipperary', the musical comedies, the unashamed sentiment, the panache of the officers and the sardonic humour of the men, all this blended into a drama, terrible certainly, and exciting, but in some way pleasurable. For the bereaved there was grief, and for the participants in the struggle there was pain and fear and discomfort. This was the war to end war, the crusade for a righteous cause, under the Union Jack. The young men went out bravely and cheerfully and their women nursed thém and fed them, knitted for them and prayed for them. And Mrs Winter made tea and sandwiches, and talked of 'her boys'.

She talked of her boys at the tea party, and Miss Luke murmured her approval, like a priestess blessing the sacrifice. She herself could not leave Mrs Luke alone, who was growing increasingly infirm, but she knitted socks which were the despair of the recipients, being made according to her own pattern, and she knitted very fast. For her the war was not a release, but a closer imprisonment. She longed to go and nurse soldiers, but instead she must nurse her mother. She would gladly have sacrificed her man to the patriotic holocaust, but she had no man to sacrifice. Once more, no one wanted what she had to give, and even her vicarious enjoyment of the drama was bitter to her. She listened to Mrs Winter eagerly, but always with discontent, because Mrs Winter had a part in the play, even though it was only in the crowd, and she herself was not even an understudy.

"So I said to her, I said," Mrs Winter continued with gusto, "I said, 'You can't grudge the boys another cup of tea, Mrs Harrow, when they're fighting for their country.' So she said, 'Well, we have to make the canteen pay.' 'Yes,' I said, 'but these boys have to pay with their lives, not with money'." Mrs Winter looked round for approbation. "She couldn't think of anything to say," she finished joyfully.

Nor, for a moment, could her audience. Then Mrs Benson murmured lugubriously, "Yes, the casualty lists get longer every day. Mr Benson says we shall have lost a whole generation of young men before the war is over."

As her husband was a jocular Christian, Mrs Benson was a gloomy Christian. And the strange thing was that although Mr Benson in person was always very cheerful, yet his wife always reported him as an incurable pessimist. Thea wondered sometimes whether he used up all his joviality abroad, and was depressed at home, or whether Mrs Benson unconsciously invested him with her own gloom.

"Ronnie says," Elsie volunteered, "that we must all keep our hearts up, and he's sure we'll pull through."

No one could ever remember Elsie Winter's married name, but Ronnie was now a subaltern, and at The Front, and therefore the military adviser of the Winter family. Whenever Mrs Winter was about to relate an unconfirmed rumour, she would strengthen it with the preface "My son-in-law, who is at The Front, gave me to understand that . . ." As though Ronnie, from his narrow dug-out, gazed out over the entire line, and various generals dropped in upon him and confided to him their strategic intentions over a bottle of wine. Most of the other soldiers from Abbot's Green appeared to serve under more taciturn superiors, or else they did not impart their information to their relatives.

"Oh yes, we shall pull through," Mrs Benson agreed

hastily. She shook her head and sipped her tea, adding, "But we must expect to suffer first."

"Well, after all, the Germans have suffered too," Miss Luke put in. "Think of the Zeppelin."

They all brightened at the words, and then sighed guiltily. They always thought of the Zeppelin in moments of gloom, and tried to pretend that the reflection gave them pleasure. But in fact the recollection of that unnatural mass of flames and men, sinking to earth over Cuffley, inspired them with no elation.

Thea in particular, thinking of the flaming Zeppelin, shuddered, because Paul's brother might have been one of those who came to destroy and instead perished horribly. She was grateful that these staunch patriots round the tea-table shuddered, too, before resuming their unreal saga of hate.

"Ronnie says that Zeppelins and aeroplanes will never be very important," Elsie remarked.

"Of course not!" Mrs Winter exclaimed, shocked at the suggestion. "It is our brave boys who will win the victory."

For to her aeroplanes were inhuman Martian creatures which appeared unexpectedly and irrelevantly over the fighting, retiring thence to their own planet. If she believed that men flew in them, she thought of them as a peculiar race of men, unrelated to the earth-bound warriors of her acquaintance.

"No," Mrs Benson agreed, putting her cup down and folding her hands impressively. "No, I'm afraid it is the blockade which must be causing our government most anxiety."

Miss Luke broke in joyously, the light gleaming on her pince-nez.

"Major Brown said at the whist drive the other day that he thought the Germans would soon stop fighting altogether, and just wait for us to die of famine."

She looked brightly round the room.

"We still have our gallant Navy," Mrs Winter suggested, but without conviction.

Major Brown, retired and living in Abbot's Green since 1900, was held to have a grasp of the military situation inferior only to Ronnie's, and considerably greater than that of the official communiqués. Moreover, the Royal Navy rarely patronised Mrs Winter's canteen.

"Mr Benson said," his wife stated, brushing aside all mention of the Navy, "that, while none of us should hoard food, still he thought that it would be an excellent thing to put a little aside each day, in case of need."

Thea was overtaken by a delightful vision of the ladies of Abbot's Green diligently secreting crusts of bread in their wardrobe drawers, like squirrels hiding nuts for the winter. Miss Luke nodded earnestly. Clearly, she was already mentally reorganising her store cupboard, to allow for a sinking fund, ingeniously concealed at once from the Kaiser's spies and from their young maid, Mabel.

" 'Put a little aside for the rainy day, and you will never want,' my dear father used to say," she murmured absently. The cupboard under the stairs, perhaps, for a few bags of flour.

Mrs Winter accepted a slice of Emily's rich fruit cake. "What makes me really angry," she said sadly, "is that those dreadful Germans who are interned over here are allowed to have as much food as they like, pounds and pounds of it." She took a bite of cake and glanced round. There was a breathless silence, in which Mrs Winter slowly realised what she had done.

Thea, looking back on that moment, always saw it as an unbearable ugliness, like one of Hogarth's pictures. Held and tortured in that silence as in a trap, Thea looked round the room, and saw Mrs Winter, swelling over her corsets, her mouth motionlessly bulged with cake, saw Mrs Benson's mild, floury face, with little eyes blinking slowly in it, like an elephant's, saw Elsie Steadman drinking tea, her little finger curled in an exaggerated attitude of gentility, saw Miss Luke nibbling madly at a sugar cake with her sharp, pointed teeth, and hated them with a violence such as she had never before experienced. She even hated Nan for her helplessness, for a straying wisp of hair, for the trembling of her hand as she poured out tea. In those few seconds of hot silence, there vanished from Thea's heart the old friends of her childhood. This moment would pass, the anger and the anguish. She would talk with these people, smile with them, see their kindness and feel pity for their weakness. She would accept them once more into her affections, house them in her gentle memories. But always there would exist behind them, larger than reality, the shadow on the wall, this momentary glimpse of ugliness.

While the flush of horror was yet flooding into Thea's cheeks, the company stirred and hastened to retrieve, or at least to repair the error, speaking eagerly and at random.

"Ah yes, it's very hard for them, very hard," Mrs Benson murmured, adding an indistinct conclusion about all human beings and prisoners.

"Ronnie says the mud is the worst, Over There," said Elsie.

"My aunt had a German maid," said Miss Luke, and then stumbled, uncertain of the good fortune of her contribution, and smiled hopefully and anxiously at Thea, as she said, "A charming girl, and so clean."

Mrs Winter swallowed her cake audibly, and said, "Of course, I mean, I wouldn't want them to starve."

"A little more tea, Mrs Benson?" Nan suggested. "Do try one of Emily's sugar cakes. They are made from her own recipe, with very little fat."

The small ship of civilities was safely launched once more, after its shipwreck. The conversation proceeded, if not easily, at least profusely, and Mrs Benson's account of their plans for the Church Bazaar, and Elsie's unflagging and totally uninteresting stories of her small daughter's behaviour and habits continued until Emily had removed the tea-table.

But there was no hope of comfort after that disaster. In each pause in the conversation, the guests could be seen examining the subject they next proposed to broach, lest it should lead to pitfalls, and glancing at the clock, with rapid mental calculations of the time yet to run before they could decently betake their shaken nerves homewards. Nan enquired after the son of a friend, only to learn that he had been killed, and Miss Luke impulsively opened her mouth, shutting it again, like a mouse-trap going off. Mrs Benson's daughter was a VAD, and an enquiry after her health led to praise of the courage of the men she nursed, followed by a silent, but none the less audible condemnation of the German shells and bullets which had maimed them. All roads led to that unhappy Rome.

At last Mrs Winter rose to go, and the other guests bounded to their feet with loud murmurs of regret. Nan attended their departure with her usual tranquil sweetness, but Thea, who had spoken no word, could only smile at them faintly, like one recovering from deadly sickness. As the door closed behind them, she sat down and put her face in her hands, shaking with exhaustion. Her anger was passed, but the weakness and sense of contamination which remained behind was harder to bear. Hatred bred hatred, she thought, like a germ which rotted the souls of men. These women in their quiet suburb were housing an emotion too monstrous for their narrow hearts, and she herself had become entangled in its coils. She had shaken herself free with loathing, but the uncleanness remained. She raised her head as Nan returned to the room, and together they watched the four hats bobbing away in the dusk, pausing at Miss Luke's gate for a brief whispered colloquy, and then separating, Mrs Benson passing on, and Mrs Winter and Elsie returning to their own house, glancing furtively at the window as they went by. Thea shrank back.

"How could they!" she cried. "How could she say such a thing?"

"She didn't mean it," Nan said. "It slipped out by accident."

"But she meant it," Thea insisted. "Knowing Paul as she

does, and having talked to him, and sung to his accompaniment, she still grudges him even his food."

"She wasn't thinking of Paul," Nan replied. "She had forgotten that he was interned."

"But, how can she hate Germans so, knowing Paul?"

Nan did not answer for a moment. She rarely expressed her opinions upon more than trivial subjects. The views she held about abstract matters, about religion and morals or human responsibilities were instinctive and inarticulate, hidden far beneath the surface of convention and civility.

"I think that, in a war," she said finally, "people cannot examine their feelings too closely. We have to fight to save the smaller countries. Germany did wrong, and we have to fight against her. But no one could fight a war unless they hated the other nation. So the people of this country have to hate Germans. They don't dare to think of the individual Germans they have known and liked."

" 'These things must not be thought on in this way,' " Thea quoted, " 'So it will drive us mad'."

Nan nodded. "And then perhaps they lose a relation, or someone dear to them, and that makes it easier to hate the enemy. And then it just becomes a habit." She sat down with her sewing, comfortable Nan, sane and untroubled in a world gone mad. "But it doesn't last long. Think how English people hated the French in the Napoleonic War. We never think of that now. It will be the same with Germany when this war is over."

"Oh, Nan," cried Thea, despairingly, "when will the war end?"

Nan looked up at her and smiled and shook her head. "It won't be long now, dear. I'm sure it won't. And then everything will be as it was before."

"I shan't be the same," said Thea in a low voice.

Nan did not raise her head from the braid she was stitching. "Mrs Winter's nephew was killed," she said gently, as though she spoke at random and without relevance, "and Miss Luke's only cousin. And Mrs Benson's daughter lost her fiancé at Ypres. And then there are those stories of atrocities. Some of them must be true."

"But . . . ?"

"No one is normal in wartime," Nan replied. "It is like an illness. Some people take it worse than others, and some people don't recover from it. But most people are cured as soon as the war ends. You will find that as soon as we have won, Mrs Winter and Miss Luke will quite forget that they ever hated Germans, and say what a *musical* race they are, just as they used to."

Thea was silent for a long time, and then began to smile.

"I suppose that in a little while I shall begin to see how funny it was," she said, "with Elsie talking about the mud, and Miss Luke about the German maid, and Mrs Winter with her mouth full, and not able to think of anything to say at all."

"Yes," Nan agreed. "Yes, it was funny, but . . ."

"But, I don't think we'll do it again," Thea finished, slowly, and they looked at each other, like two arctic explorers snowed up for the winter in a small hut, and smiled, finding the company good.

Twenty-One

I t had been during the first winter of the war, when Thea was lonely for Paul, and the dark evening seemed a long time in which to wait for his step on the path and his voice in the hall, and to know that he would not come, that Nan suggested that Thea should read aloud to her.

"Oh yes," cried Thea, "just like the old days!"

For a moment it seemed to both of them that Belle must surely stroll over to the bookcase, standing with one arm raised, in her unconscious gracefulness, and saying, "What will you have tonight, Mother?" They looked at each other with the wordless understanding that two people have who are much together, and the emptiness, which had been in the house ever since Belle left it, vanished for a moment. The room was warm with her presence, and the two people who had loved her most reached out breathlessly towards her, suddenly aware how narrow was the line of death, since memory could so nearly brush it aside. But they were neither of them in the habit of deceiving themselves. It was only Belle's memory which filled the room with her perfume, which rustled her dress and spoke in her husky voice. Thea went to choose a book and Nan broke her thread and the house was empty once more, as it always must be. Still, they liked the reading, and the evenings passed pleasantly with Grandfather's heavily-bound volumes of Dickens and Thackeray and Shakespeare. And so in the course of time they came to *Troilus and Cressida*, carefully edited by Thea for Nan's easily-shocked sensibilities.

Chaucer's Cressida said, "And women most wolle hate me of al", but Thea found that she could not hate her, poor, weak, gentle creature, swearing to be faithful "when time is old and hath forgot itself", and yet doomed from the first, in a situation too great and too demanding for her domestic soul.

Nor could she bear the story to end in such cruel hopelessness, with no promise of reunion even after death, with bitterness and disillusion blotting out even the faint echoes of their love. She read the words, "O Cressid, O false Cressid: false, false, false! Let all untruths stand by thy stained name; And they'll seem glorious," with a voice that trembled. Death was so sweet and easy a thing, compared to this.

When Thea closed the book and sat gazing into the fire, Nan remarked, in her matter-of-fact way, "Yes, Troilus and Cressida isn't one of my favourites."

"It's too cruel," said Thea.

"It's too degrading," Nan replied. "I feel that it's the sort of play that shouldn't be written."

Thea began to smile. "You mean that it is all right to show a man wading through blood to a throne, but not to show an unfaithful woman."

"Exactly," Nan answered calmly. "Exactly."

Thea, watching Nan, suddenly realised that it was from her that Belle had received not only the gift of beauty, but also the gift of laughter. Amusement was dancing in those grey eyes as it always had, for as long as Thea could remember. The griefs which had come upon Nan had aged her before her time, had greyed her hair and lined her face and robbed her of her gaiety. But still she had held to her independence, her courage, her faith in God and her sense of humour. Her courage was greater than Belle's who had fled to Monaco, far greater than Thea's who, until Paul came, had shrunk back from love lest it should rob her of her peace. Nan's was the unobtrusive strength of gentleness. She is indomitable, thought Thea.

"And then," Nan went on, "the one is likely to be within everyone's experience, but the other isn't. There is no more harm in Macbeth than there is in Bluebeard, because very few people are tempted to commit one murder, let alone half a dozen. But any woman could be a Cressida, and any man a Diomedes."

Thea was silent, thinking how strange it was that human vows made in such good faith should last so short a time. What wonder that nations broke their word, when a woman could not be true to her beloved, nor a man to his love. And as she sought for some commonplace reply to Nan's words, the doorbell rang.

It seemed to Thea that the great events of her life, both of pleasure and pain, had always been heralded by the ringing of the doorbell. Aunt Ruth's death, Paul's first visit, Paul's proposal of marriage, even her mother's death, all had begun with that unexpected sound. And whether it brought grief or joy, Thea viewed it with misgiving, because in either event it disturbed the even tenor of her life.

"Emily isn't back from her sister's yet," said Nan, tranquilly sewing still, "so perhaps you'd better go. If it's Mrs Barnes, say I'm out."

Thea went into the dark hall and opened the door. A tall man in uniform stood outside, and Thea peered at him doubtfully in the dusk, thinking that he had come to the wrong house. Then she clutched him and drew him inside, crying joyfully, "James! It's James!"

It was James indeed, wearing a small moustache, his face brown, no longer discontented, the hollows in his cheeks less marked than when she had seen him last. His hat was pulled rakishly down over one eye, there was an irresistible, devil-may-care hilarity about him, and he came into the house like the spirit of 1914, of laughing youth at war. And Thea held both his hands as though she had found something which had been lost for a long while, and never meant to let it go again.

James had come, he said, to ask Thea to go out with him that evening. She began to refuse, glancing at Nan.

"You can't leave me alone on my last night of leave," said

James, and Nan broke in to say, "Of course you must go, Thea. Run up and change."

"I don't like to leave you," Thea protested doubtfully.

"Emily will be in before supper," Nan answered. "You go along and enjoy yourself."

Thea turned to go and stopped in the doorway of the sitting room.

"It's not like James to be left alone," she said mischievously. "Did your best girl let you down, James?" He could find no reply, and she laughed and ran upstairs, feeling young and excited.

They went to the popular musical comedy of the moment and then to supper at a restaurant full of young officers on leave, filling each moment with laughter and gaiety, so that they could remember it and talk of it when they got back to the Front. Thea looked at them with maternal indulgence, with all the dignity of her married status, and James teased her in his old brotherly fashion.

"I didn't know you had your commission," Thea remarked. "When we last heard of you, you were a private."

"Yes, I got it some time ago," said James, "though," he added cheerfully, "I warded it off as long as possible. Then they stood several of us up against a wall, and said, 'Those who don't wish to take a commission, take one step backwards.' So after that, I became His Majesty's loyal and trusty and what-have-you."

"You look nice," said Thea approvingly, looking at his broad shoulders and slim waist, the Sam Browne belt drawn tight."

"Yes, that was the idea," James agreed. "They said that a private's uniform simply didn't suit me as well. I offended their artistic sensibilities." Thea made a face at him, and he added, "You look nice too," and was rewarded by her old childish blush.

"Paul said I had a funny face," she said. "Only he said it in German, and I thought it was a compliment until he translated it for me."

"I'm awfully sorry he was interned," said James gravely. "He's such a nice chap. It must be rotten for him."

"Perhaps it won't be long now," sighed Thea, but with none of the desperate longing she had once felt. "How long do you think it will be?"

"Don't ask me," cried James, laughing. "I've only been at the Front. No one knows anything there. You want to ask the man who sells papers on the corner, or one of the flower-sellers."

"It seems to have been such a long time," said Thea, and then stopped, and added contritely, "I shouldn't grumble, I know. After all, my husband's safe, and I'm living at home in comfort. You must want it to end a great deal more."

"Oh, I don't know," said James, lightly. "It could be worse. I like the excitement of it, and never knowing quite what's going to happen to you next."

"That must be the worst thing," Thea shuddered. "I should think that the best part of the war being over, would be to know that you were comparatively safe again."

"Safe!" James exclaimed. "Who wants to be safe?"

"Mother once said that," said Thea, slowly. "*I* want to be safe, but I suppose not everyone does."

"I'm not the safe type," said James, smiling, but guilty. "I'm not reliable enough for a nice steady job, and a nice quiet wife and family. God knows what will happen to me if I ever marry – or to my wife."

"I'm surprised you haven't married before."

"Oh well, I've thought of it once or twice, but you see I know too many girls. I never can make up my mind which to ask. I shall probably take the plunge one of these days. It'll be an interesting. experience anyway. Or perhaps I'll remain the ne'er-do-well bachelor uncle, and I shall strike oil or gold or something, and everyone will say that they always knew that there was good in me. But it won't be any use to them, for I shall leave all my money to my favourite nephew, and ruin him for ever."

"What will you do after the war?" Thea asked, and saw a shadow of the old discontent come back into his face.

"Go back to my old job, I suppose – if they'll have me. They were just about to chuck me out when the war broke out. So they said, 'Hero, go and get killed, and our blessings go with you. You can rely on us to back you up.' With that, they went in and shut the door."

"You were always going to go to sea," said Thea.

He laughed. "That's right, so I was. And Lydia was going to be a famous authoress, and Janey – what was she going to do?"

"Marry," Thea supplied, "and have two children and four cats."

"Or was it the other way round?" James suggested. "Well, she's married anyway. Have you met her husband yet?"

"No, what's he like?" asked Thea. She thought of Janey with her round face and blue eyes and ringlets and her habitual solemn quietness. Janey's husband was fortunate, but she smiled a little at the thought of the surprise he would get, when he first discovered the rock of obstinacy and unyielding determination which lay behind Janey's good-temper and gentleness.

"You'd like him," James replied. "He's a schoolmaster in civil life, and a very dependable sort of chap. He's my Company Commander."

"And Charlotte?" asked Thea. "I haven't seen her for a long while."

James was silent for a moment, and then said slowly, "Something's happened to Charlotte. You'd hardly know her. It's as though she's suddenly come to life."

"I've read her poetry, of course," said Thea. Aunt Mary had sent them that first cheaply-bound volume, and Thea had sat by the window and read until the light faded and Nan dozed by the fire. She had felt a personal glow of discovery and achievement, as though she had assisted at a birth and now saw the new young life setting out on its adventure. She had remembered that spring afternoon when a plain little girl had clasped her knees, sitting beside the rabbit hutches, and whispering, "I don't know. Something." This had been the secret which she had kept painfully hidden all those years, this gift of clear, lyrical, passionate song, like the voice of a thrush in springtime. And now she was free and the secret dream had become truth. Yes, Charlotte would have changed.

"She was never like the rest of us," said James. "And she was never very good-looking, but now . . ." He stopped again, searching for words to express what had happened to this changeling sister, who had stayed so still and unobtrusive in the family for so long. "It's as though there was a light inside her," he said finally. "You know she's engaged?"

Thea shook her head.

"He's a poet too, and quite mad. She met him at a Convalescent Home, where she'd gone to help entertain the patients – read to them and so on. Apparently, Lucien was reading a book of poetry, which he'd no business to do because his eyes were bad. So Charlotte stopped to tell him about that, and then she began to argue about the poetry, and that was more or less the end of it."

Thea thought that she could imagine it, the sudden, astonished meeting of two fine minds, amidst the idle chatter of patients and visitors, the way Charlotte's face would suddenly look like one of Rossetti's Madonnas, with the good bones, the widow's peak in the black hair, the thin brows over dark and glowing eyes, the tender lines of the mouth. She thought how they would forget the time, talking and arguing, and how at last they would realise that Charlotte must go, and they would start and turn to each other, betrayed, like Paolo and Francesca, into love, while they read in the same book, alone and without all suspicion. She thought how Charlotte would leave and walk home, with the smile still about her lips, no longer solitary, no longer sullen, but with a light within her which would never be extinguished.

"I saw them together when I was on leave last," said James,

"Just before he went back. They can't see anyone else at all. They talk in a private language of their own, and if somebody speaks to them you can see them blink and come out of their own world and down to the ordinary one."

"But they aren't married?"

"According to Charlotte, they 'didn't think of it in time'. I shall enjoy seeing those two keeping house together. They'll start an argument on Wordsworth, and never go in to dinner at all." He chuckled, and then added soberly, "If he comes through all right."

"Oh, he must!" cried Thea. Charlotte's life was not adjustable, like most people's. There was only one man for her, and one happiness. Nothing must spoil it.

"I think he'll be invalided out soon," said James. "He'd no business to go back this time. That's the worst of these intellectual chaps, they're not usually very strong, but they will drive themselves harder than any ordinary man." He crumbled his bread and said thoughtfully, "I suppose that's why poets so often get killed. Because they think that they can't speak for humanity unless they've experienced as much as anyone else. We shall lose a lot of poets in this war, I think."

Thea, watching him, was aware that he had pondered over the subject – James, who was believed to apply his mind to nothing more serious than football, or theatre tickets. When he wasn't laughing, he did look older than she remembered him. War, despite its excitements, had sobered him a little, after all, and his mouth, free from sulkiness or the old sardonic humour, was very gentle.

"What about Lydia's husband?" she asked.

"Oh well, he was out of it," James answered unexpansively. "He wasn't fit, I believe, and he's at the War Office. And her son's too young, luckily. She'd be throwing fits all right, if young Drew were in the Line." He was silent for a moment, and then added, "There's one thing I'm glad of, and that's that the kid didn't live long enough to be in this mess."

After all these years, thought Thea, to James, Andrew is still the child we all knew and loved.

"I didn't think it was much luck at the time," James went on, "but I suppose, in a way, it was. He didn't have a bad sort of life on the whole."

Thea quoted softly, beneath the laughter and clatter of a big party at the next table,

"Remember, O remember
How of human days he lived the better part.
April came to bloom and never dim December
Breathed its killing chills upon the head or heart."

James did not lift his head, but said quickly, "Go on."

"I don't know it all," Thea answered, blushing and shy. "But it ends, 'Here, a boy, he dwelt through all the singing season; And ere the day of sorrow departed as he came.' It's by Robert Louis Stevenson."

"I like that," said James. "It might have been written for Andy. Do you remember that ridiculous rabbit of his?"

"John Cassius?" said Thea, and they laughed together.

"You know," James said, frowning, "that day when we were all making plans and saying what we'd do when we grew up, Andy never said anything. Almost as though he knew that he wouldn't ever grow up."

"He was too busy taking things apart and putting them together again to bother about silly things like growing up."

James shook his head, still frowning, and then straightened his shoulders and said lightly, "Oh well, what's the use? Let's eat, drink, and be merry, for tomorrow . . ."

"Don't, James," Thea pleaded, and he smiled at her with the familiar sardonic gleam, and finished, "For tomorrow I may be back in an office, trying to look respectable."

As they both glanced round the room, faintly disconcerted by the serious tone of their conversation, a waiter placed a bottle of champagne on their table, saying with a flourish,

227

"With John Roydanson's compliments, Sir."

"*Whose?*" asked James, and the man gestured over to a nearby table. A middle-aged officer waved his hand and grinned at them, and James smiled and bowed in return.

"Probably a bit mad," he remarked. "Never mind, we'll drink his health." They lifted their glasses towards the major, with the inevitable result of bringing him to his feet and, somewhat unsteadily, over to their table.

"Champagne all right?" he asked abruptly.

"Yes, thank you, Sir," James answered. "It's very good of you . . ."

"John Royd of John Roydanson," said the major. James looked rather taken aback, but shook him warmly by the hand.

"How do you do, Sir," he said. "Very pleased to meet you." The major withdrew his hand in annoyance, protesting, "No, no, no. Not me." He tapped the ribbons on his tunic. "I'm Major Sands." He waved a hand behind him. "*That*'s John Royd of John Roydanson. He's getting married. Thought you were just married, too. So sent you bottle of champagne." He smiled affably down at them.

Thea studied the party he had just left, and failed to see a likely bridegroom. James, she noticed, was also searching surreptitiously for their benefactor. The major still stood by the table, swaying ever so slightly. He suddenly seemed to notice Thea, and held out his hand. "How do you do?" he said politely. "I'm Major Sands. Mind if I join you?" he asked, reaching for a chair. "Mustn't stay long. My wife . . ." He glanced over his shoulder, and then brought his eyes back to Thea. "Very pretty young lady," he said, and then fell silent, looking round the room. "Dreadful place," he said.

"This place, Sir?" asked James.

"No, no!" cried the major, irritably, "Chatham." He turned to Thea. "Ever been there?"

"Never," Thea replied.

"Dreadful place," he said. "Stationed there. Too much

Navy. Dreadful place." There was another silence, which was broken by the major saying explosively, "Shocking place!"

"Chatham, Sir?" asked James, delicately.

"No," said the major, crossly. "This place."

Thea put her table-napkin to her lips with a hand that shook. James was regarding the major with an air of bright interest and pleasure.

"I must go back," said the major. "My wife . . ." He did not move, however. "Dreadful thing, this war," he said. "Shocking thing. Mind you, I'm not in the trenches, because I'm at Chatham. Shocking place, Chatham," he added, in parenthesis. "But, Germans, very dreadful people," he went on. "Only good German, a dead German. Ever heard that saying?" And he looked at Thea intently. "Must kill them all before we're done."

"May their blood flow in streams down the rivers of commerce," said James, quietly, but with feeling.

The major stopped looking at Thea, and turned to glare at James.

"You talk too much," he said severely, and James blinked under this sudden onslaught.

The major rose to his feet, and looked towards his own table.

"Must go now," he said. "My wife . . ." He had already forgotten what he was going to say. Thea and James sat as though hypnotised, waiting to see what his next remark would be. "Have you been to France yet?" he asked James.

"I—"

"Well, you will, in time. Better than Chatham, anyway." He bowed to Thea, and for a moment was not comic or drunken, but possessed of a courteous dignity. "Good evening," he said, "I hope you'll be very happy."

Thea smiled at him. "Good evening, Major. We've enjoyed meeting you."

"I've enjoyed it too," he answered, "enjoyed meeting . . . enjoyed . . ." But it was gone. He bowed again, murmured,

"My wife . . ." and drifted away, steering an unsteady course, like a rudderless ship. Thea wept helplessly into her table-napkin, and James watched his uncertain progress with a simple gravity, betrayed only by the corners of his mouth.

In Piccadilly, as they started for home, they paused by a flower-seller, packing up her basket.

"Have you a bunch left?" James asked her, and she at once chose a sprig of white heather, pinning it on Thea's coat with her gnarled, brown old fingers.

"When will the war end?" enquired James, solemnly.

"Won't be long now, dearie," she replied. "There's white heather to bring the young lady luck, and there's a bunch for you too, my dear. No, I don't want no money for it. Gawd bless you, and bring you safe home."

They left her, heart-warmed and smiling, to catch the train to Abbot's Green.

In the train, they sat close together, and Thea leant against James's shoulder. After a second's hesitation, he put his arm round her and she remembered how once she had slept in Uncle Robert's arms, after the visit to the Tower of London. But she would not sleep now, she thought. Time was too pitifully short. In the window of the train, she could see James's face reflected, and she watched it hungrily, to make up for the long months when she would not see it. The words of the old flower-seller beat in rhythm to the train. *God bless you, and bring you safe home. God bless you, and bring you safe home.* As they drew near to Abbot's Green, she said, without lifting her face from his shoulder,

"Take care of yourself, James, out there."

"Oh, I shall be all right," he answered. "And anyway, it doesn't matter much for me. If Andy had lived, he'd 've been a useful sort of person, but I shan't ever be much good. I expect I shall come through all right, but I don't much mind."

The words Thea would have spoken were drowned in a

flood of emotion. At last she said, "We mind." James tightened his arm about her, but did not reply.

In the starlight, they walked slowly back to the house, and Thea thought how comfortable it was to have once more the support of a man's arm. At the garden gate, they turned to each other, and James took her in his arms suddenly, and held her close. She could feel his body tense against hers, and they were seized together by the same breathless passion. She could see his face in the light of the street-lamp, his grey eyes no longer amused, and her hands tightened on his shoulders. Paul had been away so long, and she had been lonely. James, oh James. She lifted her face to his. In that moment, she felt him relax his hold. He bent and kissed her lightly on the forehead, and smiled down on her, tender, amused, compassionate.

"Dear little Thea," he said.

For a long time that night, Thea lay awake, seeing James's face, his cleft chin, his hollow cheeks, his long, dark lashes, his smiling mouth. Oh James, why didn't you kiss me? Oh James, my first, my only love. As the dawn crept into the sky, she crouched by the window, still shaken by that storm of emotion, hearing James saying, "Dear little Thea," and hearing too Paul's voice, crying, with the words of Troilus, "Let it not be believed for womankind. O Cressid, O false Cressid! False, false, false!"

Twenty-Two

I n the early hours of the morning, Thea fell into an uneasy
sleep. When Emily woke her for breakfast, she felt that she
could not get up, that sleep was a refuge which she could not
bear to leave. As she dressed, slowly, and with a painful, heavy
headache, she looked down at the street-lamp, under which
she had seen James's face, lit by the stars and the flickering
gas. Rain sputtered in the puddles on the road and ran down
the dirty glass of the lamp. In the grey light, the street looked
drab and sordid, and through her weariness and distress of
mind, Thea was conscious, too, of a sense of shame, remembering how she had lifted her face for James to kiss her, how
she longed for more. Their comfortable childhood's relationship of cousinly affection and liking was blotched and marred
by the remembrance of that moment, and now, whenever she
thought of James, it would be with a hot blush, an ashamed
contraction of her heart.

She ate breakfast, answered Nan's questions, and went
about the business of the day, but always with a weight on
her mind, an insistent longing in her body, knowing as she had
known throughout that long night of torment, that if James
had kissed her, she would have gone with him anywhere to
fulfil that desire.

When evening came, and the curtains were drawn, Thea
could think of nothing but that James was already on his way
back to the dirt and danger of the trenches, that he was gone
to France, a thousand miles away, over the water, out of all
reach. She sat and mended stockings, with his face before her

eyes and his voice in her ears, desperate for the doorbell to ring, and for him to stand on the step, smiling at her.

In a few days' time, Thea was more nearly herself again. James was her cousin, she told herself, dear to her as a brother, but *only* as a brother. She felt for him a warm affection, but she did not love him, she had never loved him. As the days passed, James slipped back into the place he had always filled in Thea's heart, from the first moment when he had strolled round from the back of the house at Enfield and smiled at her. He was – James and the glow of her childhood's adoration hung yet about him, rekindled by the flaring splendour of war, of the King's uniform, of danger lightly shrugged away, of the rakish hat and the easy laughter of youth. He was the brother she had never had, the father she had never known, but she did not think of him with the tender and intimate understanding which belongs to love and marriage. But as she realised this, and found herself free of the sick folly which had come upon her, Thea also found herself desolate.

She was like a traveller who, after a long and perilous journey, returns to find cold rubble and a staring empty space, instead of the home that should have welcomed him. She thought of Paul as though he had been a stranger, without warmth, without affection, without any emotion at all. Her disloyalty made her feel guilty, but somewhere, too, was the beginning of a faint resentment that he should have married her, being a foreigner. In the first months of the war, she had looked forward eagerly to her visits to him, clinging to each moment with him, and leaving him with grief. But in the week after her evening with James, she thought that she had never hated any task so much as going to the Palace. She arrived late, but even so the time passed very slowly. She thought that Paul had never seemed so Teutonic, his eyes so blue, his face so clean-cut, his mouth so tight, his nostrils a little pinched. It seemed to her that he spoke with more accent, as though his tongue was used to the language of his own country, and

English came to him with effort, as did his conversation. The war hung between them like a cloud of black smoke, and she found herself wondering if he knew that the English casualty lists were so high, and was glad of it, and if he hoped that Germany would win. She hated to think that he lived, ate and slept with Germans, with the enemies of her country. She, who had loved and defended Germany for his sake, blamed him for being a German, shrank from the knowledge that her name was now a German one. She thought, as they sat and talked, that he seemed strange and uneasy, almost anxious for her to be gone, and when she had left him and was walking back to the house, his face was already dim in her recollection, a clear-cut, blue-eyed, German face.

A few months after James's return to the Front, he was killed in action, blown to pieces by a German shell. The news reached Thea like the final blow which breaks down all resistance. She went out for a walk by herself, and tramped the wet streets in an agony of grief and despair. As with her mother's death, she felt that she could not accept it, that the very violence of her rejection must make it not so. All the qualities she most loved in James, made him not fit for death, his gaiety, his carelessness, his laughter. It seemed to Thea that when James died, the world was an older, harsher place. The young and the beautiful were always taken, she thought. It was the old and the dull and the discouraged who remained behind. In the loss of James, she relived her mother's death, as though they had both come upon her at the same time. The old grief, so long laid aside, swept over her with all its original sharpness, sharper, perhaps, because there was not the numbness of shock to deaden it.

As she walked the deserted streets, with light rain falling on her, and mud splashing her skirts, she found herself saying, "Oh James. Oh Mother. Dear God, I cannot bear it. James. Mother," in dreary repetition. All the while, the things she had heard about the warfare in France rose up to torment her, the agony of bullet and shell, the bodies on the barbed wire.

Once she stood still and held on to a fence, shaken with tearless anguish. A woman passing eyed her curiously, stopped and asked her if she was ill. "No! No!" cried Thea, so furiously that the woman hurried away, looking back over her shoulder as she went. But Thea still stood under the dripping may tree, saying to herself, "I hate Paul. He's a German. His brother might have killed James. I *hate* Paul." And she knew that, in the turmoil and the nightmare which rocked her, the one steadying certainty, the one safe shelter would have been her love for Paul. But she no longer loved him.

While Thea thus fought out alone her struggle with despair and grief, her external life remained quiet and uneventful, as a mutinied ship sails on calm seas. She tried to conceal her trouble from Nan, and thought that she succeeded, though there were times when she fancied that she saw Nan watching her with the same unobtrusive solicitude with which she used to watch Belle. Emily, on hearing of the death of James, volunteered the remark that "it was always the 'andsome ones as was took," but she and Nan took it for granted that his loss affected only Aunt Mary, and Nan and Thea for her sake. Thea made a bad cold the excuse for not visiting Paul that week, and sat in her room watching the street-lamps, with the tears slowly running down her cheeks, thinking that Judas must have stood like this in the empty garden, with the same sick feeling of helplessness and loss. She thought of Paul, waiting for her so trustfully and patiently, and knew that she would not betray him again in this way. She never again missed a visit to him.

In Abbot's Green, people went about their business, ignoring the war as far as was possible. They talked about it a great deal, and knitted, and criticised strategy, worked in canteens or as Special Constables. But they did not forsake routine in their lives, only altered their routine to fit the wartime needs.

Thea thought that even if the enemy somehow found a way to rain bombs and shells upon them day and night, still these suburban women and elderly men would manage to absorb the bombardment into their everyday life, accepting it like a rainstorm or a heatwave. She sometimes felt almost sorry for the Kaiser, trying to make war upon thousands of people like the inhabitants of Abbot's Green, people who never drama-tised themselves or saw themselves as heroic, and so never saw themselves as defeated, people who spoke of the war in the same tone and with the same banality with which they dis-cussed the weather, people who, with their small world tumbling about them, could still pause outside their garden gates, sniff the air, and say with that genteel sprightliness which used to infuriate Belle, "Quite spring-like, isn't it?"

Then, into this neat pattern of life, came an unexpected distortion. Mrs Luke died.

There had seemed no reason why old Mrs Luke should ever die, but the quietly-beating heart had throbbed more faintly, the plump hands slowly lost their strength, and she slept silently into eternity one morning, alone in the big front bedroom, with Mr Luke's photograph sternly regarding her from the dressing table.

"Ah well, it's a merciful release in a way," said the ladies of Abbot's Green, as though Mrs Luke had been lying in bed for all these years waiting eagerly for death, instead of for Miss Luke's step upon the stairs, for the lace tray-cloth and care-fully-prepared meals.

Listening to the funeral service, Thea found herself faintly incredulous of Mrs Luke's survival into another world. It was easy to think of Belle, with all her faults, carrying her vitality and warm-hearted emotions into a finer life, but would there be a closed room for Mrs Luke, in Heaven? Would there be hot buttered toast and a glowing fire? It was possible, Thea thought, to imagine happiness in Heaven, but very difficult to imagine material comfort, and difficult, too, to think of Mrs Luke's soul as distinct from her placid face and cumbersome invalid body.

The coffin was lowered, such a small coffin, it seemed, after the great double bed. Thea looked round the bleak expanse of white stones, of marble cherubs and melancholy angels, and thanked God that Belle had died in Monaco, where the pink rocks and the blue sky and glittering sea lingered in her memory as an unchanging frame of beauty for the beauty which was gone.

"Miss Luke is taking it very well," said Nan, as they drove back from the cemetery.

"It must be something of a relief," Thea replied, and told herself that Belle's death could never have been a relief, even if she had lived to be eighty, and yet was almost glad that she had no memory of her mother, except as young and beautiful and independent. But Mrs Winter, who had come with them, shook her head.

"I expect she'll miss her at first," she said. "I know I did Maudie, though she gave me a lot of trouble, what with getting so depressed and that." Maudie was Mr Winter's sister, whose hysterical fits had so upset Mrs Winter's household for a number of years. "Still," Mrs Winter continued briskly, "she'll soon get over it. I must hurry home now. Elsie expects to be any day now." She nodded conspiratorially and hurried away to her granddaughter and to Elsie, placidly awaiting the next addition to the family.

As she followed Nan into the house, Thea was trying to forget Miss Luke's face, with the bright smile still upon it and watery red-rimmed eyes behind the pince-nez, was trying to believe that there would be some pleasures in the long years of lonely spinsterhood before her. Why, she wondered, should spinsters have become a subject for jokes and cruel laughter. One did not laugh at a woman who was blind or deaf or hunchbacked. Nan had asked Miss Luke to return to Sunnyside after the funeral, or offered to stay with her for the evening. But Miss Luke had smiled her painful smile and said that she would be *quite* all right, that she would have a quiet evening and go to bed early. So they left her to return to her solitary house, and Thea hoped that Mabel would make her some hot buttered toast and that she would enjoy the luxury of being free from attendance on her mother's needs.

By seven o'clock, they had quite forgotten Miss Luke, and were laughing over a woolly rabbit that Nan was making for Janey's newly-arrived son. Nan was stitching on the second boot-button eye and discussing whether to depict his mouth in red or fawn wool, when they heard running footsteps on the garden path, and a violent beating on the door. On the step stood Mabel, the young maid from next door.

"Oh, Ma'am, it's Miss Luke," she sobbed, hysterically.

"I'll come at once," said Nan quickly. "I knew I shouldn't have left her alone. I might have known she'd get upset later."

"Oh, Ma'am, it's not that," gulped Mabel. "She's . . . she's . . . Oh, Ma'am, she's fell over the banisters."

They found her in the hall, beneath the dim light, her dress disordered, as it had never been in her lifetime, showing her thin legs and her petticoat. She was as awkward in death as she had been while alive, and there was no repose in her attitude. Her thin grey hair was coming down, and her pince-nez hung unbroken on their chain. But from her face, the eager, questing look had vanished for ever. The sharp eyes were mercifully closed, and the contours of her nose and forehead and cheeks were softened. When they laid her on the couch, she looked, with her littleness and calm, small features, like a sleeping child. There was no need of a doctor to say that she was dead, that Miss Luke's lonely searching was over.

"I never left her but for a little while," said Mabel, awed out of her hysteria by this, her first contact with death. "I asked her if I could step outside, because I wanted to speak to my boyfriend, though I never told her that, of course, not just *now*, an' when I come back, I found her."

"It wasn't your fault, Mabel," said Nan. "She must have missed her footing." Her eyes met Thea's in mute understanding.

All night, Thea was tormented by pity and remorse. How could they have left her alone, to face and calculate the long and lonely years ahead of her? How could they, who had been for so long her neighbours, have been deceived by that smile and that weak obstinacy? She tried to imagine how the terrifying decision had been made. Had Miss Luke planned it before the funeral, known from the beginning that she could not live without the serfdom to which she was accustomed? Or had a sudden desperation seized her, when she listened to the empty house, when she heard the kitchen door slam behind Mabel? Perhaps she had known that Mabel had 'stepped out' to see her soldier, on leave from France. Perhaps she remembered the raw-faced little servant-girl whom she had engaged before the war, and was driven beyond endurance by the knowledge that this untidy child, whom she had trained to be clean and house-proud, was now blushing and giggling in the delight of a first love-affair. In what despair must she have run up the steep staircase! Had she flung herself unheeding over the rail, or had she climbed over with difficulty, and then, in a brief moment, seen the dead years behind her and the empty years before, until a wild revolt had forced her to relax her hold, to throw herself out and down, closing her eyes against the shock of meeting the ground, finding at last darkness and rest? Surely that death in the still, dark house, that pitiful, final rebellion against the life which had been so meagrely given to her, was far more terrible than the swift clatter of a horse's hooves, than a shattering explosion, than – yes, even than the cruel pain of the flames!

For a long time, Thea stared into the blackness, feeling that Miss Luke's death lay upon her conscience, that all the world should stop its warfare to shudder and grieve for this vacant life, flung down at last like an impotent challenge that no one would take up. She thought that to the end of her days, those last desolate, defeated minutes in the quiet hall would be part of her experience, impossible to disown. So she tossed and sighed all night, the pity tearing at her heart, while in the house next door, Miss Luke's body lay at peace, all restlessness stilled.

Twenty-Three

The great events of the war passed by Thea like strangers in the street. She and Nan read of the battles, of the defeats and advances, but she remembered them less than the small happenings in Abbot's Green which touched her own life. Thea only remembered the battle in which James had died. The rest of the war slipped by unnoticeably, and she wrote in her diary that she and Nan went shopping, or that she baked a cake while Emily was out, and it refused to rise. Until at last came the November day when she must write in her diary, 'Armistice signed'.

She and Nan did not go out into the street that night, when all London went mad with joy, when all griefs past and all troubles to come were obliterated by the one unassailable truth – the harvesting machine was stilled, men were not dying that night. That first rich breath of peace is like the first moment of love, uncalculating, unpractical, unreasoning. So, that night, the staid folk of England flung away their decorum and cheered and sang and danced, with only the bereaved looking on wistfully, like beggars at a feast, wondering why theirs must be the ones who would not return, and getting no answer.

Thea wondered if she and Nan were the only people in the country who, behind all patriotism and humanity, behind all right-thinking and proper emotions, regretted the end of the war. Nan, she knew, mourned for the end of their pleasant life together, of the undemanding companionship which had given them both so much pleasure. And she herself dreaded Paul's return. There had been times when she had considered writing to Paul and telling him that she must leave him, that their marriage had gone down into destruction during the war, its charred remnants passed beyond all hope of recovery. How could she, she thought, take up once more the intimacies of marriage with this man who was not only a stranger to her but also a foreigner? How could she face spending the rest of her life, sixty years perhaps, alone with a man whom she did not love? But she never wrote that letter and it was not only the realisation of Paul's complete trust in her which stopped her. In Abbot's Green, people did not have separations or divorces. They would not undergo the publicity and degradation of the Divorce Court, but behind that lay a finer and stronger deterrent. In Abbot's Green, marriages were commenced at tea parties and contracted in white satin, but they were also maintained until death. The bridesmaids wore blue or pink, the bride's father made the old, bad jokes, the bride's mother was over-dressed, the bridegroom's mother criticised the catering and the bridegroom's father the champagne, the best man pretended to lose the ring and tied an old shoe to the back of the bridal car, but from that well-worn ceremonial went out two people who were determined to hold faith with one another until their lives' end.

Thea thought of Paul as a stranger and dreaded his return. But he was her husband. And so there came an afternoon when Paul was coming home, and Thea must wait to receive him.

On the day of his release, she did not go to meet him. He said he would prefer to greet her at home. But as she sat and tried to read, her mouth dry and her heart beating uncomfortably, she wished that she had arranged to go to his place of internment and walk back with him. The meeting would have been easier in the open air, she thought, and the first awkwardness would have been lost in the brief journey home. Nan had insisted on going out after lunch, saying that she was sure that they would want to be alone together. How shocked Nan would be, Thea thought drearily, if she knew that I never want to be alone with him again.

Four o'clock struck, and still Paul had not come. Thea stood by the window, trying to remember how tall he was, and whether she would see him over the high privet hedge at the corner of the road. She recalled the morning after the Armistice was signed, and how Elsie and Ronnie had stood outside the Winters' gate, hand in hand, talking to some of the neighbours. Ronnie had been on leave when the good news came through, and now they knew that he would not have to go back to the danger of being killed, that he would soon be home to live with his wife, his daughter, and the small son. Ronnie was in uniform, and during the war he had discovered in himself powers of self-reliance, initiative and shrewdness which he had never suspected. He would return to his old job as a clerk, but in the years to come he would never lose the knowledge that if an emergency came, he could deal with it. And Elsie, with the arrival of her second baby, had laid aside her coquettish hats and frizzed hair and become the suburban matron, soon to be putting curtains up in her own home, cooking meals and seeing the children off to school. They were typical, Thea had thought, of all the little people, all over the world, who were turning back thankfully from the great events of the past four years, from the heroic opportunities of war, to their own small lives and narrow experiences. As they stood in the winter sunshine, with the little girl clutching at Elsie's skirts, Thea saw them as symbolic of the new-born peace, of joyful reunions and the promise of ease and prosperity in the future. She had turned away with a pang of envy, envy for all those women who could welcome their husbands home easily and joyously, and who could look forward to quiet years spent together in the suburbs of London, with their children about them.

She turned away from the window now, impatiently, and bent down to repair the fire. She sat back on the hearthrug, poker in hand, and stayed quite still, staring at the glowing coals. The clock was ticking on the mantelpiece and outside the window a robin was piping his crazy song, not warm and trilling like the spring music of birds, but piercing sweet and anguished.

For a moment, Thea's mind was empty of all thought. She watched the fire and listened to the robin as though she were dead and the sights and sounds of earth came to her dimly, without relevance. Then she heard footsteps on the pavement. She had not waited eagerly for those steps every evening at Rose Avenue without learning to know them from all others. "Paul is coming," she thought, and knew that she should run to meet him, but still it was as though her mind was separated from her body, an unmoved spectator of events. The latch of the gate clicked, and the gravel crunched under Paul's feet. The front door opened, closed, and there was a pause, as though Paul was listening, and then a light thump as he put his suitcase down. The same absurd impulse held her still, but now she was afraid and her mind returned to her body with a pain like cramp. I must move, she thought. I must go out and greet him. I must kiss him. She heard a faint noise behind her and turned round at last. The door had been half open, and Paul stood on the threshold, smiling at her uncertainly and diffidently. The poker fell with a clatter on to the fender, but she did not hear it. She stood up slowly, turning towards him, and saying, "Paul?" as though not sure that it was really he. He remained where he was in the doorway, and the shabby room seemed to welcome him home. His look of anxiety gave way to tenderness as he looked at her. He was smiling just as he had on the day when he proposed to her, and a stray shaft of light from the setting sun glinted on his hair, turning it from brown to gold. Thea said again, "Paul!" in tones of half-incredulous delight, and he held out his arms and stepped forward, saying gently, "Thea. Thea, my love." She stumbled round the table and into his arms, as a ship to safe harbour, swimmer to the shore, frightened child to its father's arms.

244

For a moment she held to him, and then she lifted her head and kissed him passionately, with a violence of emotion such as she had never known before, except when she raised her face to James, under the street-lamp. Paul caught her to him fiercely, and so they clung together, no longer protector and protected, but simply lovers, heart to heart, lip to lip, while the earth staggered and rocked about them and, holding each other, they found their own exquisite stability.

They fell apart guiltily as Emily kicked the door wide open and came into the room. She looked at them sternly, and remarked to Paul, "You're home then?"

"Yes, Emily," Paul answered meekly.

Her eyes went past him to the fire. "It's about time you put some more coal on," she said, and placed bread-and-butter and a plate of cakes on the table and went out again, leaving the door open.

Thea held Paul's arm, giggling helplessly. It was easy to laugh again, now that Paul was home. She was not one of those fortunate people who have within them their own spring of laughter, who, when they are most miserable, can still twist their lips in a bitter joke against themselves, and when they are happy are content to laugh alone. Thea laughed with those she loved, as responsive as a child, but had no strength of self-sufficiency when she was alone. She watched Paul kneel to make up the fire, and smiled, because when he did that small household task she was sure that he was safely home, not a German, not a foreigner, not a stranger, but Paul, her dear husband, who had never really left her.

Emily returned to the room as Paul rose to his feet, dusting the knees of his trousers. He said to her, "Why, Emily, you've made some of my favourite cakes."

Emily banged down the teapot and scowled at him. "It's about time you came back," she said. "Miss Thea don't eat hardly anything. And don't you let that tea get cold, neither," she added, furiously, and went out and slammed the door.

"I believe you take two lumps of sugar?" said Thea, and

laughed again for the pure joy of having him sitting opposite her, and of pouring out tea for him. She thought that if she could choose her heaven, it would be to sit with Paul and Belle and Nan, with the white cloth laid for tea and the fire whispering in the hearth and dusk falling outside. Paul reached for her hand. "It's good to be home again," he said, and sighed. And suddenly they found that they could neither of them eat any tea, and they looked helplessly at Emily's plate of rock cakes. At last, Paul took two and threw them as far out of the window as he could, narrowly missing a stray policeman, and then they crept like conspirators to the sofa and sat down close together, and long after Emily had cleared the table, they stayed there in the shadowy room and the glow of the fire, holding each other.

"Do you think I have changed much?" asked Thea, "while you've been away?"

"No," Paul replied, almost indignantly. "You are as dependable as the North Star."

"A very weak North Star," Thea protested, smiling.

Paul smiled too, but he said, "The North Star is not famed for its strength, but for its constancy." He was silent for a moment, and then half turned to put his arm round her, and went on. "When I was a boy, my father used to take me with him on walking tours. I remember he used to say to me, 'Paul, never be afraid of being lost at night if the stars are out. While you can see the North Star, you know at least in which direction you are walking'." He paused, and then nodded his head in the direction of the Palace. "When I was in there, I used to stand at the window and look at the North Star, and think, 'That is my Thea. While I have her, I . . . I am not lost'."

Thea sighed contentedly, thinking that when he was so sure of her, it made her feel sure of herself. Then, something in the picture of Paul standing alone at the window of his prison, clinging to that faint star in the darkness, caught at her heart. She whispered, "Oh, Paul, did you hate it so much?" and hoped that he would reply lightly, shrugging away the four years of humiliation and boredom in the joy of the present. But he did not answer, and when she looked up at his face, he was staring into the fire, his mouth a thin line, his nostrils flared, his eyes ice-blue and hard. She realised with astonishment that Paul, so modest and gentle, was a very proud man. The knowledge almost shocked her, for she had thought that in the brief time of their married life together, she had come to know him so well, yet here was something she had never known about him. For a moment she could think of nothing to say, but at last she murmured, "It's over now. We need never be parted again. There will never be another war."

Paul was silent still, his arm lying limply along the back of the sofa. Thea took hold of his other hand, saying persuasively, "It was worth it, Paul, so that there should never be another war." Paul laughed at that, a sharp, hard laugh. He drew away from her and leant forward, his hands clasped in front of his knees, his head bent. His hair and face were ruddy in the firelight.

"As I was coming here in the train," he said, softly, "there were two soldiers in my carriage. They talked about life in the trenches, and men they knew who had been killed, and one of them said, 'We'll make sure the swine don't do it again, anyway'." He straightened his back sharply and restlessly, and said, with his German accent suddenly noticeable, "If there is another war, it will be because people talk like that. And if there is another war, Germany will win it."

"Oh, no, Paul, no," cried Thea, pitifully. She spoke as though the decision rested with Paul alone. "I couldn't bear another war. I couldn't *bear* it."

Paul smiled at that. "It is surprising how much human beings can bear," he said. "They seem so frail, and yet it is the most hopeful thing about them – that they are so enduring. It makes one think that perhaps our civilisation is meant to last, after all."

"But, Paul," Thea insisted, "there needn't be another war."

He turned to look at her, and then his face softened and he put his arm round her. "Don't worry about it," he said gently. "Perhaps it may never come. I expect we shall have to fight France – Clemenceau will see to that, but probably not England. I hope not England," he added grimly.

Thea remembered how he had said, "I could not fight against your country." Her security was again slipping away from her. She sat within the circle of Paul's arm, but she felt that the emotions and distresses of all the world were being thrust in upon her, anger and humiliated pride, sorrow and vindictiveness, the whole painful disease of war, whose epidemic had swept through two generations, and might yet infect a third, whose scars were as enduring and disfiguring as those of smallpox. Nan was wrong, she thought. From this illness no one could quite recover, and it did not immunise them, but made them more ready to take the sickness when it next travelled abroad.

She saw the face of that ridiculous major in the restaurant, and how his bloodshot blue eyes had looked intently at her, as he said, "The only good German is a dead German," and thought how bitterly she had resented his words, behind her amusement. She remembered Mrs Winters' thoughtless cruelty, and how she had in a moment found herself standing alone with Paul, against all her friends and all her countrymen. Then she thought of James, going off to fight in his own cheerful, unsentimental way, because war was a joke and an adventure, but also because, beneath his carelessness and laughter, he did believe that Germany was wrong, and that he must go to the aid of Belgium and France as he had always helped anyone who was in trouble.

Thea was suddenly desperately afraid – afraid lest her new, sweet unity with Paul should be still-born, should go down into destruction in the shadow of the next war, as their former love had perished in the first war. Paul stared into the fire, seeing there his own ugly pictures of a broken and defeated country, of a surrender in a railway carriage, and of a world made viciously hostile by loss and bewilderment. Thea sat very still, listening to a train whistling outside the tunnel at Abbot's Green station, to the next-door gate banging, and to the clock on the mantelpiece, ticking away their happiness. Then she clasped her hands tightly together and did the only really brave thing she had ever done in her life.

"Whatever happens," she said, in a voice that trembled only slightly, "even if there is another war, we shall be in Germany, so at least we shall be together."

For a moment, Paul did not seem to realise what she had said. Then he turned to her a face young and eager with new hope.

"You'd come?" he cried. "You'd come to Germany now?"

"Of course, Paul. It's your country."

He took both her hands and held them hard, saying sharply and incredulously, "Now, at once?"

Thea's heart sank, but she replied, "If your firm wants you to go there."

"They do," Paul answered, and he laughed excitedly. "They want me to take up the post of Managing Director in Berlin."

"They've just offered you that?" asked Thea in astonishment.

He seemed confused. "Yes – that is – I can have it when I like. The present Managing Director is anxious to retire. He only holds the post until I take it up."

Thea caught her breath. "When did they offer you that post?"

"Some time ago. What does it matter?"

She stopped him as he tried to brush her question aside. "Paul, was it in 1913, when you asked me to marry you?"

He did not answer, but leant forward to poke the fire. Thea remembered the look on his face when Nan had asked him to wait a year, and cried out as though she had been hurt. "Paul, Paul, why didn't you tell me? I would have married you then and gone back with you."

"No," said Paul quickly, "it was better as it was."

"But, what did you tell them?"

"I asked them to hold the post for me for a year, for I thought that by then Nan would have got used to the idea of losing you. I couldn't have married you and taken you straight to Germany. It wouldn't have been fair to her. And then I saw that the war was coming, and—"

"We could have gone to Germany before the war began," said Thea, watching him.

"And left you alone in an enemy country? For I should have been fighting. You would not have known any of my family, and you could not speak the language. No, I couldn't have done that." He spoke in a cheerful, matter-of-fact way, as though the risks of lost promotion and four years of internment were hazards that any man would have readily undertaken. Thea's disloyalty hung heavily upon her, an intolerable burden of ingratitude. Stunned, she put her face down on the cushion and cried as though her heart was breaking, and when Paul took her in his arms and tried to soothe her, she cried more bitterly than ever. In those tears were washed away all doubts and reservations, all clinging to her own country and her own people, all hatred of his. She would follow him unquestioningly to the world's end like the lovers in the old romances, and, as Paul soothed and comforted her, she thought of the words of the marriage ceremony which had struck most sweetly to her heart, *Wilt thou, forsaking all other, keep thee only unto him, so long as ye both shall live?*

"Hush, my love, it is all right now," Paul said, trying to laugh. "Now, how like a woman, to cry when the trouble is over!"

But Thea only sobbed, "Don't ever leave me again, Paul. I'm not strong enough. Don't leave me alone again."

"I won't," he promised. "Dry your eyes, like a good girl. Here is Nan. I heard the latch of the gate. Take my handkerchief. Oh dear, what will Emily say if she sees you like this! I shall have to go away again."

They both laughed at that. Nan did not comment on the last of the tears being hastily mopped up, but kissed Paul warmly and welcomed him like a son, and, by the time Emily came to lay supper, all traces of the storm had vanished.

Twenty-Four

T he months after Paul's return were, for Thea, a strange blend of pleasure and heartache. When the air was frosty, and crisp with the smoke of evening fires, when the last leaves fluttered quietly to the white-grey pavements, when the lights wandered singly out into the dusk, as though the houses were just waking up and opening their eyes, Thea sometimes thought that Abbot's Green had never seemed so dear. And yet she no longer seemed to have any part in it, as she once had. It no longer belonged to her. She was in the position of a man who had taken his monastic vows but must still remain for a while in the world he had renounced, and, like him, she was anxious to be gone.

Sometimes, she would sit by the window as Belle used to, but she would look out at the fog or rain or smoke-filled air, not as though she looked through prison bars, but as though she strained her eyes to catch the last glimpse of a beloved friend, impatient for, even while she dreaded, his departure, so that she could distract her attention with new friends and new activities.

When Thea told Paul that she was going to have a baby, he tried to persuade her to remain in England.

"I don't know exactly what conditions will be over there," he said, "but I know that it is pretty bad."

"I'm coming with you," Thea answered.

"Stay here just for a little while," he pleaded. "Just until the baby is born. Then I'll come and fetch you both out to Germany."

Thea's chin stuck out in a way her mother would have recognised. "He'll be born in his own country," she replied. "We're Germans now."

"But, my darling—" Paul was beginning, but Thea caught hold of both his hands and whispered, "Let me come with you, Paul. I must come with you."

She felt that this was the first decision she had ever made for herself, the first time she had shaped the course of her life; instead of allowing her movements to be arranged for her by those who loved her. In the midst of uncertainties, one thing was clear, she must go to Germany with her husband, sharing with him the bitterness of a return from exile to a spoiled and defeated land, making a home for him in his Fatherland, and bringing his child up to be a good Christian and a good German.

"I must learn the Lord's Prayer in German," she remarked, and Paul, marshalling his arguments for a fresh attack, looked down at her abstractedly, and then realised what she had said and laughed until the tears came.

"How can I argue against you!" he cried helplessly. Thea smiled and turned to her knitting, and so the matter was settled. Paul went about the interminable formalities needed before he could return home, Thea knitted and sewed for the baby in the room where she had sewed her trousseau, and Nan went patiently on with her dressmaking and with clothes for the great-grandchild she would never see.

Often, when Thea and Nan sat in their old places on each side of the fire, Thea would try to put into words the things she wanted to say to Nan before she went. She would plan the expression of all her gratitude and affection, and just when she was ready to say it, Nan would look up and smile and make some trivial remark, some comment upon the gossip of Abbot's Green, and Thea felt herself once more defeated. She knew now how Belle had felt in the few moments before she died, and remembered how she had said, "Tell Nan . . ." and then sighed hopelessly, and added, "Tell Nan I'm sorry."

Looking at Nan's head bent over her sewing, and at the calm, humorous face, Thea thought that what Nan had given seemed beyond repayment, even in thanks.

Nan raised her head and found Thea's eyes on her. "Have you dropped a stitch?" she asked cheerfully, for Thea still brought her knitting to be set right, like a small girl. Thea shook her head, and then said desperately, "Oh, Nan, will you really not come with us? Paul says the house is quite big enough, and soon we'll be getting one of our own."

"I'll come and visit you," Nan promised.

Thea suddenly dropped her work and came to kneel clumsily by Nan, clasping the thin, veined hand, with the bone thimble on the third finger, and burying her face in the comfortable lap.

"Oh Nan," she said helplessly. "Oh, Nan."

The words were still unspoken, and she knew now that she would never say them. She saw Nan in the years to come, living alone in the ugly little house in Abbot's Green, sitting in winter behind the red curtains and in summertime in the garden, diligently collecting snails from the rockery, and then being too tender-hearted to kill them. Each year she would greet the roses with the same surprised pleasure, as though she had not expected to see them, visit her acquaintances with the same friendly reserve and bear Emily's tempers with the same patience. She would be very lonely, at times desolate, but she would do her dressmaking and her shopping, help with church work and visit the hospital, and read a chapter of her Bible every night, just as she had always done.

Thea lifted her face to Nan's and the grey eyes met hers calmly and understandingly.

"You mustn't upset yourself, dear. You must think of the baby. We've had a lot of nice times together, but now you're married, it's right that you should go with Paul. I've been lucky to have you for so long." For a moment, the pain slipped through, but immediately she thrust it out of sight. "I'll come out and see you, and of course you'll be coming back on visits." The old note of pride crept into her voice. "Emily and I will be quite all right."

Thea said urgently, "Nan – you do know, don't you?"

Nan held her close, and smiled. "Yes, dear," she answered. "Yes, I know."

Aunt Mary had written to Nan, saying that she hoped that Thea would visit her one afternoon, before she went abroad.

"We might go on Saturday," Thea suggested to Paul, during their last week at home.

Paul did not lower the newspaper he was reading, but said from behind it, "Yes. I could pick you up after tea and bring you back. I may be kept late at the office, as it's the last day."

"Oh, but Aunt Mary will want you to come to tea," Thea protested.

There was a brief silence. Then Paul repeated gently, "I think it would be best if I called for you after tea."

"We'll go and have tea at Mrs Bates's farm," said Thea decidedly. "If I go to Aunt Mary's house early in the afternoon, then you get away as soon as you can, and come for me there."

"Or I could meet you at the end of the road," said Paul.

Thea hesitated. Then, "Yes, that would give me a good excuse for leaving," she agreed.

Perhaps, for a moment, they both wondered if they must spend the rest of their lives sparing each other.

When Thea was shown into the drawing room at Enfield on the following Saturday, she thought at first that the room was full of strangers. But when she was seated by the fire, and her early flurry of shyness was over, she found that Charlotte's husband was the only unfamiliar figure. Janey and Lydia had come on an afternoon visit from their respective homes, and Charlotte and Lucien were staying with Aunt Mary while they looked for a house of their own.

Thea was disappointed in Lucien. Having read his poetry,

she had felt that she knew him, and had almost expected him to know her. But he had shaken hands with her unsmilingly, and almost without looking at her, clearly regarding her as just another female relation to be treated with distant courtesy and forgotten. Thea felt guilty at having read his poetry, as though she had read someone's love-letters, and afterwards must try to pretend that she had not. Charlotte, too, looked just as she had always done, plain and sharp-faced, and still with that air of aloofness which had always been so intriguing.

After a moment, they resumed the conversation they had evidently been having before Thea's arrival. Lydia was telling her mother about Drew's new school, Janey was asking intelligent questions, and Charlotte and Lucien maintained an ominous silence.

"And I had a letter from him today," Lydia finished, "most beautifully written, saying how happy he was."

"Take thy pen and write quickly," said Lucien, unexpectedly. Thea started and looked at him. Lydia went on, without taking any notice of the interruption, "And then I had a letter from his housemaster, saying that he was settling down very well indeed, and seemed to be a most intelligent child."

"The learned Lipsius, who at the age of four," said Lucien.

"Ho, no, sir, we are seven," Charlotte replied.

"And still the wonder grew," Lucien finished.

They spoke very quietly, looking at each other. The rest of the family ignored them completely.

"Isn't that good," said Aunt Mary. "And, of course, the housemaster would be able to judge boys immediately. How nice that he has taken a liking to Drew."

"A very Daniel," Charlotte murmured.

Thea watched them in astonishment. Charlotte was smiling faintly, and Lucien, though perfectly grave, was looking at her through narrowed eyes, in a way which somehow gave the impression of great amusement. Did they, Thea wondered, take this amusement with them wherever they went, so that the dullest company could be enlivened for them by their own nonsense-language? She thought that they were extremely rude, but felt, too, envy for the relationship which they shared, for that rare blending of mind and emotion into one personality. Nothing could touch them. They would live outside all ordinary griefs and anxieties in their own unreal world, which to them was the only reality. It was a world into which Thea could never have entered, and yet she envied it, and her marriage with Paul seemed to her for a moment a very ordinary affair, the common mating of two commonplace people, whose love was repeated a million times in the middle-class society in which they lived. Lydia went on talking, and Janey and Aunt Mary answered her, and sometimes Thea herself was forced to take part in the conversation, but she was conscious all the time of Charlotte and Lucien, serene and laughing, in their own inviolate world.

"Oh, Charlotte," said Lydia suddenly, "I saw a house that might suit you, today."

Charlotte replied, after a moment's pause, and as though she were just waking up, "Did you? Where was it?"

"Not far from the 'Leg-of-Mutton Pond,'" Lydia answered.

"Such a fantastic thing to live near," Lucien protested.

"But children sail their boats on it on Sundays," said Charlotte.

"That would be nice," he admitted. "We could go and watch them, and sail our own. What shall we call it?"

"Call it 'The Revenge'," Thea suggested.

Aunt Mary looked up sharply from her work.

"Oh yes, after Sir Richard Grenville's ship," said Charlotte, watching her mother, and Aunt Mary turned back to her embroidery.

"No, no, nothing historical," said Lucien. "We will sail her twice round the pond, and call her 'The Hope' or 'The Despair', according to whether she capsizes or not."

"If she capsizes, we will call her 'The Hope'," said Charlotte

"Of course," Lucien agreed.

258

Lydia regarded them hopelessly. "You haven't asked me about the house," she protested.

"Oh, the house," said Lucien, "that doesn't matter so much."

"How big is it?" asked Janey, taking pity on Lydia.

"Well, it's just about the right size, and has a nice Virginia creeper on the front."

"Virginia creeper, so ostentatious," Lucien put in. "It turns so very red in the autumn."

"I like Virginia creeper," said Janey, who seemed to be quite undisturbed by Lucien's conversational vagaries, unlike Lydia.

"It stops brick houses from looking naked," said Lucien, with the air of one making a great concession.

"It has a garden, and it's to be let," Lydia continued, desperately. "And if you want it, you'd better go soon, because I should think that someone else will take it if you don't."

"We'll go tomorrow," said Charlotte. "Thank you very much." Her husband nodded approvingly, evidently feeling that she had spoken with unusual social grace.

Thea was trying to decide why it was that she felt that the room was different from her expectations, what it was that was changed in it. After a time, she realised that she had always thought of the Enfield drawing room as a very quiet place. Now, they all spoke quickly and urgently, as though they were afraid of silence. She remembered her first visit to Enfield, when she had sat in that room while Aunt Mary did her embroidery and the budgerigar sang in its cage, and she could hear James's voice in the silence, speaking upstairs. She thought that her aunt was greatly changed since she had seen her last. Only the sweetness of expression was unaltered. Her dark, curly hair was now grey, her smooth young cheeks wrinkled, and her clothes did not fit very well, as though she had lost her trim, rounded figure since they were made. Above all, she had lost that air of repose which had become her so well. Thea thought that she detected a querulousness in her voice, and a restlessness in her posture, although she sat and sewed, just as before.

"When do you leave, Thea?" asked Janey, and it was as though they had all been waiting to ask that question, but had not dared to

"On Tuesday," she replied.

Charlotte said, in her cool voice, "And have you learnt German yet?"

It was the first time they had admitted that she was going to Germany. Aunt Mary was quite silent. Thea felt that she had asked her there in obedience to the demands of family ties and of propriety, but further she could not go.

"I've started to learn," she replied. "But it's such a difficult language. Paul says I shall pick it up when I get there."

"But you must learn some grammar first," Lydia insisted. "What a pity that you didn't learn it at school."

"Oh, I think you learn a language better from living in the country," said Janey.

"No, it's best to read a little first," Charlotte put in. "Not grammar, but novels, with ordinary speech in them."

They spoke as a family, covering up their mother's silence, and trying to make Thea feel that she was one of them, as she had been before. Even Lydia was taking her part in the involuntary conspiracy.

"Paul's a very good teacher," said Thea, obstinately determined that her husband should be recognised as a member of the family.

The girls glanced at their mother, and there was an infinitesimal hush, as though they all caught their breath. In it, Thea heard the voice of Major Sands, saying, 'The only good German is a dead German'.

Then Lydia said, as the eldest, "Yes, I should think he would have the patience for teaching. And probably, when you hear everyone talking it, you will pick it up quite well."

"Have you a house yet?" asked Janey.

"No, not yet. We are to live with Paul's father and mother until we can find one. I believe it is almost harder to find a house in Berlin than in London."

"Yes, and I should take plenty of warm clothes," said Lydia. "The winters are cold there."

Thea's trunks were packed and closed, but she said gratefully, "Yes, I will. Paul's mother said that things were very bad there for food and clothing."

Aunt Mary spoke, without looking up. "They must expect to suffer," she said.

Oh James, thought Thea, is this all that is left of you? Are you, with your generosity and kindliness, to be remembered only by an ineradicable hatred in your mother's heart for the whole German nation? This, then, was to be the imperishable War Memorial of a million men who had died for peace.

"You must write and tell us how you get on," said Janey quickly, just as James would have spoken.

"Yes, I will," Thea replied, but she did not think that she would. She looked round the room. The birdcage was empty. A photograph of James in uniform stood on the piano, beside a vase of spring flowers. He was smiling a little, looking out upon his family with the old gentleness and humour, and it was strange to Thea that his mother could not hear his voice, lightly accepting death, speaking so kindly of Paul Bruner, his father's friend and her husband. She glanced at the clock, and got slowly to her feet.

"I think I should be going now," she said. "I'm meeting Paul at four o'clock."

"But, you'll have some tea first?" Aunt Mary protested, laying aside her embroidery, and speaking for the first time naturally and hospitably.

"No, I don't think I can, thank you. I arranged with Paul to have tea at Mrs Bates's."

She took Aunt Mary's hand, and said with a tremor in her voice, "Say goodbye to Uncle Robert for me."

"I will," Aunt Mary promised, and kissed her with the old

kindness. She could not forgive Paul for being a German, but she could forgive Thea for marrying him. "And don't worry about Nan," she added. "We'll see she doesn't get lonely. She might come here on a visit when you go."

"Oh, thank you, Aunt Mary." Thea paused, and hesitated. Would Aunt Mary not send one message of friendliness to Paul? Should she herself say anything about James? Aunt Mary smiled sweetly. "Goodbye, dear," she said.

Thea turned blindly away, and found Lucien in front of her. He took her hand and smiled down at her, his eyes meeting hers.

"You'll like the Germans," he said. "They're the most friendly people, when you get to know them. And give my regards to the German beer." He pressed her hand, and added, "Berlin is wonderful in the spring."

"We'll see you to the door," said Janey, and took her arm, Charlotte and Lydia following behind. They stopped in the hall, and stood close round her. Thea thought that they were trying to make her feel one of the family, trying to send her out to the strange land with some sense of security in the unbreakable ties of home.

"You must write to us, Thea," said Janey. "Write to us *soon*."

"Of course, we shall hear from Nan about the baby," said Lydia.

As Charlotte kissed her, she said very softly, "Mrs Bates's son was killed in the war. Wasn't it a shame?"

Her eyes met Thea's, not with detachment, but regret and understanding, and Thea nodded, and answered, "Thank you." Mrs Bates's farm was now closed to her and Paul. On the doorstep, Janey put her arms round Thea's neck and kissed her. Her three cousins stood and watched her as she went down the garden path. Suddenly Charlotte called after her, in her clear voice, "Don't forget to give our love to Paul."

Thea turned to glance back, and the other two smiled and said, "Of course." She nodded, and waved her hand, and then turned to go, blind with tears. Her tears were not only in gratitude for the kindness and loyalty of her cousins, but in grief for the old days that were gone and would never come again. She thought of the apparent indestructibility of family life in the nursery and the schoolroom, and how it crumbled with the passing years, beneath the rough winds of death and misfortune and broken affections. She thought, too, of Uncle Robert, and how he would have grown grey and stooped with the loss of his second son, and with the knowledge that he had quarrelled with James in his lifetime, and the more bitter certainty that he would still have quarrelled with him if he had not been killed. She thought of Aunt Mary, clinging desperately to her daughters and to her grandchildren, and perpetuating the memory of James in an implacable hatred that was pitifully alien to her nature.

Thea shook the tears away, and walked steadily up the road, moving slowly and heavily because the child was already a burden. At the end of the road, Paul was waiting for her, and he came to meet her, taking her arm. She leant on him gladly. He did not speak, and they walked for a while in silence. She knew that there was no need to tell him anything about her afternoon. At last he said, "Shall we go straight to the farm?"

"I think I'd rather have tea when we get home," said Thea. "Let's just go for a walk."

"If you aren't too tired."

"No, I should like to see the fields again. We could sit on the little seat."

She remembered the sturdy little boy, and the big, dark-haired young man, who had gone from the Middlesex farmhouse to die in the fields of France. How the old days had been dispersed by the deep whirlpool of war! But, I have finished with the old days, and the old people, she thought. Paul is the only person who matters to me any more, Paul and the baby. She glanced up at him, and he looked down to smile, anxiously.

"We have each other, Paul," she said. "Nothing can touch us as long as we have each other."

Twenty-Five

T hey sat on the little wooden seat, which was set down a slope from the stile. The sun was giving its first real warmth since the winter, and all over London, people were turning to each other and remarking encouragingly that summer would soon be here, as visitors tell a patient that he will be better soon. The hedgerows behind the seat had budded long since, but now the tiny green leaves were opening, tracing the black twigs with delicate colour. In every front window in suburban London, the long-cherished bowl of bulbs displayed its hyacinths, blue and pink and yellow, or its daffodils and narcissi. The mysterious smell was in the air, which combined certainty of spring with promise of summer, and women began turning out cupboards, and men the tool shed and lawnmower, with the same automatic purposefulness with which birds and animals move from their winter quarters. There was hopefulness abroad, too, because the war to end all wars was over. The blind and the maimed were hidden from sight, fighting their own still battles, away from public pity and regret, and all other citizens set peacefully to work to restore the life they had once known. With so much hope, and such resolves, how was it possible that the world should not become a better place to live in?

Thea was thinking of all this, as she sat beside Paul on the small wooden seat, below the place where she had stopped him from proposing to her. She herself would be in Germany, and there, too, surely, people would be turning gladly to their peacetime occupations, forgetting hatred and cruelty. A sudden doubt came to Thea's mind for the first time.

"Paul," she said, "Your mother and father won't mind my being English, will they?"

Paul hesitated. It was evidently not the first time he had thought of that.

"Just at first," he said, slowly, "there may be a little difficulty, because of Fritz. But they will soon learn to love you."

"Fritz? Your brother?" Thea was frightened. She thought of the photograph on the piano, a constant reminder of grief and anger. "But, he wasn't . . . wasn't . . .?"

"Yes, killed in action. At Ypres, I believe. I didn't tell you, did I?"

"No, Paul. No, you didn't."

How well he could keep a secret, when he liked. How silent he could be upon matters which concerned him closely, and her too. Then she looked at his face, and forgot everything but sorrow for him.

"My darling, I'm so sorry."

Paul shrugged his shoulders. "Just one more," he said. But Thea knew that it was not so, to him, that Fritz was for him the only casualty in the war, just as James was to her. We are oppressed by a million deaths, but we can only truly grieve for one or two.

"He was younger than you?" she asked.

"Yes, he was younger, and more clever, and more daring. He was all that I wasn't. When we were skiing, or skating, or just climbing trees, it was always Fritz who risked his neck. I took the safe path, always." He spoke bitterly, and Thea thought how those four years of safety in British internment would stay with him for the rest of his life, and that they were on her account. She clasped her hands tightly in her lap, but could think of no words of comfort. Paul went on speaking.

"He was always very strong, much stronger than I was, and much braver. I remember seeing him on dangerous runs, when

266

we were skiiing, with his yellow hair and blue eyes, and his rosy cheeks, and always laughing. He often got into trouble, and once he broke a leg, but as soon as he was well again, he'd be off on some other mad scheme. My mother used to say that he'd drive her to distraction, but she liked it really. She was very proud of him." Paul laughed, and then stopped.

Thea remembered that he had once shown her a photograph of Fritz, a big, blond, handsome boy, with thin lips and clear-cut features, who showed very white teeth as he laughed, and seemed, even in a photograph, to give an impression of almost overpowering vitality. She had been glad that she was to marry Paul, and not Fritz.

"When we fought," Paul went on, glad to talk of his brother, now that the silence was broken, "I usually won, because Fritz would use up all his strength in one great exertion, but I used to conserve my energy until the end, and then it was quite easy to overcome him. Then he used to yell, and then my mother would come and scold me for treating my little brother roughly." Paul smiled, and shook his head. "But we didn't fight very often. He was irritating at times, but no one could get really angry with him.

"When Fritz was five, he cut his arm open with the wood-chopper. I'd been left in charge of him as my mother was out, and I just bundled him into the wheelbarrow and ran round to the doctor with him. The neighbours always said how funny we looked, with me red in the face and out of breath, and Fritz sitting in the wheelbarrow, crying, with blood pouring out of his arm."

"But you saved his life," said Thea softly.

"Yes," Paul agreed. "I saved his life at five, so that he could be blown to bits at twenty."

"Oh Paul, you mustn't think of it like that!"

"How else is one to think of it?"

"We can't tell what might have happened to him if he'd lived."

"Then why didn't he die at five?"

267

"He had fifteen years more of life, of being loved and admired, and of enjoyment. The first day you came to our house, you told us that Fritz wanted to be a soldier. Perhaps he would rather have died that way than any other. Perhaps when the war was over, he would have found that there wasn't much else that he wanted to do. He might have found it hard to settle down in a peaceful world, and been unhappy, and made all of you unhappy for him. You said that first day that you didn't know what he'd do if he didn't go into the army."

Paul was breaking a twig up into tiny pieces and throwing them on to the grass. He gazed away down the meadow, and Thea thought that he was half-convinced of the truth of what she said, and yet the only thing that mattered to him was that he would never see his brother again, that Fritz, with his immense vitality and energy, had been swept meanly away in the common carnage of war, unnoticeable among so many dead. She, too, was silent for a time. From the questioning and searching and pain of the past years, some sort of certainty had emerged in her mind, as the rounded vessel appears after the helpless spinning and turning upon the potter's wheel. But it was imperfect and unfinished, and she was afraid to show it to Paul, lest her fumbling words should do less good than her silence.

"It's all so unreasonable!" Paul exclaimed, violently. "If Fritz was going to be killed at twenty, why should he be born at all!"

"But, don't you think," Thea began diffidently, "don't you think that perhaps we're wrong to worry so much at what age people die? Because eighty years is nothing out of all eternity. I sometimes think that the sad life isn't that of someone who dies too soon, but someone who lives too long, like Miss Luke. And perhaps all lives are complete, if we only knew it. I'm sure that Andrew wasn't meant to grow up, to go to war, to be wounded, perhaps, or gassed. But there wasn't anything cruel or ugly in his death, and his family will always remember him as he was, with his baby-rabbit smile and engaging ways, and his naughtiness and obstinacy."

"But, if you are right," said Paul, after a moment, "what of those who *were* maimed in the war, or gassed, or mentally shattered?"

"I don't know," Thea replied, helplessly. "I don't think you can generalise. Perhaps there's a reason in each individual life, if we only knew it. Perhaps they're given the courage to bear it, and even needed something like that to show how brave they were."

Paul shook his head. "I cannot believe that such things should ever be right," he said, "or that there is a merciful Providence that arranges such things. No, we may as well admit that it is men who make wars, and that Englishmen killed Fritz, just as . . . just as Germans killed James."

Thea caught her breath, and he put his arm round her, the old jealousy stilled at last.

Thea said slowly, "I have often thought, since, that it was better for James to be killed, that it was what he wanted. He could never have settled down to become a solid, prosperous businessman. He would always have made his mother and father unhappy, and made himself unhappy too. Probably he would have married, and then he would have had constant worry and failure in trying to support a family, always giving away more than he could afford, and spending too much, and borrowing money to give away to someone else. And in time, people would have forgotten his generosity and his lovable ways, and thought of him just as an elderly ne'er-do-well, always wanting money, and never paying it back. But, this way, we can remember him at his best." She saw James in his uniform, going gaily off to war, laughing at danger, content that his future should be uncertain, since the plans that had been made for him in the past had always gone awry. She saw him, with his old gentleness and thoughtfulness, forbearing to kiss her, as though in that moment before he went away for the last time, he returned her, kindly and affectionately, to her husband, himself stepping into the shadows.

"And Mother too," said Thea, and stopped. Not even to

Paul could she say what was in her mind. While she had been at Monte Carlo, she had only partly understood the people and events, young and inexperienced as she was. But much that had before dimly troubled her was now clear. She thought of Belle, rejoicing in her beauty, loving the unconventional, and yet subscribing all the time to the middle-class morality from which she had fled. She saw, and shuddered to see, Ambrose, always at her mother's elbow, Ambrose, who did not love his wife, but could never marry again, Ambrose, who flattered her and made her laugh, and who always got what he wanted. In the casualty-list where she had seen James's death, Thea had come upon the name of Ambrose. At the time, she had hardly noticed it, thinking perhaps it was coincidence, but now she wondered whether the unquiet messenger had come to him and to James in the same hour, and whether he had ever thought of Belle Lawrence, in the torn fields of France.

"Mother wouldn't have wanted to grow old," she said aloud, and knew that that, too, was true.

"But, do you believe, then," said Paul, "that everything that happens to us is predestined, that our lives are planned for us, and that all we have to do is to follow the set pattern, and try to believe that it is the best one?"

"No, not quite that. But I think that there is a pattern for our lives, and that if we make wrong decisions, then we twist the threads. But God's hand is always ready to make a new pattern, when we have spoilt the old one. I think each life has, perhaps, a dozen different patterns, according to decisions made at different times, but I think that God's hand is upon them all."

"I wish I could believe that," said Paul under his breath. "I wish that I could see God as the master weaver, as you do. To me, life is a great machine, clacking away without guidance, and we are the helpless threads, twisted and racked and finally broken, without any finished cloth resulting."

"I couldn't go on living if I thought that," said Thea. "I

270

couldn't endure to see life as a succession of narrow escapes, with death the final accident that no one could escape. That would mean that there was no safety anywhere." She turned to look at her husband with pain in her eyes. "Paul, try to believe that there is a God," she said.

He laughed a little and held her to him. "While I have you, I can almost believe it," he said. "Yet I would rather believe that there was no God than believe that He is so bad a craftsman that He should allow someone like Fritz to be wasted, with all his gifts, his strength and charm, in a war that will do no one any good."

"We don't know what might have happened to him if he'd lived after the war," Thea repeated. "We can't look forward, or try to change what happens. We can only look back afterwards and see part of the reason." She leant her head against Paul's shoulder, and went on, "Mother once said that life was like a jigsaw puzzle. We can't fit all the pieces in, and we haven't the complete picture to guide us. But if you come back to a jigsaw puzzle after leaving it alone for a while, you suddenly find that you can do it, and wonder how you could ever not have seen the pattern of it."

"Perhaps in time," said Paul gently, "I shall come to think as you do."

They were silent, both gazing away down the meadows, golden in the spring sunshine. Thea felt upon her a great peace. She knew now, she thought, why old men delighted to write their autobiographies, looking back at their lives with smiling detachment, watching the pieces drop easily into place, the death of a beloved wife, the loss of an only son, fitting into the inevitable pattern. She had left the old world behind her, the world of Abbot's Green and Enfield, and this quiet field was the resting place allowed to her before going on to the new world of Germany and of the Bruner family. And she was fortunate, she thought, in that she went with Paul and with the baby. She saw this child, conceived in England and born in Germany, as a symbol of unity between the two countries, of peace and kindness. If it were a boy, he would come to England, as representative of his father's firm, and perhaps he would meet Janey's children, and walk in these fields. If it were a girl, she would marry a German, and teach her children to speak English and to sing English nursery rhymes. For Paul and for the Bruners, these children would take the place of Fritz, drawing the bitterness out of their hearts, the boy who would be strong and blond and courageous, and the girl who would have red-gold hair and blue eyes and the spirit of laughter.

Paul said, without looking at her, "You will miss Abbot's Green."

The gaze softened. She would miss the ugly houses and the beautiful gardens. She would miss the Mountain Ash, the home-made trellises with their roses, the little businessmen mowing the lawns in their shirt-sleeves, and trimming the privet hedges. She would miss the suburban ladies, with their impertinence, their curiosity, and the kind-heartedness that lay underneath. She would miss the plane trees, with their mottled trunks, and the may tree at the corner of the road, and the magic which the wet streets had in the gaslight, "Yes," she murmured, "I shall miss it terribly at first."

Paul looked down at her, his face troubled. "Sometimes I am so afraid that I should never have asked you to marry me. If I had never returned to Abbot's Green, if we had never met again . . ."

"Oh Paul, Paul," cried Thea, between laughter and tears, "how can you think of such a thing! You've brought me the only real happiness I've ever known. I never wanted to be great or famous or rich. All I ever asked was to love and be loved, and to live quietly and safely. When you took me in your arms, that afternoon before the war, I felt for the first time since I was a child that no harm could come to me. As long as you love me, I shall never be afraid again."

It was in Paul's mind to tell her something of what he knew or feared of the state of his country, the starvation and despair, the anarchy on one side and the apathy on the other, the dangers into which he was taking her and the unborn child. But Thea was holding the lapel of his coat, smiling as though at a private joke, and whispering, "Safe, safe, safe!"

When the sun turned red and round in a delicately-tinted sky, they turned away from the quiet meadows and climbed the slope together. Before them were two more days at Abbot's Green, the parting with Nan and Emily and the last journey to the station from the dark little house called Sunnyside. But, to Thea, pausing by the stile, it was as though, in leaving the field where she had flown her kite with her cousins, she left behind her the old life, and stepped forward into the new life, with her husband.

Epilogue

On a spring afternoon in 1937, Paul Bruner sat alone in his Berlin office, looking at the calendar. Each year, he determined to let this date pass unnoticed, and each year it crept upon him like an enemy, dreaded, but always taking him by surprise. He knew that this yearly surrender to memory was like a drug. It brought him dreams of beauty and horror, and left him weak and shaken, but relieved. When it was over, he could turn again to his work, with his marriage thrust far into the past, almost forgotten.

Beside the calendar, there used to stand a photograph of Thea, with the name of the funny little photographer from Abbot's Green below her smiling face. But he had married an Englishwoman, and it was best if some of the callers to his office were not reminded of that fact, and so he had taken the photograph home, trying to convince himself that by so doing he did not hurt Thea, but feeling uneasy and degraded.

I must work, he thought. There is no sense in going through all this again.

He could hear his secretary's typewriter from the next room, but he did not turn to the pile of papers on his desk. Instead he drew out his pocket-book, and looked at the snapshot which he always kept in it. It was taken in the back garden at Abbot's Green, beneath the apple tree, with an ugly brick wall of the next-door house in the background. Thea was dressed in a skirt and plain shirt-blouse, but she was laughing at him in the sunlight and he remembered how she had turned her left hand to make the engagement ring glint,

275

and how Nan had stood and watched them from the flagged path, and how Emily had pretended to be washing the tea-things at the kitchen window.

"Oh God," said Paul. "Oh God."

He put his face down in his hands.

His wife sat opposite him in the railway carriage. She had taken her hat off, and he watched her sleeping features: the small nose, the soft, curved mouth, the unexpectedly firm little chin, the fine, silky fair hair, which looked as though it might tumble at any moment about her face, yet which kept miraculously smooth and tidy. She always looked, he thought, like a child pretending to be grown-up, who has tucked up her hair with fortunate skill, and displays a demure dignity, at variance with her small stature. The curve of the child she carried added at once to her childishness and her dignity. The old painters were wise, Paul thought, to paint their women with child, catching that air of defencelessness and repose, of simplicity and ma-turity, which every woman wears as she awaits a birth. The fast train jolted through the night, past the sleeping villages of Belgium, and Paul watched Thea's face, sick with dread for what they might find at the end of the journey. Once he rose to take her hat from her loosened fingers, and she awoke and smiled up at him sleepily, and pressed his hand. At last, he, too, went to sleep, but before he closed his eyes, he saw her face, calm and peaceful, with a faint smile still upon her lips. That was the last time he saw her alive.

The moment of the crash was not in his memory. He found himself running and stumbling along a bank beside the train, which was half upon its side, and half crushed, as though it had been a cardboard model. There seemed to be a great silence and darkness everywhere, and in it he heard himself shouting for Thea. He bumped into a man, and caught his arm, crying, "Where is she? Where is my wife?" The man threw him off and spat, saying only, "*Sale Boche!*" and Paul realised that he had been speaking German. The shock of those words acted like cold water. He pulled himself together and went up to a group of rescuers, asking them coolly enough for his compartment. They pointed up the train. He had been running away from it. He walked back, clenching his hands and fighting against his panic, praying under his breath, as he used to when he was a small boy, frightened by mice in the attic above his room. He was in time to see a stretcher lifted into an ambulance, and he knew it had to be Thea. In a moment, his coolness vanished. He ran up and tried to climb on board. A doctor reasoned with him, but he struggled violently, and at last he was roughly pushed aside, and the ambulance drove away. He started to run after it, and someone from the group behind him called after him, but he paid no attention, only kept the red light of the ambulance in sight as long as he could, and came on to a main road before it turned from his view. Then he dropped into a stumbling walk, and so came to a small town.

It was in the early hours of the morning. The streets were ill-lit and deserted. The houses were all shuttered. Like a man half-mad, his only idea was to continue to walk until he found Thea. He staggered from street to street, gasping for breath, with the sweat dripping down his face. Sometimes he muttered to himself and called on God, sometimes he would stop and lean against a wall, moaning in an uncomprehended pain. He had no clear idea of what had occurred, only knew that some disaster had come upon him, and that he must find his wife. After some hours had passed, he came upon a policeman standing on a corner, and collected his wits sufficiently to enquire in French for the hospital. The stolid Belgian looked at him with some curiosity, but took him by the arm and led him two minutes' journey to the hospital. He believed that he had passed it more than once in his wandering, indeed, could hardly have avoided doing so, in so small a town.

They took him straight upstairs, and there a doctor, the very one who had thrust him away from the ambulance, told him that his wife had died without regaining consciousness.

277

"How long ago?" he had asked.

"About twenty minutes," the man replied.

It was as though a nerve in Paul's brain leapt and broke, leaving him very cold. He thought that the Belgian doctor viewed him with some sympathy, tempered with dislike of his nationality, but he preferred the Frenchman who had called him '*Sale Boche*'. He was taken to Thea's bedside, and found her with her hair about her shoulders, as he had seen her first, and a calm upon her, as though she still slept, but there was no smile upon her lips. His Thea, his little wife, who had trusted him, who had said that with him she found safety – had he brought her away from her own country for this?

Paul Bruner lifted his head from his hands, and his face was haggard, the face of an old man.

He rose to his feet with an impatient movement and went to the window. He stood looking down at the broad street, with its trees coming into leaf, but the memories forced themselves upon him still. The doctor had said with a clumsy attempt at kindness, "We could not save the child. I am very sorry, but he was too young." Paul had thought, it is one more dead German. Why should you care? But he said nothing. Since that day, he had rarely spoken at all, unless he must. He brought Thea and the child to Berlin, since she had so desired to come to his country. "Berlin is wonderful in the spring," she had quoted to him, laughing at the remembrance of their first meeting.

When they returned from her funeral, his mother, her round cheeks oddly sunk and paled, had said only, "Fritz was buried in France."

Paul had replied, "Yes. That was a pity," and they looked at each other for a moment like enemies.

When he had unpacked his trunk, he found in the top some of Thea's possessions, which she must have pushed in at the last minute. They were such treasures as a child keeps, a cheap, gaudy kite, a tawdry ring out of a cracker, a tiny purse with one shilling in it, a sprig of dusty heather, a newspaper cutting, a pine-cone wrapped in a lace handkerchief. He had knelt on the floor beside these things, trying to guess why they had been dear to her. The newspaper cutting was easily understood – a list of war casualties, with her cousin's name in it. The kite she had perhaps saved from her childhood, for her own children to fly. But what of the rest? He thought how he would have teased Thea about them, and how gravely she would have told him their history. But now he would never know. Their secret had perished with her and with their son. He stayed for a long time, looking at these foolish trifles and sniffing the faint perfume on the handkerchief. He had not known that it was possible for any man to suffer so much.

Paul took up his life again in Berlin, with a fierce determination to forget all that had gone before. He was made a director in his firm. The other directors were all old and tired, and he soon had almost complete control of the business. He found, as time went by, that judicious friendships with members of a certain not very reputable political group gained privileges for his firm which were worth having. He decided that to join the Nazi Party was a sensible move, even as he smiled contemptuously to see their rise to power, and the crazy devotion of their followers.

At home, his mother and father were old and dispirited. His mother put fresh flowers each week under Fritz's photograph, and grumbled about the shortages – but not too loudly, in case someone should hear and think that she criticised the government. Neither she nor his father approved of the new Reich, but when Paul spoke jeeringly of the 'mad little corporal', his mother hushed him fearfully, as though someone might be listening, even in their own house, and might report his words. Paul did not care who governed Germany, as long as order was brought out of anarchy and strength out of weakness. There would be a war, of course. If Germany was to be strong, there must be a war, but what should Paul care for that? If Thea had lived . . . But Thea had died before these new gods came to Germany. There was a strange feeling, almost like relief, in Paul's mind, but he thrust it away, as a sick man refuses medicine.

From the street below came the sound of marching feet. Paul smiled with twisted lips as he watched the little band of youths strutting beneath their banner. Of course, he thought, it was one of the holy days of the new religion. There were to be parades of power and exhibitions of strength, purely for the people's amusement. He started and leant forward, as he thought he saw among the stern young faces one which reminded him of Fritz. But, if Fritz had lived, he would have been in the Gestapo, no doubt of that. If Fritz had lived, he would have been beating up Jews and dragging people out of their beds to answer unanswerable questions, with the same reward for speech or silence. If Fritz had lived . . . But Fritz had died when he was thoughtless, but not cruel; prejudiced, but not sadistic. His mother wept each year, at the anniversary of his death, but she had never learnt to fear him. It is not possible! Paul exclaimed to himself. It is not possible that I could have been mistaken for so long, that there is in truth a merciful Providence who ordains these things. What have I to do with God – I, a man without a god, in a country of mad gods?

The parade of Nazi Youth had been succeeded by a body of stormtroopers, the pride of Germany, boys of nineteen and twenty, with their Teutonic regularity of features and fine physique, marching with the magnificent precision of a machine. When the war comes, thought Paul, how they will sweep through Europe, and through England! In England, he thought, people are still content to think that there will be no war. He thought of the English people now with contempt, their wilful blindness to unpalatable truths, their obstinate refusal to believe that anyone would ever want to fight them. He had not returned to England again since he left with Thea. He wanted to remember the two soldiers in the train who had talked of Germans as 'swine'. He wanted to remember the lost look on Thea's face, when she came away from her last visit to Enfield. He did not want to be reminded of the kindness that could be met within England. He did not want to see Abbot's Green again, or the little red-roofed house where he had lived with Thea. Nan had written to him regularly, but he had been glad when she died, leaving him in her will her own father's heavy gold watch and chain. He had worn it ever since, to his mother's resentment. When the stormtroopers marched victoriously through London, he need not worry about Nan.

If our son had lived, thought Paul, he would probably have been one of those preparing to fight for the Fatherland. He might have marched into London, or piloted one of the great bombers that Paul's firm was helping to produce. At school, he would have learnt to talk of the Treaty of Versailles, and to hate France and England. He would have had to show particular enthusiasm for the Party, since his mother was English. Paul stood and watched the stamping boots below and the expressionless faces under their helmets. Would Thea have liked to see her son marching in that army, she who loved peace and dreaded cruelty? The great swastika outside the window of Paul's office flapped in the breeze. Would Thea have been proud of her husband, thought Paul, offering assistance to the men he despised, and accepting in return the protection of their crooked cross? He began to tremble. He could not part with the bitterness he had cherished for so long. He could not live without the anger which had supported him. He flung away from the window, and walked restlessly up and down the room, but he could not escape from the truth.

If any country should muster enough strength to bomb Berlin, the industrial quarter of the city had crept out to join the district where he lived, and his house would be one of the first to be destroyed. He thought of his timid, gentle wife in danger of aerial bombing. He thought of her having to endure the food and fuel shortages which would soon grow more stringent. He thought of her weeping for her son, torn between loyalty to her husband and grief for her own country.

He thought of the dangers she would have undergone, being English, when the war came. I will not believe it! he cried. But suddenly, he knew that he did. He sat down at his desk, feeling very tired, but contented perhaps for the first time in years.

From the next room, the typewriter had never stopped, and from the street came still the sound of marching boots. But Paul Bruner sat and looked at the calendar, and he was smiling as he had smiled on the day when he proposed to his wife. If I believed in Thea's God, he thought, I would believe that He took her that day because it was kindest and best for her. If I believed in God (and perhaps I almost do) then I would think that in His very mercy He did not let her son grow up in this new Germany. He remembered Thea sitting beside him in the sunshine, making her own innocent plans for their happy future, and thought that she had never known that they were not to be fulfilled. He remembered how she had smiled as she slept in the train, sure, as she had always been sure, that he would protect her from all dangers. And at last he remembered her as he had seen her in the hospital, with a great calm about her, in that final protection which was stronger than his – as ship to safe harbour, swimmer to the shore, frightened child to its father's arms.